Belinda Castles won the *Australian*/Vogel's literary award for *The River Baptists* in 2006 and was one of the *Sydney Morning Herald*'s Best Young Novelists for 2008. Her next novel, *Hannah & Emil*, won the Asher Literary Award for 2012–13. She has recently returned from teaching in the United Kingdom and is currently a lecturer in creative writing at the University of Sydney. Belinda lives with her husband and daughters on the northern beaches of Sydney.

Also by Belinda Castles

The River Baptists
Hannah & Emil

June 2018

BLUEBOTTLE

BELINDA CASTLES

Sam!
Thank you for making Exeter
such a friendly &
nourishing place for me.
And for helping me fix
the ending!

Love,

Belinda x

ALLEN&UNWIN
SYDNEY·MELBOURNE·AUCKLAND·LONDON

First published in 2018

Copyright © Belinda Castles 2018

Allen & Unwin
83 Alexander Street
Crows Nest NSW 2065
Australia
Phone: (61 2) 8425 0100
Email: info@allenandunwin.com
Web: www.allenandunwin.com

 A catalogue record for this book is available from the National Library of Australia

ISBN 978 1 76063 284 7

Set in 12/18 pt Minion by Midland Typesetters, Australia
Printed and bound in Australia by Griffin Press

10 9 8 7 6 5 4 3 2 1

The paper in this book is FSC® certified. FSC® promotes environmentally responsible, socially beneficial and economically viable management of the world's forests.

For my brothers and sisters

CHRISTMAS DAY

There was a house on a honeycomb cliff above the Pacific, perched over the beach in air as scrubbed and softened as old linen. A deep scoop of land in front had fallen away and sat in rocky clumps in the water beneath, surfacing at low tide. The house was humble: made of apricot fibro, its roof dull and rusted, the scrub on the escarpment reaching up towards it, ready to pull it down. When storm heads built out to sea, you could imagine it in pieces, splintered slabs jutting from the surf, like those rocks that were once land in the sky.

On Christmas Day 1994, a bright mist filled the sunny bowl of the beach and gully and gave the day a nostalgic feeling even as it unfolded. The Christmas visitors under the cliff moved sleepily, a little tipsy perhaps from picnic champagne, wandering between the baking orange sand and the cool, invigorating surf.

Some, drifting down to the rusty shore, dodging the skittering kids and their trenches and castles, noticed a small pink-shouldered man leaping about at the water's edge. He galloped one way and then the other along a five metre stretch of sand, like a coach on the touchline, raising his fist to the sky, calling out to the sea. He jumped in the air. He leaned on his knees and shook his head.

People eyed him curiously as they pushed into the swirling waters towards the sandbar. The swimmers let out their waves of delight as they rode the peaks and his booming voice carried above them, calling out names: *Lou! Jack! Phoebe!* A strong-looking girl on a striped board teetered and crashed near the shore. Her board shot out towards a swimmer and stopped just short, caught by her leg rope. She emerged from the foam, her long blonde hair in strips across her face, smiling. 'Sorry,' she said, before turning to the man on the beach, her hand resting on her board as though it were a piano and this was the moment of silence before she let loose her voice. The man too seemed like he was waiting for her to sing, looking up into the misty sky and then back at the girl, aqua eyes made of the same stuff as the sea.

The day, endless as it felt, began to wane. The lifesavers were packing up their shelter, pulling up the flags. 'Merry Christmas!' one called into his loudhailer from the beach buggy. 'Stay safe.' He started the vehicle and called to the man at the shore, 'Watch the rip,' but he didn't seem to hear, absorbed by the sight of a chubby little kid leaping sideways laughing off her board into the messy pond at his feet.

As the beach emptied there was a tiny movement from the top of the cliff. The man caught it and looked up at a figure on a balcony, waving a piece of cloth from side to side as though a small plane flew overhead and she was hoping to be rescued. She waved from the apricot house, the one that looked ready to join the rocks at the base of the cliff.

The visitors trudged to the carpark on the warm sand, the air smelling of sausages and suncream as they queued to wash the sticky sand off their feet and boards. No need for the family on the beach to tackle the carpark, or fill the car with sand. A walk up the track, a warm shower, a cold drink from the fridge out on the breezy deck.

The beachgoers drove back to their apartments in the suburbs, their homes in the green hills. Walking the dog in the quiet streets in the pink dusk, watering the tomato plants on the sill, they thought of that man down at the beach. What was it about him? Him, of all the people packed onto the shoreline on a dreamy Christmas afternoon. Some had pulled their towels a little closer to the water after their swim, kept half an eye on him as he called out to his children from the shore. Those girls, the Amazonian, the most natural surfer, with her strong legs and shoulders, her long hair streaming behind her; the little chubby one, laughing and clowning. A boy, who seemed a teenaged replica of the man with his slight body and wild sandy hair, but nervy and sweet, his triumphs and failures written in the set of his shoulders, the tilt of his chin.

It was the father they remembered though, oblivious as he was to the atmosphere of the beach, its softness, its air of gentle pleasure. When one of his children wiped out, or caught a wave and rode it in, something drew your glance back again and again from the child in the water to the man on the sand. Irresistible, the spectacle of him, feelings surging through him like a heavy swell pushing towards the shore.

BOXING DAY

After midnight the heat swelled in the house on the cliff while the cool surf pounded below. When daylight spread across the gully, the tin roof began to shimmer and throb. Jack Bright lay close to the ceiling on the top bunk in the children's room, twitches flickering across his face. Then his mouth opened and he lurched into the morning gasping. Closing his eyes, he took ten deep breaths, counted to five for each breath in through the nose, each release through the mouth. He hoped that his sisters were up already, out in the world; counted until he was calm.

Awareness of the day broke through: the heat radiating from the tin roof not a metre above him, murmurs and crockery chinks from the living room. He leaned out over the edge of the bunk and dipped his face into the stream of cooler air below. The wider bottom bunk was empty but for the girls' crumpled sheets, their quilt in a heap on the floor.

What is it? he allowed himself to wonder now that he could breathe. You know where you are. You're in the new house. He allowed the slow gravelly rush of the ocean to settle him in place.

At some unknown hour in the night, beneath the roar of the waves, heavy footsteps had moved back and forth along the floor of the den below, approaching and receding endlessly. Was that why he had woken as if from drowning? But then, listening to the creak of the floorboards, he had told himself to follow instead the rhythm of the waves, and within moments he had lost the line between his breath and the sea and sunk back down into sleep.

Jack leaned forwards and placed his hands on the ceiling above his head as though bracing himself to make a parachute jump from the back of an open plane. The plaster was warm, his skin was slick. He settled in to tell himself the story of how he came to be here, right here in this bed on this day, remembering events in sequence so that they were logical, so that everything was in place. The past would be made to lead directly to now, without chasms opening up, dark gaps in time. One bright moment to the next.

He began with an image of this house on its crumbling orange cliff. When he saw in his mind the house from outside, perched, tenuous, his chest tightened.

Your old room. Start with that. And so he was there, amid the smell of turpentine, looking out through a wall of windows to red gum forest, painting at his easel. A horse and rider passed slowly along the trail, the horse's huge flanks catching the light amid the trees. Through the heavy days at school—the jostling stink of adolescent boys, the persistent fear of disgrace—the dappled, changing light on the trail was always there, waiting for him. He saw his hand holding a brush dipped in a dark bush green, dotting leaves onto the dimpled paper. Out there, the flicker of animals, the movement of branches. Recently, the sense that there was something more than the animals among the trees, something that thought in language.

One spring Saturday he decided to skip his usual bike ride along the trails, spooked into risking the atmosphere at home. He and his sisters lolled in front of *Rage* in the lounge, eating endless bowls of Fruit Loops, their parents nowhere in sight. They all loved *Rage*, fought about every single song, often physically, someone sitting on you to force a confession, that you liked Céline Dion, that you *loved* Bryan Adams, only to retract it the moment you were free. The children were heaped on the couch, slack-jawed in horror at some boy band in matching sweaters, when their dad took up a position between them and the television.

Jack grew still and ready, studying his father for a sign of intent. Charlie twitched in front of the TV in a tatty T-shirt and running shorts, waiting for the girls' attention. He clamped his lips together, preventing something from escaping, a humming bird or mouse, and held his hands at his chest, cycling his fingers as though he were playing the harp at manic speed, happy with whatever tune came out, like a toddler. He'd bought something, probably, just so that he could create this moment of suspense and then awed appreciation. Like the Mustang, the pinball machine, the boat. The Megadrive. The divers' watches.

Fat little Phoebe was off the couch, making ready to launch, and then bam, she slammed into Charlie's legs, flung her arms around his waist. She tried to scramble up him like she had when she was tiny and nimble, her feet sliding down his thighs, bare below his shorts. She pulled his head down to her mouth and whispered loudly, 'Tell me, Dad. I won't tell those knuckleheads what it is.' He winked at Jack, his sandy hair electrified by the ideas pulsating beneath. Louisa was trying to peer around Charlie's legs—Silverchair had just come on—and he rose on the naked balls of his feet and finally spoke. 'In the car, kids! Something to show you. Might want to wear your togs.'

'Yes!' Phoebe said, and ran upstairs. Lou gave a theatrical sigh, leaning forward to shake out her bleached swimmer's hair in preparation for whatever foolishness she was to be made to endure. But neither Lou, nor even their mother, lugging the beach chairs through the den wearing an inscrutable expression, was going to sit out one of Charlie's schemes. Jack thought about raising a hand, saying he'd give this one a miss thanks, Charlie. Head out into the bush on his bike. The chink of bell miners, the rustling of leaves. You could be out there for hours without seeing another soul this early in the season. Until you did, and what then, with no one else around? A shiver blew across his neck and he followed the others upstairs to find his swimming shorts from last summer.

In the driveway, in their togs, towels over shoulders, Lou said quietly, 'What do you reckon it is?'

'I honestly don't care,' he replied, and yanked open the heavy doors of the Land Cruiser, scooting along the back seat into the middle to avoid a fight.

It was a blue day, cloudless and warm with a light breeze carrying a lemony eucalypt smell into the open windows. They drove up out of the widely spaced suburban streets, past horse paddocks and steep burnt bushland. Hugging the trees were bright green boas of fresh growth. When he saw the poles of black bark,

Jack could smell last year's burning summer, recall closing his eyes at night to see a perfect circle of advancing fire.

The girls pressed against Jack on either side, Phoebe's squishy thighs, Lou's bony hips. Silent, all of them, waiting, his sisters' faces resting against opposite windows. The two bowls of cereal Jack had eaten sloshed in his stomach and he kept his eyes on the horizon.

In the front seat, Tricia leaned her shimmering blonde head towards Charlie. 'What is it?' she whispered. He waggled his head from side to side and gave her a grin, looked at Jack in the mirror, his pale green eyes iridescent. She laughed and murmured, 'Charlie *Bright*.' Jack kept his gaze on that band of deep blue beyond the bush. What was it now? A helicopter ride, a swim in a famous person's pool. He refused to get worked up about it. Whatever it was.

By the time they turned north at the bottom of the hill and began to crawl through the beach suburbs with the Saturday traffic, Phoebe had cracked. She leaned across Jack towards the front seats, smelling of Fruit Loops and suncream, her fingers soft and hot on his leg. 'Is it . . . whale watching? Is it . . . free diving? Is it . . . rock fishing? Is it—'

'It's nothing you're going to guess, pudding.' Charlie laughed. 'Never in a million years!' The car fell quiet as they continued to speculate in private.

Up the hill and down its long wide slope they trailed a red and cream Kombi into Newport with its surf shops and deli, its teenage kids in their swimmers on bikes on this warm spring day. The crowding greenery on the hills was dotted with fat purple jacarandas. Jack loved reaching the Newport strip; it was like entering another dimension in which people moved slowly, ate amazing fruit with their dazzling teeth and didn't have to worry about the normal things. He watched the line of Norfolk Island pines roll out along the long beach. He couldn't see the water but it gave off its own light, a glow between the trees. They climbed up the slow bends round the headland, a hang-glider just lifting from the broad lawn, and turned off to go down steeply through scrub, the ocean glittering beyond to the horizon. The road wound down through the shady gully, past a beach carpark and up again to a couple of rows of houses, set up the slope like bleacher seats.

Charlie crunched the handbrake next to a *For Sale* sign filled with the view and cut the engine. Jack's heart knocked at his ribs. Tricia placed her long fingers on the dashboard and leaned forwards as though she were about to begin a piano recital.

'Get a wriggle on,' Charlie said, twisting towards the back seat, and the girls cranked open the heavy doors, not speaking. Jack slid along the seat, hot from Louisa's bum. The street was silent except for the grainy roar of the ocean below. Plants that could survive the wind and salt lined the driveways; they were spiky, shiny, with flowers of vivid pink and red. As his foot hit the hot tarmac Jack felt heat rising in his face and a tremor in his leg. He smelled something sweet, these flowers perhaps, the salty air and dampness rising from the shady driveways, a weirdly thrilling mix. Breathed in the salt mist and decided then and there that it had special properties, the power to fix him, to make him like other fourteen-year-old boys.

Charlie—Phoebe and Tricia on either side—headed down a mossy drive towards a man in a dark suit standing with his legs apart, chest and shoulders puffing at the cloth of his jacket. Lou and

Jack followed, a strange gravity drawing them on, down to the front door of the ugly house on the cliff.

Charlie laid an arm along the man's swollen shoulders and gestured with the other towards the squat salmon fibro behind him. 'I've brought the gang.' The man smiled at them, his eyes hidden behind aviator glasses. He jangled a cascading bunch of keys and opened the door. 'Welcome to Bilgola.'

Jack, here and now, sitting in his hot bunk on Boxing Day morning, tried to place himself back in that moment, balanced between thrill and hurtling panic, standing on the shady driveway, breathing in the sea and the dark, earthy presence of the house.

Phoebe had bounded inside without hesitation. 'Are we getting a holiday house?' she called out behind her. 'Ariana's got a shack, with a sleepout. Bunks on the verandah!'

'A bit more than a holiday house. This is it, the big one. Wait till you get a look at the view!'

Tricia whispered in the doorway: 'You're a dark horse, Charlie. What are you up to?'

Jack stepped into the hall behind them and felt the thick green carpet brush the sides of his thonged feet, the smell of meaty dinners puffing up like spores with every footfall. 'Holy baloney,' Lou murmured. At the end of the corridor light fell on a dark green Formica bench, pale green kitchen cupboards. Jack followed the others into the living area, where Phoebe stood in front of a brown-framed sliding door with netted security screens, still and silent. She looked like a captain on the bridge, elevated against the wide blue stripes of sea and sky.

Louisa leaned over Phoebe, her arms on the glass above her head, but Phoebe couldn't stay still for long. She wriggled out from her spot, the floor trembling as she threw herself down the stairs to whatever lay beneath this room. Charlie followed her, two steps at a time. 'What do you think of your old man, now?'

'My old man's a genius!' she called, and they thumped across the boards below, laughing.

Tricia stood in the kitchen, leaning on the bench. Jack and Lou waited for her to say something. The room was filled with the boom of the waves. Jack spoke quietly, not knowing where the real estate agent was. 'Has he bought it, Mum? Or is he seeing what we think first?'

'I think he's actually bought it,' she whispered quickly. She bit her lip, trying not to smile.

'He'd buy a house without talking to you about it?' Lou said.

Tricia leaned forward on the counter that divided the kitchen from the dining area. 'You know your dad. Loves to surprise us.' She giggled, then made herself serious. 'We talked about moving. I said I might like to, now. I might even have suggested it.'

They waited for her to say more.

'Things don't feel the same any more, do they?'

Jack, caught in their whispering habit, said quickly, 'Shouldn't we stay, though? Do you think . . . we should wait and see what happens?'

His mother gave him an impatient look—don't spoil it, Jack—and he looked for the words to explain. A trembling preceded the others returning up the stairs and Phoebe launched herself across the living room at the scruffy old couches, jumping on the springs. The agent appeared from the corridor. Tricia straightened up and clasped a skinny elbow with her other hand, the way she often did when she was smoking. 'Phoebe! You'll break the furniture.'

Her tone in front of others was deeper, smoother, her enunciation more precise, a dusting over of childhood tracks. Jack and Lou had found themselves in front of Jana Wendt on TV one night and giggled without having to say why.

'Don't worry,' the agent said. 'No one's worrying about those any more.'

'They're her couches, when it comes down to it, hey?' Charlie said to the agent.

'That's right.' He laughed.

Lou gave Jack a brief conspiratorial glare, and he opened the sliding door to the sea, having to joggle it over a bump. The noise of the waves came roaring in with the breeze. He creaked out onto the small deck at the top of stairs leading down to the strip of bindi-swirled lawn between the house and the cliff edge, feeling Louisa's weight behind him. They sat on the top step and considered the beach beyond the lawn and descending scrub, its orange sand a deep bowl, a glassy ocean pool lying beyond, under the next headland. The red and yellow flags were up and a few kids were surging into land on boogie boards, voices rising softly into the air.

'What do you reckon?' Jack said.

Charlie and Phoebe called triumphantly from inside the house above. Lou looked out over the rippled sheet of ocean. 'Smells of old people. They probably died here, on those couches.' She paused, put on a boofhead voice. 'No one's worrying about *those* any more.'

He laughed, quietly, and she went on, 'What about our friends? We've got lives.' She gave him a sideways look, grinning. 'Or some of us do.'

'Check out that pool,' Jack said. 'No more six o'clock bus.' She'd fit right in, queen of the beach, with her pale hair and tan and her fifty laps a day. 'And he'd build a new place, right? Now's his big chance.'

'Listen to you. Thought you didn't care.'

'I didn't know it would be *this*.'

'Yeah.'

The air was filled with mist and thunder. The clean green waves rolled onto the beach in a long broken line, massive shoulders making butterfly strokes, over and over again. Jack watched that moment of bulging water, held the last moment before the wave tumbled and felt a tension that ran like shivers through his body. He tried to conjure his room at home, the bronze angophora trunks in the changing light, to think properly about what it was he'd be giving up, walking away from, but the sound of the ocean washed over memory.

A movement caught his eye, a runner, a slow ant, coming off a path that emerged from the base of the cliff onto the beach. He saw himself stepping off that track at the start of the day, the cool sand of morning beneath his feet, the beach and sky pink. The water would be dark and smooth, swelling. He could grow to contain it, that feeling of being poised at the crest, about to fall. All this air, all this water, no one here but you.

~

Jack, in his brace position on the bunk, his palms on the ceiling, felt the heat spread through his fingers. What then? How had that day unfolded? You had to work through everything, get past it, not let things loom. It made him slow, this continual piecing together of his life so that it made sense to him, but he had nowhere to be. He was in a strange non-time, between the relief of walking away forever from the sly idiots at his old school who watched him sideways for signs of trouble, and the pristine possibility of the next place, where he was not known, and might yet manage to get through the days and weeks of his last few years of school without having to lie down on the classroom floor in the middle of maths.

On that first day, after Charlie had made Tricia take a picture of him pasting the *Sold* sign over the board, as they clambered back up into the Land Cruiser on their new street, Jack had said, 'There's a rock you can jump off, into the surf.' He had not planned to say it but was overcome for a moment by a Phoebe-like urge to draw attention to himself, to mark the heady unreality of this day.

The kids slid into position and Charlie turned from the front, his arm trailing Tricia's seat, his pale eyes bright, hair mad, and beamed at him, ignoring the others. Jack did his best to resist the surge of joy this brought him. A Buddhist monk had visited his school last year and Jack had since developed a belief that the key to his survival was to learn to receive the praise and disappointment of his father with equanimity.

'Jump Rock,' Jack said calmly, 'up at Palm Beach. The guys all talk about it. You go round past the pool. You do backflips and that, into the water.'

'You're on,' Charlie said, turning the key.

'Sounds a bit lethal,' Tricia said, but she was smiling.

'How often is Jack the ballsy one?' Charlie waved at the real estate agent backing out of the drive and started the motor. 'Let's see this rock.'

Tricia glanced back at Jack and then craned her neck to peer up at the glamorous large-windowed houses on the hill. Jack took in the shifting configurations of cliff and water, practising non-attachment. They threaded their way through the houses sliding down the hill to Pittwater, clouds massing above the ridge beyond, and rounded the point towards the surf beach, everyone quiet in the car, even Phoebe suspended in a dreamy moment. A football field of glittering water lay before them in the middle of the ocean, sun funnelling through a circle in the clouds. The sea around it was dark grey-green, opaque after the glassy surf at Bilgola. If something slipped beneath the surface, you'd never see it again.

Charlie parked at the southern end of Palm Beach and they sat in the car and faced the sand, silent. 'So, when are we moving?' Tricia asked eventually.

'By the Christmas hols if the solicitor pulls his finger out.'

'What about their schools? And our neighbourhood?'

In the back seat they listened, waiting, pretending not to. Jack took in the long curve of the beach, the lighthouse on top of the hammerhead of rock at the far end. Across the river mouth the sun fell on white waves crashing at the base of glazed charcoal cliffs. Jack mixed paint colours in his head. Where would you even begin?

'Our neighbourhood, Tricia?' Charlie said. Then quietly, 'Will we just wait around for someone to grab Louisa? Is that the plan?'

Tricia flicked a glance towards the back seat. Jack and his sisters looked out the windows, careful not to catch her eye. 'What about my tennis club? The kids' schools?'

'Those women have had enough of you thrashing them by now, surely. Give someone else a shot at glory.' He turned towards the back seat. 'Do you want to live on the beach?'

'Yes,' they said together.

Tricia sighed. 'That house, though.'

'The house'll come down soon enough. Get those magazines out and start choosing taps.'

Charlie opened the door and the girls were a second behind, jumping down into the sandy carpark. Most of Phoebe disappeared except for her round shoulders, her curly dark head, turning sideways, seeing what was next. Jack looked at his mother's bony back beneath the straps of her sundress, her thoughts a mystery to him.

He dropped down behind the girls onto a scattering of long bendy sticks from the pines that felt like dried-out sea creatures beneath his feet. Behind them was a surf club—not the usual kind, with an ice-cream kiosk and gritty-floored toilets. It looked like the grandly shabby beach house of a movie star. He imagined immaculate girls serving drinks to hide-faced old men who laughed intimidatingly. He saw Charlie look at it for a few moments, considering.

The sun cleared the clouds as they headed onto the sand. He spotted the place he was looking for, beyond the pool at the south end of the beach. There was an anvil shape jutting out from the rock platform. That was the one. His stomach shrank; it was tiny. As he stopped to take it in Tricia passed him laden with the esky and striped fold-up chairs. Charlie and Phoebe were up ahead, Charlie greeting people as he passed, as though everyone knew him already. Phoebe skittered around him in her orange sundress, a blur in the kicked-up sand, always coming back to face him after her cartwheels and tumbles. Tricia stopped, looking about her. 'Do you think this'll do?'

'Mum,' Lou sighed, a hand on her hip.

'All right, madam. Better to make sure now than have to shift it all later.'

'Send him to me if he gives you a hard time.'

He looked at his mother, fussing with the folding chairs, pursing her lips. He felt he should stay, get her talking about the house, or laughing at Phoebe falling on her backside. Ignore Lou, he wanted to say. Thinks she's the bee's knees, like you know who. He opened his mouth to speak but the hunch of his mother's shoulders kept him quiet. Louisa was already several paces further on. He ran across the sand to catch up.

'You can be nicer to her,' he said.

'I'm trying to encourage her to grow a spine.'

This is what he'd have missed on his bike ride. The excitement of the house, yes, but also these jabs and spikes like stepping on Phoebe's Lego as you crossed the floor of the lounge.

A couple of girls in bikinis reclining on their elbows checked Lou out sourly, turning to say something to one another. Lou was not quite a year older than him but a head taller. They would be, for a month over Christmas, the same age; this year, fifteen. As he walked beside her, they looked straight ahead, picking their way towards the pool amid the scattering of bright towels and lunging toddlers, pretending that the whole world was not watching her as she passed with her long body and limbs, her summer blonde hair, her blank face that saw something beyond the realm of these nobodies. He knew they wondered what she was doing with him. I'm her *brother*, he wanted to tell them. She's *obliged* to hang out with me.

Out at the rocks, past the pool, the anvil rock seemed more significant, jutting up and out a couple of metres above the foam like a diving platform. Charlie tapped Phoebe on the shoulder and bolted ahead, in and out of stone gullies, splashing through rockpools.

A feeling gripped Jack, and Lou too. She leapt gracefully from rock to rock. Jack hung back, his head pounding, planning his trajectory.

Phoebe sprang out of a dip ahead of Charlie and flung off her sundress without stopping, soft body in her first bikini, skin glinting pale gold with down. She scaled the rock like a monkey and hurled herself straight off the highest peak without looking, soaring up into the light as she clutched her legs in a tight bomb. There was a splash and shriek and then her low laugh as she came up, curls flattened, triumphant. 'You little legend, Feeb,' Charlie called out. She clasped her hands together in the air, boxer style. 'The greatest of all time!' she managed to say, shivering, before she swallowed a mouthful and had to use her arms to swim.

Charlie sailed over her head, water pluming high. Lou turned to Jack and held up a hand—*Witness!*—and jumped; spring, fold, plummet, like a bird into a river, vertical, heart-stoppingly close to the rocks. Jack's breath leapt and tumbled with her.

Charlie was already dunking Phoebe, her face surfacing rigid with glee. Jack closed his eyes, ready to try a somersault, to begin the countdown, and opened them to see Louisa's face below him sunlit against the green water, creased in pain. 'Jeez, Jackie,' she said, voice tight.

He took a step towards the lowest edge of the platform and a small patch of foam bloomed pink as her bleeding thigh broke the surface. She scrabbled at the wet rocks and Jack kneeled on the mossy curve, grasping at her smooth shoulders, shoving his fingers into her slippery armpits. The blood, the wet skin, all too close. She rose slowly, heavy, muscular, from the water, her long leg gashed to the knee in a dark red line spreading pink across the blonde hairs on her thigh. Jack squatted, queasy, the rock shifting beneath him like a boat.

Charlie propelled himself from the surf and onto the rock shelf next to them. The smell of him, always the faint tang of sweat, and something else, oily, metallic, like a car engine, even now, after swimming. He shoved Jack aside. 'Jack, *Jack*, out of the way!' Lou's eyes were closing. Jack stared at her thigh, thinking, *shark*, a space in his chest flaring open. For a panicky second he saw through her leg, grey rocks and bubbling sea foam where there should be skin and muscle. But it was a line drawn down her, black-red and jagged, thin and deep, not a bite taken out.

Charlie hefted her into his arms and straightened with a couple of knee bends like an Olympic weightlifter. Then he was away, picking over the rocks, her legs trailing almost to the ground, the nearest of them bright, slick with red. Jack was panting, as though Charlie had emptied the air from his lungs with his shove. He drew in a breath and pushed himself forward onto his knees towards the water. 'Feeb,' he gasped, leaning down towards her, hands on his knees. Her face was as dark as the sea beyond its turquoise borders. 'Watch where you put your feet. There's oysters.'

He turned away from the surging water and focused on the stable platform at his feet. Phoebe pulled herself up onto the rocks, watching Charlie and Louisa disappear amid the people at the pool. She wore an expression he knew well, the one where Charlie and Lou—Jack and Tricia too, though it was rarely anything to do with them—were dead to her, until the world was rearranged the way she liked it, with her at its centre.

~

Jack sat on his bunk, the heat of Boxing Day morning radiating through the iron roof onto his skin's salty crust. It was just an oyster cut; he'd known that, but the blood and panic had done their work on him quickly and he had sat alone for a few minutes, hands and feet in a cool rockpool, before joining the others. Phoebe settled as soon as she got an icy pole. They had fish and chips for dinner, sitting on the Palm Beach ferry wharf, their legs dangling above the clear shallow water and moored boats, a white bandage wrapped around Lou's thigh. Wrapped around slowly by a bronzed kid from the surf club, a bit older than Lou, kneeling on the ground beside her bench. Plenty of staring on both sides. 'You're gonna have a mental scar,' the boy had said, and Lou had laughed while Charlie shot them daggers, hands on his hips.

On the wharf, Tricia looked out across Pittwater's shimmering evening skin and said, 'I can see us in this life, Charlie. It'll never be the same up there now.'

'I know, love,' Charlie said, and put his arm around her, the afternoon sun spangling off the water, their faces aglow. 'There's a taint, isn't there? Fresh start. That's what this family needs. A new adventure.'

And so Jack had come home from school every day to a growing pile of boxes, the only house he had ever lived in emptying of the stuff that made it theirs, until the final day when he stood in his bare room, the sky beyond his large windows dull, the bush grey and quiet. He had stood there, looking for movement between the trees, wondering what he should feel and when that feeling would arrive.

Now they were here, had had Christmas in this house, so it was officially home, even if it was to be knocked down as soon as

Charlie could arrange it. Jack swung his legs around to the ladder, setting the bunk bed rocking and creaking like an old boat. Charlie had knocked it together on a blowy day a few weeks before, out on the strip of lawn. When it was done he'd sat on this top bunk above the cliff, sandy hair in tufts like a cartoon character, raised a beer to the misty gully and laughed. Then he'd had to partially dismantle it to get it up the stairs and through the doors, but even that wasn't enough to knock him off track. He'd been bullet-proof for these first weeks of his new life—cashed up, free of his work worries, free to run on the beach and spear-fish and plan his magnificent house on the cliff. Perhaps life really could change. Perhaps all Dad needed was this, fresh sea air and a project.

Jack could hear Phoebe singing out in the lounge as he dropped off the edge of the bed, foot spasming with the impact, into a pile of her clothes, shed repeatedly for swimming, surfing. Lou was already up and out, training at the ocean pool at the far end of the beach, a big sexy robot, mowing down dithering breaststrokers, shaking her wet hair as she emerged from the water.

Charlie loved her best, he showed them every day. They stepped around this fact of their lives as though they didn't know. Even Phoebe never said it aloud. And really, who could blame him? It wasn't just the swimming and the way she looked. It was the way that she was just like Charlie, *doing*, instead of all this thinking, this endless weighing and measuring.

He padded along the hall on the dark green carpet, pausing in the soupy stirring of air under the fan. The light felt strange, the ocean quiet. It was early but hot, everyone driven from their beds. At the table, Charlie, ignoring the view before him, leaned over the open newspaper, his burnt shoulder blades drawn together as though his back were scowling. Tricia floated between the kitchen and the table, skinny tanned limbs sticking out of a floaty white dress, bearing coffee, juice, milk. She set a jug down next to Charlie's paper and he looked up briefly. 'Where's the sugar?' She fetched the bowl from the bench and brought it back to him without comment, humming a Joni Mitchell song. She was doing what Lou called her Lady Bountiful, in which she might fetch and carry for you, or at least for Charlie, for twelve hours straight with no hint of a scowl or sigh. Then he'd go off somewhere and you'd ask her to pass the butter and she'd throw it over your head and walk out of the house.

Jack sat down opposite his father at the round dining table and tried to get a reading on him, but his face was obscured by the paper. Maybe he was just concentrating. He had been easy, mostly, here. Jack was almost forgetting to keep a look out. Christmas was perfect, a promise fulfilled. Charlie had bought them beautiful new surfboards with sleek stripes and they took them down to the beach and practised until they could all stand up. A pretty girl in the surf had actually clapped when Jack had ridden past her, and Charlie had caught the moment and lifted a fist in the air. At dinner he had toasted their cleverness and Tricia's fabulous meal before passing out with the whisky bottle in the downstairs den. Jack had found himself standing between his sisters in a row looking at their father lying on the oldest couch in the world. They wanted to watch a video and were assessing him to figure out the odds of getting him to move. There was a space between snores, his head thrown back, his face scalded by sun, in which he seemed briefly dead, disarmed. His stillness was a moment of relief, somehow filled with tension. They had turned away from the couch without speaking and traipsed up the stairs.

Phoebe's curly head appeared at Charlie's elbow and she squished herself into the too-small space between his lap and the table. The paper was crumpled at the edges, damp-looking, where he had gripped it too tightly. He looked up from the paper, over her head at Jack, eyes pink-rimmed and bagged. Jack recalled that pacing in the night. Phoebe rested her head on Charlie's bare chest, as happy as a kitten sleeping on a cushion in a square of sun.

Charlie let one side of the newspaper fall and pointed at a head shot of a girl, the girl they all knew, the picture upside down to Jack. 'They've found her schoolbag, in the bush up near our house. They'll probably dig her up any minute. What are we going to *do*?'

He waited for Jack to respond while Phoebe nicked bits of bacon off his plate. Charlie jabbed at the girl's face in the paper, and Jack felt heat rise from his neck. Don't bring this here, was his first thought; fresh start, you said, but he put it aside, ashamed. The boys at school had talked about her, his neighbour Monica Kazmi, started making jokes not a week after she'd disappeared, telling naked lies about what they'd done with her. Their phrases injected themselves into his head and an extra shot of shame unfurled in his blood like poisoned ink.

'What do you mean—do?' Jack said quietly.

'We should get up there, help search. What use are we sitting around down here working on our tans?'

Phoebe twisted towards Charlie, sensing his involvement elsewhere. Tricia threw more bacon in the pan and the salty meat smell and sizzling filled the hot room. Bent over the stove, she swished her head lightly from side to side, singing quietly, her sundress rippling around her legs in rhythm with her hair like something from the sixties, but Jack caught a glimpse of her expression. She was peering into the pan with a look of concentration. He knew the look. Stay quiet until he gets off the subject. Wait it out.

Charlie shook his head at the newspaper. 'Police letting everyone else do their job for them. Useless is what they are. It was a bush-walker's dog who found it, dragged it out from under some leaves.'

Jack's bowels clenched. 'Phoebe,' he said, 'want to play with my new car?'

'Yes! I do!' She slithered off Charlie's lap and disappeared down the corridor.

Charlie rested his head on his hand, looked into Jack's eyes so he couldn't look away. 'Imagine what might have happened to her.'

Oh my God. No, Dad. No thank you.

Tricia leaned forwards over the table, retrieving Charlie's plate from under the newspaper, glancing at him, then Jack, before heading back to the kitchen. His friend Lachy had a fat cheery mother who sat around eating biscuits and doing puzzles with the kids. He wished Tricia would stay, sit down for once, absorb a bit of Charlie's intensity. You married him, Mum. He's not our fault.

'When her parents went on the news, oh God. That old Iranian fella from across the road, raging at the cameras? Hamid. Imagine what he'll be like now.'

'But they haven't found *her*.'

'Christ, it won't be pretty when they do. That sweet little girl. What if it had been your sister?'

Charlie picked up the paper and flipped it around towards Jack so he could do nothing but look at Monica's picture, though he had done his best to turn away since it had begun to appear everywhere in spring. Her face had been outside the newsagencies and on the evening current affairs shows all summer, the same smile forever. He tried to resist the way it replaced his memory of her, moving in the sunlight through the school corridors, talking to her friends. The details were right, her shiny black hair, that toothy smile, the same checked school dress as Lou's. He wondered if her mum and dad felt like this, though, unable to look at that picture, that cheap replica of a true person. Charlie flipped the page and carried on reading.

Her mum—he'd once had to sit down on her nature strip to sort his breathing out, had looked up into her face as she'd approached quietly and touched his shoulder. She'd thought he was diabetic and made him eat some unbelievable Middle Eastern pastry before she let him cross the street to his house. The dad was an older guy, a scientist, quiet, solemn, except for that amazing moment on TV, when he had stood from the press room desk and shouted, pounded a fist theatrically into his open palm until the police had persuaded him to sit down again.

Jack turned away from Charlie and the picture and conjured memories of the times he and Monica had said hi to each other on the street and at school, willing her into movement, life. Her dark glossy hair caught the sun as she moved. She was very slightly plump in a way that made her seem friendly and well loved. She raised a hand when she said hello, even if she was right in front of you. A big unguarded smile and then she dipped her gaze, left you with that little wave, like an apology for being too much, as though she knew when people looked at him for too long he felt a hundred tiny punctures in the skin along his shoulders and he didn't know what would come next. Once when he'd passed her outside the gym, stopped to ask her about her hockey match, she'd been standing with two friends and they'd leaned together as he moved on, laughed in a way he did not believe, then or now, to be unkind.

Jack stepped out onto the platform of the wooden staircase in the hazy morning, leaving Charlie hunched over the paper and Tricia encased in her protective shell of endless activity. He spotted Louisa straightaway, striding among the flabby mortals to the goat track at the northern end of the beach. He breathed out. It was a relief when she was here too, his own form of protection. Some days, when Charlie spoke, or looked at you, a portal opened in the air and through it was a world where anything might happen.

~

Louisa faced the ocean pool, her toes gripping its concrete lip, arms raised above her head. She looked down into the foam of the waves crashing over the wall, felt the weight of the sun on her skin even at this hour, and plunged down into the cold water, so much thicker and wilder than an indoor pool, as though it had its own plans for you. Pushing forward into it, her body came to life, bubbles streaming from her nose. She surfaced in the seaweedy surge, the pool sparsely populated at this hour on Boxing Day, and shot past a young man with a triangular torso, shoulders like the blades of wings about to open.

The way those surfer guys checked her out in their little clusters in the beach carpark as she walked by—she'd seen it. The older ones, in their twenties, filled their shiny wetsuits, gave off pulses of something dangerous and cool. Then there were the teenage boys in their summer packs, mimicking the older ones but failing with their shoves and loud laughs, their watchful cheeriness. These thoughts led to Dean, nothing like them, skinny as a hungry dog, body long and white, hair unnaturally black. If you put Dean in among this lot, what would happen? Some sort of negative reaction, a repellence, or a fight. His strangeness was what drew her, what held her attention.

She turned at the end of the pool, zipped smoothly past an elderly turtle-like man, patiently repeating a butterfly stroke so slowly he seemed to be dancing strangely on the spot. She swam free and remembered. Dean had walked into her maths class late in the long dull winter term, brand new, with his black hair and skin like a ghost, and taken the empty seat next to her. She was aware of him there for that long hour, of his cigarettes and soap smell, of the quiet noise of his breathing. She let her hair hide her face on that side. That hour of her pen scratching on the paper, the teacher's voice smoothed of meaning, ended with the bell and the scrape of chairs and she began to shove her pens back in their case. He dug her gently in the soft space beneath her ribs and she froze. 'I've seen you. Your yard backs onto mine,' he said, so close to her hair that it shifted against her cheek.

His long back was passing out of the doorway before she allowed herself to look up. So then, he was one of the new people in that house of horrors beyond their fence, with its overgrown garden, the asbestos-roofed shed falling down on one side. They made up stories about it at dinner, that house, Charlie egging them on. He called it the humpy, the paedo lair, pretended to play a boondocky banjo.

That afternoon, she sat at her desk in the window in a daze and realised he was out there, leaning on the bottom fence, looking up at her room, not even pretending to be doing anything else. It was like she had conjured him. Power tingled in her fingers.

She had waited for a while, was not aware of thinking anything, just holding his gaze, easy at this distance. Her garden was long, he was just a small figure at the end of it, not even real. Then something jolted her out of this drifting moment and she went down to him, giving in at last. The words they'd spoken over the fence, the mozzies biting, hadn't mattered. They were just passing time until they got to the next part where he leaned over the fence and kissed her in full view of both their kitchens. He tasted of cigarettes and after he'd kissed her she turned away without saying anything and walked back to the house, her bare feet feeling the damp garden, her eyes down, looking at her painted blue toenails moving through the blades of grass.

As the weeks went on, she and Dean would sneak home from school to his place and hide in his room, carving out whole afternoons from life. They had made a deal once to take off their T-shirts for half an hour on his narrow bed and touch whatever they wanted to that was bare. As he tilted the blinds she saw her mother in her tennis whites, standing at the kitchen bench, staring out into the dark bushland that bordered their houses. That was what Tricia did these days, looked into the bush as though it would attack one of them. She lay back on his bed and heard movements beyond the bedroom: the kitchen blinds clattering, the dog whining and buffeting the door. She set her alarm on her waterproof watch and laid it on Dean's pillow, giggling. His skin was chalky, his ribs, front and back, were like the frame of a boat: delicate, fascinating.

He trembled when she traced her thumb along them and she felt dizzy for a moment when he slipped a finger inside her bra. The beeper sounded. She turned and pulled on her T-shirt quickly.

Now she was reliant on phone boxes and buses for even a taste of that feeling he gave her, something wrong but good, like holding a battery on your tongue or the taste of gin. He said he could get her a mobile phone from his mum's work at the electrical store. Maybe he'd have it today. She'd have to hide it, somewhere Charlie wouldn't find it, charge it in the carport maybe, and take it to the beach to talk. She imagined herself talking into the phone in a public place as those surfer dudes walked by, looking like she had important business, like she was doing a deal.

She lifted herself up out of the pool with trembling arms. Behind her, she imagined the crocodile eyes of rotating freestylers lifting briefly above the waterline to look, and steadied herself. She would turn sixteen in three weeks and had decided to make a gift of herself to Dean, to bind him to her. Then perhaps it would be him figuring out how to reach her by public transport on a forty-degree day.

Louisa saw her morning unfolding, stepping onto the bus, her hair slipping over her bare shoulders, walking down the aisle as they curved around the Bends, away from the beach. Then of Dean's dyed black hair, grown past his T-shirt collar, his long fingers, the heat of his thin chest, pressing.

~

Jack was on the lawn in the strange morning light, a minia-ture of Charlie, slight and mad-haired with those otherworldly

29

green eyes. If only she'd got those; they'd be a weapon in life. She gave her brother a sideways look and carried on, limbs shattered, drawn up the stairs by the smell of bacon. Sweat broke through her salty pores. Jack was retreating, travelling elsewhere, as he sat on the lawn looking out over the beach and murky sea. Her scalp prickled.

She took the stairs slowly with her eyes closed, a cartoon character, drifting upwards, borne aloft by the smell of food. In the lounge an electric buzz revved up and faded and then started again. Charlie was sitting on the couch, scrolls of paper curling in front of him on the coffee table, while between his feet on the floor Phoebe drove Jack's new remote control Ferrari into the stand of the yellowing Christmas tree. Mum wiped the benches, boned chest slick with sweat, singing, fooling no one. Louisa hovered by the dining table. 'Breakfast finished?'

Tricia gave a little shake of her hair and threw the cloth in the sink. 'Bacon and eggs?'

She nodded and snuck a glance at Charlie, assessing whether she could clear the lounge without getting snarled up in his weather. He was leaning back against the cushions, looking out the window to the hazy sky. Coppery stubble poked through the skin of his jaw. Light fell on his eyes; they seemed even paler than usual. Last night Louisa lay squeezed between Phoebe and the wall and heard over her sister's little squeaks and farts someone—Charlie—creaking back and forth along the downstairs floorboards endlessly. It had not kept her awake; after swimming in the morning and surfing in the afternoon, nothing could, but you could see it in him, a way he had of tapping his side teeth together. The need to release something.

Charlie noticed her presence and came to life, sitting forward. He patted the spot next to him. 'Lou-Lou. Check this out. You always see what I'm driving at.'

'Wet cossies, Dad.'

'Don't worry about it. Sit down.'

Her foot skidded on Phoebe's car as she crossed the floor. 'Bloody hell, Feeb!'

'*Louisa* . . .' Tricia said quietly as she reached up to the cupboards for the pan.

Phoebe clutched the car under her arm like a puppy and stomped down the corridor. 'It's Christmas,' she was saying. 'You're supposed to be *nice* to your sister at Christmas.'

Louisa squeezed between Charlie and the coffee table to the empty spot on the couch and made to sit down. 'Up, up,' Tricia was saying behind her, flicking her on the shoulder, handing her her beach towel. Louisa wedged it underneath herself and looked at the scrolls of paper, lifting gently at the edges in the breeze from the ceiling fan. On the sheets, torn from Phoebe's roll of rough drawing paper, she saw triangles, rectangles, a massive hump like a child's picture of a hill, stick figures inside the shapes, scrawled notes followed by multiple question marks.

'What am I looking at?'

Saliva filled her mouth as the bacon sizzled. She tried to concentrate on the shapes, the smell tormented her. She could think of nothing else. It took her several seconds of sitting there, Charlie electrically still beside her, to understand that this was the house he was planning to build. Those stick figures were walking through rooms. That hump was the cliff. The only thing that made sense was a graceful staircase swooping up and out from the shapes and down to a curve of shore. As if you could do that, though. The whole thing was mad, unbuildable.

'What do you reckon?'

She looked at him warily. 'You'll have to talk me through it.'

'Okay, so drawing's not my strong point. Don's coming for lunch. He can have a look, pretty it up.' He pointed at two of the rectangles. 'I want it to feel like it's moving, flying.' He stood up and jutted out his arms behind him, like a plane, grinning, and then wiped his face and sat down next to her again. 'Awesome, right?'

'But it's . . . a house?' She glanced up at her mother, who was looking at them with a hand on her hip, giving her a warning look, unhelpful in its lack of particulars.

'Okay,' Louisa said. 'What about this staircase though? No one else has got stairs that land on the beach. It can't be allowed, can it?'

Silence emanated from Charlie. He was very still.

Then he leaned forward and began to roll up his plans. 'I thought for sure you'd be smart enough to get it.'

She sighed. 'Come on, Dad. Don't do this.'

'I want you in the house today.'

'Just explain to me how it works.'

'We have a lunch at one. I expect you to be in a presentable state.'

'That's like five hours away.' She had *known* as soon as her backside had hit the couch. Before, when she'd seen Jack. She opened her mouth to speak but he cut across her.

'You shouldn't be roaming about the way you do, dressed in next-to-nothing. Those lads out there. I know how they think.'

She looked down at herself in her cossies. 'I've been swimming?'

'That dress I bought you in Tokyo.'

'What about it?'

'Wear it for lunch. It's a celebration, for my retirement.'

'Food's up,' Tricia said sharply.

'No more bacon these holidays,' Charlie said. He meant Phoebe, but they'd all have to keep to it, for as long as it lasted.

Tricia held Louisa's plate in the kitchen, pursed her lips, waiting.

'I mean it. That kid's porky enough. Doesn't have the Bright metabolism. Passed right over her.'

'Come on, Dad. Chill, would you?'

She could sense her mother shaking her head in the kitchen as Charlie stood up, thrust the scroll of his drawings at her. 'Get a clue, Louisa,' he said, as though she'd started the day drunk in a ditch or had announced she was pregnant, and went down to the den.

She stood up slowly and approached the dining table, where her mother placed the plate in front of her and opened the sliding doors, the gravelly sea, the beach voices rushing in. 'Mum.'

'We just need to let it blow over, all right?'

'He's gonna do it for days. Jack's already spazzing out on the front lawn.'

'Don'll snap him out of it.'

'What set him off?'

'Since when does he need a reason? But anyway, there was a thing on the news last night, you know, about Monica.'

'What, Mum? Have they . . . found her?'

'No, nothing like that. You know how hard he took it.'

'We barely knew her!' She began to shovel bacon in.

'Evidence of evil, you know.' She looked at the ceiling briefly.

'But he's been so happy. He doesn't have to work or do anything. I'd like to retire from school. I'd walk around with a smile on my face from dawn to dusk.'

'Lou, come on. Don't stir the pot. We'll just tread carefully for a day or two and he'll be back on form. Take an interest in his plans. That'll do the trick.'

'Mum.'

'Don will sort it out.' She giggled, leaned forward, laid a hand on Louisa's arm. 'He'll come up with something amazing and Charlie'll think it's all his idea.'

'You'll be saying next it was Don who made Dad's company so successful.'

Tricia withdrew her hand and watched Louisa eat for a moment, hands on her hips. 'Well, no, but he certainly helped smooth the way,' she said eventually, before retreating to the kitchen to wash up.

~

The brightness in her parents' bedroom made it difficult to see what was in the wardrobe. Striped laundry bags were piled high, not yet emptied from the move, clothes and ties and shoes spilling from them. There was a small blue velvet bag she wanted, the perfect size for her purse and lip gloss. She didn't like her chances of finding it but if she asked Tricia directly she'd have to get into why she wanted it. As she delved in the bags she thought of bringing Dean down here, to the house, when they were all out, but Charlie now had no routine, and Tricia had stepped off the suburban tennis circuit to think about tiles and taps. She could go the formal route, imagined introducing him formally to Charlie and Tricia. *Pleased to meet you, Mr and Mrs Bright.* Charlie would look him up and down and look away, then start the process of chipping him down to size until he fled the place, never to return. Part of her knew, too, that even if she did manage to clear the house for a couple of hours, something would change between them the second he stepped through the door, saw how life was for her now, how it was going to be.

In one of the shoe bags her hand closed around a soft, thin velvety strap. She tugged gently and it came loose, dragging some-thing hard, a necklace, that knocked against the wardrobe door. She caught it in her hand to silence it and shoved the tangle in the little bag.

An urge was rising in her, to go down to the den and have it out with Charlie, nicely, but still, to just sort this out. She had a knack of setting him straight. 'You and me, Dad,' she'd say. 'Let's figure out your plans. We'll drive around the beaches looking at houses we like and find out who designed them. Then we'll make something better than any of them!'

She would love that, actually, but if he took her up on it, he'd want to do it now. Today, not tomorrow. This minute, not this afternoon. And then she'd miss her bus and they came too rarely on a public holiday for her to squeeze her trip in before lunch if she waited for another. She retreated quietly from her parents' room with the bag and gathered her clothes from their neat folded piles in her drawer, an island of order in the chaos of this room she had to share with the grottiest kids on earth.

As she stood in the antique shower, making out a pattern in the chips of the tiles, Charlie's plans appeared to her again, arrows shooting off into nothing, little figures caught in the scribbled lines. You looked at them and could feel like Mum was right, that with a bit of down-to-earth thinking they could be tidied up, and amazing things would happen. That, or he was mad, and you'd all been walking around kidding yourselves for years.

She closed her eyes, water drumming on her eyelids, felt for a moment that she was standing on that staircase made of nothing, that moved in the breeze like paper.

~

The bus let her off outside the gates of her old school and she stepped carefully out into the heat. 'Don't do anything I wouldn't do,' the driver called after her.

'Thanks for the tip, wanker,' she said under her breath.

Across the sun-baked oval the glaring light bounced off three police vans parked in front of the bleachers, the crackle of their radio just audible as she walked along the tacky asphalt. There were no people among the vehicles, the only movement over there a fluttering stretch of tape catching the sun, disappearing into the bush track next to the stand. She stopped for a moment to wonder what news there was, why they were here again. If it were her missing they'd find her in Dean's shed, hiding from her parents. Perhaps that's where Monica was—in a squalid hideout, wondering how to face her mum and dad.

When she reached Dean's house and started up his path she caught a trace of an old feeling, that his house hid some shame. But she knew these people now, his mum, pretty in their old photos, with a flirty smile, a bit fat these days, tired, gentle, and the amazingly loud toddler cousin she'd taken in because of some chaos and mishap at home. Some dark night of shouting, Dean told her, a near accident with the baby and the bath. Lou had to pick her way carefully to the front door, Casey's faded plastic cars and action figures lying scattered on their backs across the lawn as though a miniature action movie had just been shot here.

Her hair had dried salty stiff and she had sweat under her arms. Maybe she could have another shower here, if his mum was out, but there was no lock on the door, and it wasn't the cleanest bathroom in the world—you would really need thongs to be able to relax, standing on those grotty tiles, the blackened grout. She knocked, setting off the dog in the yard. Who was living in her house now? She'd see it in a minute, from Dean's room. She looked at her watch and knocked again. A muffled thump came from inside the house and she leaned her head on the frosted glass, trying to see movement in the dim hallway. After another minute a shape loomed and shrank, the door opened and there he was, a thin boy, lurking indoors, reheated Chinese wafting out of the house.

He put his fingers through his hair. 'Lou? It was today?'

'You knew that.' She laughed. 'You were counting the days, right?'

'What time is it? Feels early. Come in.'

As she stepped inside, he flattened himself against the wall and she passed without touching him. He smelled of stale pot. There was a crackle in the air, as though he was about to tell her he'd had enough of her, or been with someone else. After a moment he turned back and kissed her on the cheek with dry lips. They went through to the kitchen, where the remains of last night's takeaway sat on the bench. 'You had Chinese on Christmas Day?'

He plunged his hands deep into his tracky pockets. That strangeness he had, that she'd liked, his thinness, his dull black hair, looked a bit . . . seedy.

'Mum was working.'

Out the open back door was the square lawn, the fibro-roofed shed, and beyond that her house. Its white paint was flaking. She'd never noticed that before. She didn't notice her house at all really when it was hers. She'd had hopes with their move for the sort of house you noticed every time you walked into it. Charlie's plans, though. They'd left something like a tender spot in a muscle she was trying not to put pressure on.

There was a small girl with orange hair at her window, with something in her arms—a kitten? A teddy?

'My room's kind of trashed.'

'It was always today, you know. I took two buses. I had to sneak out on Charlie.'

'It's cool, Lou. We can hang here. Or in the yard. I've got some Pepsi left from last night. Want some?'

She nodded, starving again, but the thought of eating anything here turned her stomach. She wondered whether he was going to touch her, but it was as though the moment had passed and could not now be returned to. 'Don't you want things to be nice?'

'Yeah, sorry. You have a drink.' He opened the fridge. 'I'll stack the dishes. Mum loses it when I leave it like this anyway. You've saved me a freak-out.'

'Don't bother.'

Dean stood in front of the fridge with the door open. It made a grinding sound and juddered into silence. He seemed to have lapsed into a trance.

'I mean, really, don't bother, if it's too much trouble. It only took me an hour to get here. I wouldn't want you to go out of your way.'

'Relax, would you? We don't all get the rockstar treatment. Mum's busy, you know?'

'I bet you didn't even remember about the phone.'

He folded his arms and let the fridge door close. There was a mean look on his face, his tongue pushing against his top lip.

'Don't worry about the drink.' She stepped back into the corridor, a hand in the air. 'Don't worry about anything.'

He followed her into the corridor. 'What is up with you?'

'I've got to get home anyway. There's a lunch for Charlie. People are coming. It's kind of a big deal.' She was going to have to get hot chips from the shops. She tried to suppress the irritation that built in her when she let herself get this hungry, to get things back on track. 'Gonna wear that dress you like.'

'Oh, fucking *Charlie*.'

She turned around. She could barely see him in the dark hallway after the bright kitchen, but still, the way he was looking at her, she felt as though she was peering into a dark cave. 'What is that supposed to mean?'

She felt him pause in the shadows, then his breath on her face, the smell of food and smoke as he spoke. 'Why doesn't he make you call him Dad?'

'He does, sometimes. I mean, I do. It's just, you know, he says I'm an adult, near enough. I can use his name.'

He spoke slowly: 'Creepy fucking Charlie.' There was a long static-filled pause. He reached down, encircled her wrist with his long fingers. 'Charlie wants to fuck you, Lou. That's what I reckon.'

Her body felt the words before they reached her brain. She shook off his hand, was out the door, running down the tiled steps, passing into the treacly heat, and then the words arrived properly, like a balloon smacking into her head filled with something nasty, thick.

'Lou!' he called.

She lifted her hand behind her as she ran, gave him the finger. If she were still in front of him she would smack him in the face. She had strong shoulders and hands, a swimmer's upper body.

'Lou, I'm sorry! Didn't mean to say that. It's not what I meant!'

She didn't stop running until she reached the bus stop at the strip of lame shops where she and Jack used to buy iced coffees when they were in primary school and think they were sophisticated. The life she was leaving behind in that terrible house: punching cones, cleaning up his dishes, reminding him to change his filthy clothes once in a while. I was doing you the biggest favour of your life, you fucking loser.

At the bus stop the bench was out in full sun and it was meltingly hot, so she balanced on a patch of kerb under a tree, longing for submersion in a cool blue pool. The street was dead, the only sound the swelling throb of cicadas, but then from a crappy passing car flew a pile of change, a coin bouncing off the tarmac and stinging her calf. She thought she heard her name. After the car had passed a dickhead she knew from school leaned out of the back window and shouted, 'Give you twenty cents for it!'

The bus arrived a minute later and she recognised the smart-arse driver who'd dropped her off. He raised an eyebrow, but took a look at her face and kept his thoughts to himself.

~

She walked down her driveway into the shade, sweat between her shoulders. The key she pulled out on a string from inside her shirt was damp. She imagined for a moment as she opened the front door that she was stepping into the house as it could be—wide cool tiled corridors, seamless windows onto a huge terrace, a pool that bled into the horizon.

The hallway was smoky and the house was loud with daggy music—Mum's easy jazz, she had a little sway she put on to it while she served drinks—and voices; Charlie and a young woman laughing. Don's girlfriend? A model apparently. Louisa paused in the corridor as the girl shouted, 'Don told me you were *crazy*, Charlie!' Pure bogan, she could tell from here. She should introduce her to Dean.

Louisa slipped across the corridor into the bedroom to change, a hot wind stirring through the open window. Was Jack out there already, checking out Don's girl? She wanted to rate her and then get Jack somewhere on his own to evaluate in detail. She was ruthless in these interrogations, because to analyse boys' preferences she needed data: is it about the boobs, the clothes, the walk, the hair? What is the relative weight of these things? Like, do big boobs cancel out the need to blow-dry your hair? Do eyes even figure?

In the wardrobe her Japanese silk dress hung, a luscious shimmering blue, a swathe of ocean glinting from the dark, chosen by Charlie to match her eyes. When she wore it they were startling; it was like pulling on a magical cloak. But—it would be stooping. She kept on her denim cut-offs and changed out of her little top into a Smashing Pumpkins T-shirt that came down to her thighs, messed up her hair. In the mirror she saw the look in her eye. Try me, it said.

She moved down the corridor towards the smoke and music and sound of the laughing girl. Tricia was hunched over the chip pan, her head obscured amid a greasy cloud. Although the fan above the stove clattered manically, the smell of hot oil was so strong that Louisa had a vision of the house exploding, black smoke billowing from its red core on the cliff and out over the beach.

At the table the girl's tanned back glistened beneath her thick drape of toffee-coloured hair. Louisa stared for a moment at the girl stroking it slowly. Don and Charlie were tucked in close on either side, poor old Don melting in rolled-up shirtsleeves, Charlie in his faded orange running shorts and a tatty grey T-shirt. Imagine if she was standing here like a loon in that stupid dress. She would have died. Charlie said something that Louisa couldn't make out over the exhaust fan, leaning towards the girlfriend, and she threw her head back way further than necessary to laugh, her hair reaching down to her buttocks.

As Louisa moved towards the kitchen she checked Charlie out. He seemed better now, his skin plump, eyes bright. Perhaps he'd had a nap, or a swim. Jack, sitting opposite the adults, seemed puzzled and slightly alarmed. He glanced at her helplessly and then turned back towards Don's girl, to whatever the spectacle looked like from that side of the table. The whine of an American tween from the television drifted up the stairs from the den, followed by Phoebe's unselfconscious echo, eerily perfect. No one paid any attention to Louisa as she joined her mother behind the kitchen counter. She could cartwheel her way across the room, like Phoebe would, and it would make no difference.

Tricia lifted the French fries out of the chip pan, trickles of sweat seeping from her tied-up hair. 'What's the model like?'

Louisa asked, in no danger of being heard over the fan and the music. Tricia glanced over her shoulder towards the table. Louisa looked too, seeing the girl almost front on from this angle. The shape of her—the plumpness of her lips, her cheeks, of every-thing except her tiny waist and long limbs—was a lot to take in. There was something about the way she was stroking her hair that made her look like she was going to fuck herself—right there on the dining table. That kind of model, then. Don must be a bit more amazing under that Kelly Country suit than you'd give him credit for.

Tricia said in a reedy voice, 'I'm stunned no one followed her in off the street,' and began to pile chips high on all the plates but one.

'You have some too, Mum. It's not as though he'll notice.'

Tricia gave her a look, mouth small, and handed her two plates, one overflowing with chips, a massive bloody steak seeping pink into them. She reached forward and wiped the other with a tea towel, handing Lou the larger one. 'This is for Mariah Carey over there. The other one's for Don.'

Phoebe appeared for her burger and carried it very slowly past the girl on her way back to the den, almost walking backwards by the time she reached the stairs. Lou had to push her way inside the girl's bubble of perfume and hairspray to deposit her plate in front of her. She turned her smile on the girl and sat down opposite her, examining her slightly flattened nose, her newsreader makeup. The girl gave her an unfriendly once-over before diverting her dis-approval to the enormous plate of food Louisa had pushed under her rack. Charlie stopped talking—he was bragging about his last big land deal in the city before he'd sold up—to look at the girl looking at the food. The air at the door moved but did nothing to cool the room.

They ate reluctantly, except for Louisa, shovelling away, in the incredible heat. No one spoke for a while over the music. This close to Jack, she could hear the difficulty he seemed to have with breathing. Phoebe's TV show blared from downstairs; the occasional shout from the beach drifted inside with the sounds of the sea. Louisa watched their rate of drinking, the adults emptying their glasses quickly in the heat. There was a glass in front of her and she took a large swig, no one noticing. Real French champagne. She took another, felt the warmth of the room, the awkwardness of the adults fizz together in an amusing bubble.

Finally Don registered her presence. He wore a mournful look on the best of days, with his navy suits in summer and his strands of hair combed carefully forwards, but right now, melting in the heat next to a girl way out of his league, he looked like death would be a relief. 'How's the training going, Lou-Lou?'

'Loving the pool, Don. Getting stronger every day.'

Don peered around his girlfriend's head at Charlie. 'This girl's going to the Olympics, no question.'

Charlie pointed his steak knife in the air and gave Lou a meaningful look. 'I'm not seeing the focus required, personally. Too easily distracted.'

Lou looked at her mother open-mouthed. Tricia raised her eyebrows and absented herself, staring out at the haze above the beach and sea.

'What is that supposed to mean?'

He had returned to sawing away at his steak, ignoring her. Still sulking about your stupid plans, are we, Charlie? She imagined picking up her side of the table and tipping the food all over him, him and that girl next to him.

'Charlie's going to take us all spear fishing!' the girl said, and giggled as though it was cute to laugh at nothing, and not totally moronic.

Tricia, plate barely touched, lit a cigarette and looked unimpressed by this proposal. Louisa recalled her at the sink last weekend, in her bra, bony arms and back tensed around the fish she was gutting with a huge curved knife that looked like a medieval weapon, her fury clearly emitted to all but Charlie.

He put his cutlery down and appeared to reanimate. 'Let's go for a swim right now! Bit of practice. It's hot as Hades in here.' He turned to the girl. 'You'd be a swimmer.'

'No danger of sinking with those inflatables,' Louisa murmured in Jack's ear.

'I need lessons!' the girl said. 'I can't do the proper breathing— I just have no lung capacity at all.'

Fantastic, Louisa thought, and pinched Jack's thigh under the table. His leg twitched, the table jumping with him, and she punched him in the arm. He dropped his fork with a clatter onto his plate. The girl looked at them as though they were a boring TV show. Nothing, just noise.

'Kids,' Tricia said, blowing out smoke, clearly done with fetching and carrying, or just unwilling to lift a finger for Don's girlfriend. 'Clear the table, please, would you?'

Jack and Louisa, and Don too, stood at once and began to heap cutlery onto plates amid Tricia's smoke. Lou was having trouble not laughing, though beneath the thin layer of fizzy weirdness was a grey exhaustion. If it were cooler she would sleep for days.

At the sink Don and Jack seemed fixed on making as much noise as possible, banging the crockery on the bench, opening and slamming cupboards to find the washing-up liquid. Don turned on the taps full bore and scraped the plates violently. 'Awesome about your training, Lou,' he said. 'Sounds like moving down here was just the thing. And when you're covered in medals I'll brag I knew you when you were just a nipper.'

She leaned on the bench to watch the ones at the table, her parents and the blow-up thingy. Charlie laid his hand on the girl's arm. 'You know they found her,' he boomed over the noise of Don throwing the dishes about.

'Volume, Charlie,' Jack said quietly, wiping a plate dry.

'Who?' Don's girl's bloody chips sat on her plate, completely ignored. They had left them in front of her, as though to tell her to eat up. Lou would give anything for Tricia to say to her, as she would to any of them, They'll be there for breakfast, love. Better to get it over with now.

'Monica. You know that sweet girl? She was our neighbour.'

'Oh!' The girlfriend sat forward. 'Did they? Was she . . . alive?'

'Well, it's not actually her yet. It's her bag, in the bush, right next to the kids' old school. She'll turn up soon,' he said with an air of weary knowledge, 'one way or another.'

Tricia stood from her chair and took her cigarettes and lighter out onto the deck. Don sloshed cutlery about vigorously, but Jack, standing at the drainer, was motionless, listening.

'Oh my God! She was only a few years younger than me. It could happen to anyone.'

Charlie held the edge of the table. 'I know. Can you believe it? This bloke's allowed to just walk the streets jumping young girls.

Police sitting around on their arses while we wait for it to happen again.'

'They found her bag?' Louisa whispered to Jack. He nodded thoughtfully, watching Charlie.

Those police cars, up at the school, that was what they were doing there. Last term, when she and the others smoked in the bush after school, or went off into the trees to kiss some boy against a flaky gum tree that shed all over your uniform, Monica's bag had been lying there in the leaves. She was a nice girl: true, somehow, amid the sarcasm and casual cruelty of school. Disarmed you with her clear sincerity when she said hello. Maybe it was something to do with her family background. Her father had fled his home, that was the word used, not long before Monica was born, but Lou barely knew from what, beyond the pictures she saw on the news of men with beards. Whatever the story was with her family, there was no cynicism, no teenage performance to Monica, and it made her stand out. She really dug Jack, that was clear. Was she there, still, among the trees?

Louisa felt the champagne and the heat of the room and the prickly atmosphere all at once, an airlessness.

Deep thuds rose from under the floor. Phoebe ran from the stairs into the kitchen and threw her arms around Don's legs. He lifted his foamy hands from the water and hesitated, smiling down at her dark head.

She finagled chocolates out of him and ran off down the stairs with the box, Jack following, leaving Lou stranded with the adults. Charlie and Don's girl were murmuring to one another, heads close. Then he stood up, spoke at full volume. 'Come on, I'll show you. What's the matter? Don't want to get wet?' He was leaning

47

over her, pulling at her hand. She pretended to resist but then they were teetering across the carpet, her painted nails in her heeled sandals looking like they might bleed on it, and out the front door, laughing up the driveway.

Don stood at the sink, shoulders hunched over the dishes, frozen. She couldn't bear to be left alone with him, the false cheer he would quickly resume if she stayed in the room. Tricia was at the top of the outdoor stairs, lighting another cigarette and blinking into the haze. Louisa joined her in the incredible still heat. Beneath them the dense strip of umbrellas and towels and people stretched down the deep beach to the water. She couldn't help but check repeatedly the point where the sand met the track, and sure enough after a few minutes out they stumbled, the girl moving awkwardly in her ridiculous dress, Charlie pulling her after him. They seemed to step right over people, lurching onwards. From this distance it was as though Louisa could see him more clearly, as others might.

'He's not normal.'

'Thanks for the update.'

'Why do you let him do this shit?'

Tricia looked out at the sea rather than down at the beach. 'We can't complain, can we? This is your father. When it's good, it's great.' After a moment she returned her gaze to the hilarious lurching couple and they both watched them track messily across the sand.

'That's the deal, is it? He gets an idea into his head and off he goes and that's all fine.'

'Do you want one of those dads that potters around in his shed till he dies? Just let this blow over and enjoy the good stuff.'

'He needs to *shut up* about Monica. What's wrong with him?'

'Oh God, Louisa. Don't. Don'll take Chicky Babe home eventually, your dad can go for a run or something, and we can all get on with our lives in peace.'

'You know what? It's you that makes me mad. Running round after him. Letting him do whatever he wants. *Pretending*, all the time.' The words flowed out easily, as though they'd been waiting there, leaving her free to watch her mother's reaction. 'He makes things happen at least, big things. You just scurry around like a slave, waiting for the next little present.' Tricia watched her daughter's mouth as the words gushed out, her own tightly closed. For about half a second Louisa felt the sweet drunken pleasure of having spoken without restraint.

'If you knew the lengths I go to to make sure everyone has a quiet life.' She was aiming for an exasperated kind of sarcasm but her voice was cracking. 'Thank you very much, dear.'

Oh, spare me, Louisa thought, yanking back the door to go inside.

~

Through the square of her viewfinder Phoebe saw bits of bodies and clothes, the brown-painted timber posts of the outside stairs, slivers of ocean and crumbly orange headland. The focus settled and she saw a finger in a pocket, the finger of a man's big hand, coated in black hair, pushing its way into the pocket of a woman's dress, her mother's floral dress, covered in huge flowers with frightening stalky centres.

Don's finger was rubbing her mother's leg inside her pocket. His hand disappeared into the fabric, up to the wrist.

They were standing on the deck, beyond the screen doors, Phoebe crouching on the stairs down to the den. She bumped her bum up a step so that her head lifted higher above the lounge room carpet. Down in the den Lou and Jack were watching the end of *Jurassic Park* for the millionth time. She could see Lou's hand hovering above Jack's arm ready to make him jump in the scary scene where the velociraptors chase the kids around the kitchen.

When Phoebe lowered her camera and looked at her mum and Don directly, she couldn't see what his hand was doing. They had turned back into what she always saw, just grownups, talking about their grownup stuff. They stood very close to one another on the platform against the white sky. She lifted her camera and found the connecting point again, the area where they touched. There was no movement now but the hand was still in up to its hairy wrist. Mum's smoke drifted across the viewfinder and then evaporated.

She looked a little longer, to be sure. Someone would say, if she told them: Did you *really* see that? And she would be able to say: Yes, I really did. And then she realised she was being dumb—she could get evidence—and pressed the button. The click and whirr seemed loud but at least now she could prove it. No one ever believed anything she said.

Her mum turned to face Don and Phoebe ducked her head, slipping down the stairs, still on her bum. She ran in front of the TV and waited for Jack and Lou to pay attention. Behind her, on the screen, the ginger kid was slamming a huge steel door on a dinosaur's head.

'I can smell your feet, Jack.'

'What are you doing?' he said. 'We're watching this.'

Louisa reached across him for the remote. They were doing everything slowly, as though the heat was making them stupid. She looked at their faces. Sometimes it was like she didn't know them at all. They looked the same as usual, their faces matched their real selves, but they might be cyborgs, plotting things together, sending messages between themselves. She pointed her camera at them in front of her chest as though she could control them with it.

Lou pointed the remote back at her and pressed the buttons, zapping her into oblivion. Phoebe saw that rubbing again, that she had seen through the viewfinder, the hand disappearing. She didn't know how to say it, or what the picture she had taken would show. It was shaming, even to have seen it, even more to have Mum and Don's body parts nestled inside her camera.

'Mum's a skank!'

Jack snorted and covered his mouth.

'Feeb!' Lou said.

'You say way worse things. You're always saying fucking this and fucking that. I'm only telling the truth.'

'What happened?' Jack said. She looked at his messy hair, his pale eyes and she didn't know him, he couldn't help. Plus, if you got him too worked up he'd just faint.

'They're getting a fucking divorce.' Before this moment she had never said that word and now she'd said it three times. It was a lovely word to let yourself say, that little cracking k at the back of your throat.

'Keep your voice down. And don't be an idiot,' Lou said, but she was looking at Jack while she said it. As usual they snatched whatever she brought to the conversation and kept it between them, like a ball you took into the playground at school and then never got to touch again.

'Is she all right?' Jack said quietly. 'What's going on up there?'

'Don loves her.'

Louisa rolled her eyes. 'Big deal.'

'I don't think he does, Feeb,' Jack said. He was being kind but he talked to her as though she was still a little kid.

'He so does,' Lou said.

Phoebe heard a rushing inside her head. 'I'm telling my dad about this.'

'Oh, what are you going to tell *your* dad?' Lou said. She stretched her arms backwards along the back of the settee, as though she'd never in her life been so bored. It was enraging.

'I don't want to see your horrible armpits all the time!' Phoebe turned away from them, banged open the screen door and dodged between the bindis in her bare feet to the dusty path between the lawn and the cliff. Her camera dangled from her wrist, banging her hip as she ran. Above her on the deck, she knew, was her mum with Don, but she wouldn't look at them. She saw everything now. She had thought he was so handsome, with his dark hair and his suits. He had only ever been nice to her to show off to Mum.

The air was thick and hot and slowed her down. Music came from the houses, shushed by the sea, and barbecue smoke hung in the air. Her eyes stung. She would take her camera to the rockpool and get pictures of jellyfish for her project. Dad was going to build an amazing house, with her own room again, and he'd promised she could have her pictures made into huge posters for every wall. She wanted jellyfish everywhere: the little clear round ones you chucked at each other when they got left behind by the tide, beautiful bluebottles with their stingers trailing, and those monsters you sometimes saw off the boat, with massive rubbery bodies, huge clusters of trailing tentacles that made your breath stop to look at them. Still, if you could touch them, you would, just to feel, and see what it was like. She'd like to throw herself into a wading pool filled with them, to squeeze and pop them by rolling around hard on their bodies. She had jumped on a bluebottle on a trip to the South Coast when she was seven. It was dead, one of hundreds lining the beach. How could anything dead hurt you? She still remembered the feeling, like someone was pressing a blade against her foot and moving it, just enough to maintain the pain. Jack held her still while Lou chucked stinky vinegar over her foot. She had carried a tender red whip mark across her heel and ankle for days afterwards, but when the pain was gone it was gone, and she loved the bright blue creatures as much as ever. When she saw a long blue stinger half-buried in the orange sand, her admiration was tinged with awe at the damage stored up in those delicate tendrils.

She reached the path down to the beach. Up higher was the section that met her street further along, snaking up through the shade of twisting trees with hanging vines and spiky palms. There was a smell of things growing in the dark, rotten and sweet. She stopped for a moment to breathe it in, this dense patch she called the jungle, that felt so different to everything around it. Then she clambered downwards in the glaring haze, bristly grass turning to hot sand.

She walked quickly down to the edge of the surf to cool her feet and made her way among the couples, Jack and Lou's age, showing off in their bathers, walking hand in hand through the wash like something off *Home and Away*, checking with secret glances to make sure that everyone was looking at them. The little kids were digging holes where the water would run in, climbing inside as they grew deep enough. Last summer she would have pestered Jack and Lou to bury her. She was too big now for that stuff—she was out surfing with them yesterday on their new boards—but for a moment she imagined that feeling of being in up to her neck, the wet cold sand clamped around her shoulders and thighs, giggling till it cracked around her chest.

It was crazy with people at the pool but the concrete bench alongside it was covered by the shade of the cliff. The warm air still billowed even in the shade but it was lovely to be protected from the flame of the sun, to feel the coolness of the wet concrete under your thighs. She pressed her legs down into the feeling, willing it to spread through her. In a minute she'd head back out into the glare and explore the rock shelf for stranded jellyfish and pipis, but for now she sat in the shade and looked through her view-finder, watching kids on the far edge of the pool holding on to the swinging chain railing as white waves crashed over their heads. Mum had told her never to do that in case she got swept away, but she and Jack and Lou had stood out there beyond the pool the first day they were here, she in the middle, their hands over hers on the chain, the waves crashing over them, while Mum and Dad were back at the house unpacking boxes. She had held her screams in, let them race around her body like the wave was inside her.

Oh, there was Dad! Sitting on the far side of the pool with his legs in the water, right where the waves were hitting. *Dad, Dad, Dad*, she thought. She began to raise her arm but he was turned away towards that Bree who came to lunch with Don. He was standing up, yanking on her arm, and she was getting to her feet, but pulling back away from him, laughing. Phoebe grappled for her camera clumsily, held it up and pointed it, hoping for a space to remain clear through the jumble of smooth brown arms, jiggly white thighs, bright floaty rings. She pointed and clicked, the view-finder telling her nothing in the dazzling light.

Dad had hold of her now, scooping her up like an enormous baby, swinging her back, throwing her in. Click click click. Then she disappeared and a fountain of water shot into the sky above the beach as though a whale was in the pool among the kids on Li-Los and old ladies in swimming caps.

Phoebe lowered her camera to look at her dad. He was diving in after the girl, doing one of those sideways, show-off dives that big boys did, but Bree was already heaving herself out of the pool. There were grown-up women around her, sensible swimmers in caps and goggles, staring at her in her wet dress. You could see her little red undies and the exact shape of her: massive boobs and butt and tiny waist, like a girl in a music clip.

They were walking away now, down the concrete path towards the surf club, Dad pulling her along while she tried to smooth her tight wet dress down over her legs. You could still see her bra and undies from here though. People turned as they walked by as though the girl was a big horseshoe magnet and they were paperclips.

Phoebe too felt the pull of them, the urge to run after them and jump in front of her dad, to surprise him and get scooped up, tickled, kissed roughly, his stubble scratching, but she was pinned to the cold stone step, heat rising in her face. Sometimes, if you picked the wrong moment, he said something mean. Getting too old for puppy fat, hey? Time to start you swimming like your sister. It would be like that now, while his attention was on that person.

What was all this? Was there a swap happening? Was this woman, this girl who was fat in embarrassing places, going to be her mum? Could Phoebe then try on her dresses and lipstick? Only secretly, because she could tell already that this Bree girl would only love Dad and would never think she was a classic or a little legend. Her big swivelly eyes would slide right over her, like she didn't even exist.

AFTERWARDS

Jack, in adulthood, had come to love this: the quiet when others were asleep, the early golden light and the shifting shadows of trees brushing across the wall of his hut. Not all the fear of childhood waking had gone, but he had learned where he was in a way he never managed then, and could hold the knowledge while he slept. Waking up was no longer like the trauma of being born every day. There was just a brief spill now, a momentary tilt before righting himself on the plane, opening his eyes and letting himself fill with the anticipation of the people he loved stirring and filling the house, the quiet and peace before they did.

If the people he loved were not with him then he worked out, as slowly as he could make himself, when he was going to see them again, what they would be doing now, thought through some method for filling the days or hours.

This morning there was no need. From the springy couch where he lay he saw through the bedroom door his daughter's hand clutching the sheet and her dark blonde hair, a fat swirl like a hazelnut on the pillow. He would wake her soon—not yet—and they would walk out into the cool autumn morning and down through the forest of angophora, cabbage palms and glistening dewy sandstone to her school in the village.

Then some small piece of knowledge arrived, not fully, a dark hole opening up at the edge of his vision and closing again. He put it aside, not knowing if it was anything other than the fear that had tailed him all his life, hiding sometimes for so long he forgot it was there.

He felt the urge to get up now from the exhausted couch and touch each of Indi's fingers, draw the line of her cheeks with the trail of his thumb to absorb her realness and solidity, to settle himself and store up the feeling of his shed in the morning with Indi in it. He couldn't bring himself to break this moment though, the heat finding a funnel through the trees onto the tin roof, the kooka-burras unleashing that sly laughter, his girl asleep in the bedroom, resting her body and brain, gathering her strength, humour and energy before flinging herself headlong into her day.

~

He did everything right, carefully. No to Coco Pops. Yes to a berry smoothie. He packed brown bread sandwiches into Indi's scrubbed lunch box at the short clean bench. As they stepped down the creaking sloped stairs of his shed he squinted into the slanting light between the palms. Time to spare.

On the steep driveway she gave him a flicker of a smile, lifted her forefinger and said, 'Watch this, Dad.' She kneeled on the tarmac, facing down the hill, and leaned back slowly onto her chunky backpack. She was hinged flat, almost parallel to the slope. 'Guess what I am.'

'A nut job?'

'A paperclip.'

'Of course.'

Then she stood up and faced him, shoulders quivering for a moment, creasing and straightening, ready for business. He held her hand as they took exaggeratedly careful steps down the steep drive to the shaded road.

She found the world and herself hilarious. Thank Christ for that, given the alternatives. Her anarchic streak came in a diagonal line from Phoebe, minus the bottomless craving for attention. Indi's mother's family communicated in pissed-off stares and car-door slamming. The genetics were strong in that regard, at least until they got to Indi, fingers crossed.

'So I've been working on ears?' she said. 'I was going too pointy and it was all a bit Pokémon.'

'Right.'

'So I'm doing just a *tiny* curve, at the top, like a mini wave.'

'Is that working?'

She smiled, her freckles sunlit, and blinked slowly. 'It so is.' She held up her finger and made tiny waved points across her sightline.

'I can't draw animals at all. Or people.'

'I know. It's all the bottom of cars and weird empty bedrooms.' He held his breath for a moment. 'I don't mind. They're cool.'

'Thanks, Indi.'

'Mum *hates* your pictures. She says they make her skin crawl.'

Georgie said it was like you could hear one of those old-fashioned camera flashes going off as you looked at them, like they were a crime scene. There was always something missing; it was what had happened here.

'It's true.'

Then he knew what it was, that dark spot, just out of sight. It was last night at Lou's place that the new piece of knowledge had lodged inside him like a flinty stone.

A steady painful tugging nagged as they clambered down through the reserve, rocks shining, the sea and the breeze in the trees rushing. They tumbled down towards the school, children's voices audible through the bush. The next few minutes held inside them the bell, the disappearing of her back and legs and hair into the short throng in green gingham and grey shorts. The stretching out of the silent week; still, quiet hours painting out the strangeness, coffees with Lou and Phoebe and Tricia, their homes tent pegs securing the shelter of this suburb.

They reached the shady road of houses on double, triple blocks with plantation shutters and summer houses screened by grevillea, those lush endless lawns he mowed. Indi stopped and waited for him to look at her, grinned slyly. 'Surf check?'

'Oh God, I don't know.'

'You so want to.'

'I do and I don't. It'll be just perfect and then you'll have to go to school and I'll have to get to work and we would have been better off not knowing. Right now, we could just go off into our lives believing it's flat as a tack out there. Shhh. Listen. I can't hear anything. Can you?'

'I can hear the surf.'

'That's traffic.'

She tugged at his hand. 'Quick sticks.'

'Double maths is going to be torture, and it's your own doing.'

At the headland carpark they turned briefly towards the blond units behind them, looking for Phoebe. Her place was two floors up at the front; she liked a good spot for a surf check too. *Surfer* check. No sign of her this morning. Sleeping it off, perhaps. They stood side by side and looked out over Avalon: black figures on the frothy-edged swell trying their luck at the north end, a couple of runners, a boot camp class in front of the concrete block of the new surf club.

'Mmm,' Indi said. 'You were right.'

The movement of the glassy waves induced in Jack that tugging. The sea slowed as he watched it, ultramarine lava, fire in it though it was cool and blue. A thick slow movement, surfers' boards wedged beneath the spilling crest. He allowed himself to be absorbed in this vision, for it to be all there was for now.

He felt her fingers in his pocket. 'Dad?'

He dragged himself into the next moment, looked down at her with what he could manage of a smile.

'It's first bell.'

'Bugger.'

He took her hand, led her quickly down the hill to the crossing, Avalon Parade stretching ahead of them past the shops and on into the bush and hills. A boy in a green polo shirt whizzed past on his bike, shoulder-length hair streaming behind him. Jack once. All speed and purpose on the outside, internals a clanking mess. Though this boy might be proper boy all the way through, of course.

As they passed the glary forecourt of the servo he couldn't quite come out of his dream. The smell of coffee drifted in bursts from the corner café across the road where men older than him with short silver hair and skinny pants nursed toddlers and laptop bags. As they passed the lane down the side of Woolies a girl laughed, standing with a couple of checkout kids smoking in the shadow of the skip.

'What you doing after you drop me?' Indi said as he tried to steer her across the mad intersection, a black hole of traffic rules.

'Painting maybe? Bit of work.'

'What are you going to paint?'

'You know. Cars. Weird bedrooms. Saw an ugly garage the other day I might have a crack at.'

'Maybe you could try a kitten.'

He laughed and squeezed her hot hand.

They were the only ones walking towards school now. The traffic was all the other way, mums with their smaller children or empty-handed, light-footed and almost smiling. Free, unloaded of their burden. He made himself take in the clammy reality of Indigo's fingers, curved around his own.

They turned the corner into the steep lane that ran alongside the school and slipped between the parked four-wheelers climbing up into the bush. The school was quiet as they approached but for a loudspeaker in the playground. It was assembly. Good, Indi could sneak in among her class on the tarmac without having to get a late pass from the office. No record. Home and hosed.

Except there was Georgie, half in the shadows, stiff and yet brimming somehow, volcanic. Oh God, he thought, his feelings charged as always with a shot of wanting, for her, the exact shape

62

of her in the dappled light, furious or not. The perfect shape and sound and movement of a person. Although, . . . her head looked strange, small.

She kept her eye on him as she bent from the waist to kiss Indi on the top of her head, patted her on the backpack. Pointed through the gate. Go. Indi's face reached up towards Jack out of the cool shadows, her freckled cheeks cresting into the light. He breathed her in as he kissed her. Weetbix and dirt, a secretive dot of pink lip gloss sticking to her buckteeth.

She rounded the corner out of sight and the shadowed passage past the classroom became like one of his paintings: empty, something missing.

When he straightened to look at Georgie, a mingling of excitement and dread in his gut, he could see now what was wrong with her head. It was an odd shape: hard and small, raked. She'd had those braids put in, like a kid back from Bali. The cornrows of a girl on *Sesame Street*. She was still leaning forwards. She put her face close to his and said quietly, 'What. The fuck.'

A glam mum towering over them, all blonde and interestingly textured fabrics, something in fashion or PR, smiled apologetically as she squeezed between them out of the gate.

'It's assembly,' Jack said. 'She's good.'

'Why would you push it? This is thin ice you're on.'

He watched her face crease and uncrease and felt in spite of everything a couple of seconds away from her laughter. It was just the other side of a membrane he used to dissolve with the touch of a magic finger. 'She wanted to do a surf check. We had a bit of time.'

'Except you didn't, did you? Next sleepover's off.'

'George, come on. It's not a "sleepover".'

'Be realistic.'

'I am!'

'I can't believe we have to discuss this.' Her face, magnetic to him. Old with worry but young, Indi's gorgeous goofy teeth. If either of them ever tried to get braces he would lay himself down in front of the dentist's door and refuse to budge.

She lifted a hand in the air and walked up the hill, away from him. Her legs were strong and brown, her walk graceful. The beads in her silly hair rattled. He wanted to reach into his chest and settle his beating heart with a firm squeeze.

~

Jack stood outside Lou's tall gate for a moment, unseen from the house, catching his breath after the walk along the ridge of soft sand and up the track to her street. When he closed his eyes he held an image: small waves breaking in a line like an underground detonation, a seamed explosion repeating itself. He was sweating, ready for a swim, but calmer for the walk. Still, that phrase, 'Be realistic', bothered him like a mosquito bite somewhere hard to reach. And something else, a disturbance beneath the skin, a nervousness about seeing his sister.

When his breath had settled he fed his hand through the gate to lift the latch, passing into Lou's world of lush serenity. The driveway was a continuation of the thick bright lawn with its underground sprinkler system; he followed it past Lou's car and the deep verandah lined with comfy daybeds, through to the backyard and its perfect rectangle of turquoise, glinting pacifically under a row of palm trees.

'Lou?' he called as he opened the back door off the deck. She was here—he'd just walked past her Volvo—he didn't want to startle her though, by being in the house before she'd had a chance to register his presence.

The kitchen and the living room were empty, the acres of marble benchtop entirely clear, the oak floor in the living area glistening in small patches that disappeared as he watched. Space and calm, plenty and comfort. Framed photos of Lou, Magnus and Aart, and Indi too, with Jack. A couple of his paintings in a gap between the fridge and the doorway: storm clouds, waves—the less 'dark' ones. In the living area immense low grey sofas, baskets of colourful cushions, shelves of cookery books, interiors magazines, board games.

Every now and then the people from one of those magazines came to photograph the house and Lou put the board games away. When film companies came to make ads for breakfast cereal she took them out again. Indi made him have the TV on for hours up at Tricia's place, in case one came on. Every now and then she'd get lucky, glimpse a picture of her cousin on a wall and squeal.

Lou emerged, a glimmer of blonde hair and pale clothes in the dark corridor and that hesitation about seeing her made the air solid. She stopped in the doorway and a knowledge passed between them from opposite ends of the galley kitchen. He pushed through it, that feeling, and they moved towards each other, smiling.

Last night, when he'd been round here with Indi, they'd sat on the tattier sofas in the den, the television news on quietly. They often gravitated like this to some quiet corner of the house or garden, away from the splashes and chaos of Indi and Lou's teenage son

Magnus, leaving Aart to his bright screens of flickering numbers, every hour a new market coming online, always something to keep an eye on. Tonight he was cooking, something fragrant, Asian. He'd spent his childhood in Indonesia and made incredible food whenever he had time.

Jack hadn't been able to make out anything on the news except for the odd familiar word over the calls of their children and others, on trampolines and skateboards, drifting in through the open doors at the back deck. The Prime Minister was biting into a raw onion. Lou laughed, a quick, dirty chuckle he never heard in anyone's company but his. Aart came in with two bowls smelling of ginger and lemongrass. He smiled absently at Jack. 'Indi is eating it. She has decided to be crazy brave, she says.'

'Fucking yum,' Lou said after he'd gone. Then a man's face appeared on the screen and there was a knowledge in the room, a quickening of attention, although neither said anything. Jack made himself take a mouthful of noodles, barely registering the flavours and textures of Aart's famed cooking.

A startled mugshot, wild hair, red eyes, filled Lou's flat screen TV. The sort of man you'd learn had locked girls in his basement or picked off hitchhikers on the highway for years. Something was already holding them still and ready—the name of their old suburb, perhaps; and then her name, after all this time—Monica Kazmi. The pictures moved on, a man, the same man presumably, in baggy high-waisted jeans with a grey blanket over his head outside a police station, being extracted gently from a van by fit, efficient police officers, their backs to the camera.

Jack carried on eating. He felt the heat of Lou's arm rising and falling next to him but continued to look at the screen as gargantuan diggers tipped back and forth across a red landscape, cut into terraces as though a human colony were being built on Mars.

They had got through their meal, watched a movie with Aart and the kids, Indi chloriny and gorgeously warm in a towel in his lap, and kissed goodnight, nothing said. But it was there now in that look, in the kitchen, and even as it passed there was a strange ghost of the man's wild-eyed stare in Lou's features, though her hair was sleek and dried, her skin lightly tanned and plump with good health and plenty of rest.

There had been nights when no one in the family had slept but they were long ago. Even now, with Indi only parcelled out in hours and minutes, he mowed lawns and surfed and walked until his body could do nothing but sleep when darkness came.

'What's up?' she said, smiling, laying a hand on his arm on her way to the coffee machine. 'Indi get off all right?'

'Yes. No. Define "all right".'

~

Early this morning, the sky still pinkish above the roof line of the shopping strip, Lou had parked in front of her shopfront and leaned back in her seat for a moment, looked at the sign: *Louisa Bright Real Estate*. A lovely clean white font against the colour of a tropical sea. That's my girl, said Charlie's voice in her head. But then she might hear him say, on a day when she was tired, felt her famous nerve wobble: This is what you made of yourself with all your brains? A suburban real estate agent?

She unlocked the door and passed into the office, nothing like the other real estate agents dotting the shopping strip. The long room was filled with chunky trestle tables and colourful chairs. She'd wanted it to feel like a hip café, hip but friendly. Later on the tables would be scattered with smart young people gazing into the screens of silver laptops. Their clothes would not exactly match but there was a colour theme, the palette of the peninsula she called it in their contracts. She hadn't thought to take that section out of Jack's paperwork for doing the lawns. She knew when he'd reached it. He looked at her, deadpan, until she said, 'Yes, okay, Jack. That doesn't apply to you, obviously.' He'd given a tiny shake of his head and carried on reading.

Her office at the back was fully visible through a glass wall. She took a folder off her desk and headed back to the car. She fumbled her keys as she retrieved them from her bag and they fell with plenty of time for her to watch their progress towards the grille of a drain next to her car door. They sat there, hooked on a thread of iron, and she retrieved them slowly, watching her hand with its faint tremor. Are you right to drive, Louisa Bright? Of course she was, it was Avalon on a Monday morning. Who was going to stop her?

She retrieved her bag from the passenger seat and left the car where it was. Give herself another half an hour. The café was only a couple of minutes' walk, and there was a lovely autumn chill at this hour. You could arrive cool even after a walk in heels. Arrivals were important, Charlie had taught her that: they'll decide about you as soon as they lay eyes on you. Whenever she arrived at an open house, still, there was a tiny electric spark as she climbed down from her gleaming car and gave her hair a shake, walked towards the client with her hand outstretched.

The café was a daggy old diner, well away from the beach. How did these joints survive with all the artisanal coffee places sprouting like mushrooms up and down the strip? Louisa had never even set foot in it before. It was next door to one of her rivals and she lingered in front of their boards for a moment, sensing movement inside, counting to twenty before she moved on.

The café was empty. It had a bit of retro Italian charm: Formica tables, padded chairs, a serious-looking coffee machine. A bit of spit and polish and the place would shine right up. She ordered her coffee, sat down facing the door and spread her materials in front of her. Phoebe's photos grew more beautiful by the day—those patches of light that made you want to own them.

As she reached the last mouthful of her unbelievable coffee, strong, strong enough to set her straight, she let her mind drift from her plan for the day, for her week, the things she wanted for her life, and gazed out the window to where a line was forming on the pavement between the shade of the awning and the brightness beyond. Her mind cleared and she was outside, walking down that shady strip towards the beach wearing a new straw hat from the chemist, with Charlie, laughing. She was in that body of hers in youth, the heat of Charlie's presence beside her. She felt that heat in her face and neck and then a breeze gusted into the café and a broad, tall woman walked in. She'd seen her before around the place, noted her presence. She did her best to look at the woman's face, wide, flat, serious. Her chest was distracting, enormous beneath her cream chiffon blouse. She was a large woman in every dimension, tall, broad-hipped, with a large head and thick layered hair. Not fat. The right shape, just . . . big.

'Louisa, right?' She was American.

Louisa stood up, quiet for a moment. You'd weigh three of me. 'Mrs Beringer?' She held out a hand. The woman shook it firmly.

The proprietor appeared at the table and leaned towards the woman as she sat down, clasped her hands as though praying. 'Mrs B, I have some fresh orange cake. It is too early?'

'Been up for hours, Angie. We'll call it brunch.' She turned to Louisa, who felt she too had assumed an air of attentive obedience, ready to do this person's bidding. 'What do you have for me?'

Louisa imagined sitting her down in a tilting chair in the middle of a closed hairdressers. She'd start with her hair, get a girl to soften it into a bob, give it some highlights, then light sparkly makeup and a swishy suit. No one said you couldn't look nice while you were chucking power about. She spread her palms across the open brochures of recent sales, felt the thick stock of the paper beneath her fingers. 'I've brought you some comparisons to look at, but mostly I'd just like to hear your thoughts. If your views are decent you might consider an auction.'

'I'll be honest with you up front, the house is humble. We moved in, we were always super busy with work, then my husband got sick. Renovations never happened. But the position is a dream.'

'That's all I need. Can I ask what your plans are?'

'I've already gone. Beautiful retirement complex on the North Shore, three minutes' walk to the station. I can go to shows, galleries, catch up with old co-workers.' She leaned forward and whispered behind her hand, 'This place is kind of insular, you know.'

'It's a blessing and a curse.' Louisa's face felt damp. This woman, with her nineties newsreader style, it was like she had no interest in your approval. Her eye was on Lou, throughout the chitchat, and now, waiting. The tiniest splash of vodka would give her the fuel she needed, that little kick you could ride through anything.

'So you said you'd bring pictures?'

'Sure.' Mrs Beringer reached into her handbag on the seat next to her and pulled out a yellow envelope.

Lou smiled and took it, reached in and laid the pile of photographs on the envelope to protect them from the table. The one on top showed a view out over the sea, a little bit of orange beach, the corner of an ocean pool. 'That's the view from out front,' the woman said. 'Nice, huh?'

'Oh!' she said and then stopped. She made herself look directly into the woman's dark, calculating eyes. 'I can sell a view like that any day of the week.'

She tucked the top photo underneath the others. The next one was the same view but from inside the house, inside the living room, and there it all was, a strip of green carpet, the brown sliding doors, the flimsy wooden platform at the top of the outside stairs. She closed her eyes briefly, a breath before a dive, and looked at the next one: the ugly carport dipping towards the house, the steep mossy driveway, the salmon fibro walls.

'I want you to know what you're working with. She's no oil painting.'

'You haven't changed anything? How long did you and Mr Beringer live there?'

'Twenty years, give or take. You know, you stop noticing the gruesome carpet after a while. That view was all I saw. Never got used to it.'

Louisa concentrated on the details of Mrs Beringer's face, the new hair growth, like a toddler's, at her temple. 'You don't want to stay and fix it up, now you have a little more time?'

'Like I say, I've moved on. They weren't happy days there, toward the end. But some lucky banker's wife can make it real cute.'

She nodded. 'I rarely see places with such potential. It's a blank slate.'

'Sure. Although the house is solid. Nothing wrong with it at all.'

Come on, lady. It was always a day or two from the wrecking ball. 'No, of course. It looks fantastic.'

Mrs Beringer's coffee arrived along with a massive slice of cake, moist and dense. Louisa ate it in her mind, one of the tricks of thinness, the experience without the payback. It wasn't working this time, she was in danger of dribbling on her chin. The woman nodded at the proprietor and took a large bite from her tiny fork. 'I've seen everyone round here now. Saved you till last because I like the photos you do. There's something wistful about them. Yearning—is that the word I want? I was in travel for many years. Yearning's worth big bucks.'

'My sister, Phoebe Bright, does those. Check her out on Instagram.' She leaned towards the woman, but not too far, because of the size of her chest. 'But you know it's not hard to stand out around here. These guys are living in the eighties.' Louisa gathered her things into her leather folder. 'It's been so good to meet you, Mrs Beringer. Should I call you tomorrow to see what your thoughts are with this?'

Mrs Beringer reached inside her blouse. It looked as though she was giving her left breast a squeeze. Louisa waited for the world to right itself and out came her hand, pulling on something tied around her neck. She lifted it over her head, a loop of string, a key dangling. 'Go check it out, tell me what you see.' Louisa reached out to take the key, closed her hand around it, still warm from Mrs Beringer's chest, and smiled, a flood of heat rising through her body.

On the cool sand of Avalon she found a private spot against the ridge in front of the surf club and crammed in a chocolate muffin as fast as she could without choking. The surf was smooth, pale. This was the most perfect time of year—summer lingering, the water warm, the crowds cleared. When she closed her eyes she saw not the house but the man she had seen on the news with Jack, that unavoidable stare. She kicked away from it from as though it were the dark water of a rip. She stood, a little too quickly, brushed the sand off her jeans and walked into the shade of the trees in the reserve, her strength returning.

~

Jack leaned on her kitchen counter with his arms folded. He didn't look at you, when he was worrying.

'So what happened?'

'Georgie reckons Indi can't stay over.'

Oh, she thought. *Georgie.* Okay. 'You've got a deal. She's got to stick to it.'

'She told me to be realistic.'

She opened up the jar of coffee and turned the machine on. 'I'm struggling to remember what you saw in that woman.' She did remember. Enormous breasts and always laughing, once upon a time. Also that nurse thing men seemed to go helpless around.

'You sound like Mum.'

She turned to face him, pointed at his chest. 'Don't.'

He managed a half smile. She saw him as he had been, the night before, bending over Indigo in the back seat, doing up her seatbelt. She was asleep so he had had to prop her up carefully and then go around the other side and settle her against the closed door so she wouldn't tip over on the drive up the hill.

'You've got an arrangement. She can't just decide to bully you because she's up on blocks.'

'Jesus, Lou.'

'You know what I mean. Stick to your guns. Don't let it spoil your time with your girl.' She passed him his cup and they went out onto the deck and reclined on the teak loungers.

'Do your lawn today?'

'Magnus can do it.'

'Let him go to the beach. All that homework he has to do.'

She'd been wondering whether to say anything. Now she was sitting up on the lounger, her elbows on her knees. 'You'll never guess what.'

'You're running for mayor?'

'Maybe next year. I met a woman this morning. Wants to sell her house.'

'Well, that's good.'

Her mouth was dry. She swallowed. 'It's *our* house.'

'She wants to sell your house?'

'Don't be an arse. *Our* house. On the Serpentine.'

He watched her, his mouth slightly open.

'And, and. She hasn't changed a *thing*. She's the only one there's been, her and her sick husband.' She pulled down the corners of her mouth, trying not to smile. 'Dead, now, sadly.'

He shook his head. 'She bought it off Mum?'

'Right, and it's all still the same. She showed me a photo of the lounge. That carpet! And you could see a bit of the green kitchen and the sliding doors. It's fucking incredible!'

Jack picked up his coffee from the deck and looked out over the pool. Closed his eyes as he blew on his coffee.

'What do you reckon?' she said.

'About what?'

'How nuts is that? That she brought it to me? Although, you know, she's a player. She's been to everybody.'

'You're not going to take it on, though.'

'You bet your life I am.'

'Why?'

'I want a stickybeak. Come with me. I've got the key already.'

She caught a glimpse of a look that passed quickly. It reminded her of Magnus as a little boy, when she placed food in front of him he couldn't believe he was being asked to eat. 'No thank you, Louisa.'

'Oh come *on*. You'll never get another chance.'

'I always hoped someone had pulled it down.'

'Come on. You must see it every time you go for a swim.'

He said nothing.

'You don't go to Bilgola? You don't take Indi? That's child abuse.'

'She goes all the time. Just not with me.'

'You've never gone? In twenty years?'

He drank his coffee and stood up. She scratched at the last square of blue nail polish on her big toe. 'I prefer Avalon,' he said.

Oh, *Jack*. Get on with your life, would you.

~

Louisa had Aart's MacBook open on the counter. She entered his password and his balances opened up in front of her. He'd been doing a bit of selling recently, getting as close as he got to antsy about Greece and China. It looked like plenty to her, a very agreeable amount, but no doubt he had plans for it. She logged out and snapped the laptop shut, looked out at her pool, remembered the yard before she'd got to work on it, a patchy lawn with a two metre long cement slab at its centre like someone had stashed a body under there. A crowd of people standing around with auction paddles, a feeling rising in her blood that this place was going to be hers, observing Aart's utter calm as their competitors fidgeted and whispered.

She took a swig of Diet Coke from the bottle on the bench, a tot of vodka knocking the edge off the fizz, and picked up the laptop to carry it back through to Aart's desk. She stood for a moment in his dark office, in its awkward south-facing corner of the house, blinds down because it looked straight onto the neighbour's brick garage. She had never liked this room. There was never anything to be done about it, this and Magnus's room above it. For long months she was able to ignore it, the house's imperfectability. Then it returned, a needle to the brain.

Back in the light of the kitchen, the key to the house dug hard against her hip in the pocket of her jeans. She reached in and squeezed it until it hurt her fingers, then laid it out on the bench. An ancient copper key on a loop of tangled string. It must have been the spare, all these years. She remembered the way the string scratched her, keeping her alert, alive to the nerve endings in the salty skin stretched smooth across her bony teenage chest. She fed her fingernail through the tangles until they were gone and pulled the string over her head, tucked the key into her shirt. That was it, that scratchy feeling.

She downed the last of her Coke. She knew how much was enough, for warmth, the loosening of ideas, the boldness necessary to live this life, do the deals. She wrote down the figures from the laptop screen onto a Post-it, tucked it in her bag and the key string rubbing against her neck, climbed into her car. Backing out over the grass she imagined the house, being in it.

Her sleek car moved onto the street, the wide lawns and deep decks rolling away behind her as she reached the main road threading its way through the beach suburbs. She kept to the speed limit even as a plant-shaped tingle moved through her breasts like the first inkling of carrying a child.

~

The light was changing, Phoebe had caught the best of it already from up here on the sandy ridge. The ocean was losing its opaque blue, becoming lighter, more daytime and ordinary. The green swell was pretty, good for Lou's marketing shots, but it was not what she was interested in. Secret times enjoyed by a select few, private worlds not clearly visible.

Straightening from her camera on its tripod, she waved goodbye to Reef and Mattie, bobbing over the ridge of sea. The area around them was filling with dads, tubby in their wetsuits like seals ready to be eaten. Chomp.

Reef was still looking back over his shoulder towards the beach. She threw her arms in the air and fell sideways into the sand. The beach in front of her was dotted with people, but they all had their backs to her, mesmerised by the brightening sea. He held up a thumb and she got to her feet, smiling, dusted herself off.

She folded her tripod, began the walk along the shore to her unit, energy fizzling out of her with every step through the white foam. She tried to identify the little black figures waiting out on the swell. The boys and girls she photographed, she knew plenty of them inside their wetsuits, or had shared joints with them on the balconies of unit blocks with the mosquitos biting whenever you passed the joint on. This morning she'd opened her eyes on a couch in a Whale Beach shack, woken by someone knocking things over in the bathroom. The door was open, it was Reef, snapping his wetsuit up over his perfect white arse. He caught her eye and grinned. They walked down to North Av together mostly in silence, smiling at each other as they passed through the empty pink streets. He nudged her gently with his board every now and then, neither speaking much. She stripped down to her undies when they reached the cold sand and they pushed themselves in past the breakers and bobbed about, hangovers clearing.

She'd gone to fetch her camera, he'd picked up his board, and she'd watched him for an hour through her viewfinder. Whatever it was between them, nothing more than a silence, a glance light as a long blonde hair, stretched and snapped as she walked the length of the beach towards the rock pool and the row of units and the busy village.

By the time she reached the cool mildewy shade of the stairwell at the back of her block she was a sleepwalker making for home. In her apartment she dusted the sand off her bare feet and fell into her crumpled sheets, a moment of pleasurable sensation before her brain wiped itself clean.

Her phone vibrating hard on the tiled floor woke her what felt like moments later, though the sun was high and strong at the edge of the blinds. A message lit up her screen, from Lou. *Come and check out a house?*

She texted back through half-shut eyes: *Where?*

Bilgola. Meet you at the roundabout in 15.

By the time she'd stood under the shower for thirty seconds she was returning to life, pleased to have a job, even if it was out there in the blinding light. She was broke this month, waiting for a trip to WA later in the autumn. She made a coffee standing naked at the messy bench and poured it into a travel mug, stuck her head sideways under the cold tap to drink, rubbed some of the water through her curly hair to rough up the parts flattened against her pillow. Found her bikini, dress and sunglasses on the floor and walked up the hill, camera around her neck, brain pressing against her skull with every passing bus. And yet she was elated. The sun, the grind of traffic, her sister, in some pristine casual get-up, fresh from the gym or the triumphant demolition of some bloke thinking he could cut an easy deal. That brilliant exterior, and yet she always gave something away, if you knew what to look for.

It was still only ten-thirty as she approached the bus stop at the roundabout. After this she could catch a lift back with Lou, sleep until the afternoon, work until dark and then go out. There was a party in Whale Beach at a share house some friends of Reef had just set up. Someone's foolish parents' place. Nothing had happened with him, but this was her favourite part, when you knew something was sparking away beneath the surface of life, ready to catch fire. All flirting and power and anticipation, even if it was just a night in the end, five minutes in the dunes even, with a joint and a crowd of noisy louts about to stumble over you as you kissed your mate, blissed out and greedy.

As she came down the short path connecting Barrenjoey Road and the Serpentine, the dappled light fell on Lou's silver T-shirt. She was walking down the middle of the bright street towards her, moving as though the world had its eye on her but she didn't care. No, wait, as though there was a bowl on her head, filled to the brim with piss.

A few steps away from the main road the sound of the sea rushed up through the trees. This place, she'd turned ten and then arrived here, as though the first part of childhood you just had to wait and then it was all yours, forever. This winding street of oleander and birds of paradise, these houses tumbling down the cliff towards the sea.

Lou stood in the street, head cocked, trying not to smile.

'Something on my shirt?' Phoebe said.

'Just pleased to see you.' They continued to look at each other for a few seconds more, a habit of assessment, of updating the picture you had. Lou's perfume smelled herby, like Thai food before you cooked it, lemongrass, basil. Phoebe felt her misdemeanours rising from her skin after her hilly walk. Lou stepped back, all business, except for that look in her eye.

'So, shithole or drug palace?'

Lou gestured towards the street behind them and they walked out into the sunny street between builders' utes and BMWs. Lou's Volvo was perched on the ridge that sloped down to the houses on the ocean side fifty metres ahead. The street gave off wafts, occasionally rising above Lou's perfume, of that old life. Some sweet plant, the salt of the ocean.

They reached the Volvo and Lou stopped, facing the driveway, hands on her hips. 'No!' Phoebe said, shoving her. 'No way.'

Nothing had changed, the weedy tiled driveway, the low salmon fibro at the bottom, the iron roof, all intact, in the past and present at the same time. She rode past here on her scooter sometimes, had a taste of the drug of memory, but this was the full hit, standing here, smelling it, breathing it in.

Lou pulled a string necklace out from under her silver T-shirt, a key dangling on the end. Phoebe leaned forward, squinting at it. 'That's *your* key.'

Lou nodded, face turned up towards the sun, radiant with excitement.

'Been in yet?'

'Waiting for you, pudding.'

Phoebe took a deep breath, filled her lungs with salt and the plants of this street that clung to the cliff in the mists and breezes. She put her hand on Lou's arm, as they teetered on the brink of the drive. 'Oh my God. What about Jack?'

Lou lifted a hand. Forget that.

'Let's go, Lou-Lou.'

They started down the drive, descending into the shade of the road, high at their backs. This had seemed like the steepest driveway in the world when Phoebe was ten. She liked to bomb down it on her bike and only squeeze her brakes a metre from Charlie's car at the bottom. She recalled that feeling, the bike tipping forward on its front wheel, her hand on the tarp-covered bonnet, heart hammering.

They stood in the alcove together, the front door the same, the white paint flakier now. Louisa fumbled the lock.

'Get a grip.'

'All right, you.'

The door pushed open against a bunched mat and they took a small step into the corridor. That smell: dinners that never quite came out of the carpet, familiar in an old, old way. The doors into the bedrooms were shut but the carpet beneath their feet was thick and green, just the same, and they could see down the corridor the Formica kitchen bench, the pale green cabinets, the brown aluminium sliding doors out towards the sea. All this time she'd been living her life, going to college, travelling, running around the beaches, and it had been here, unchanging. As they moved towards the living room and kitchen they saw that there was no furniture, just small shapes pressed into the carpet where it had been, recently or years ago. Nothing to say that anything had happened here for twenty years.

A voice came, deep and urgent: *Feeb*. Him, Dad. His voice sounded as clear as Lou's but she knew it existed in a different place to this one. She opened the sliding door and the salt air rushed in, a cold shroud against her face. The rock pool glinted beneath the far headland, the surf churning over the wall at the northeast corner.

Behind her Louisa was walking around, opening cupboards, brushing a hand along the counter. Phoebe turned around and felt them all here: Mum, young, pretty, in the kitchen, a blonder, brittler version of Lou; Dad rampaging about the place in his old peach-coloured running shorts, sweaty-chested. She succumbed to it, these people of her past wandering the place, passing through Lou in the kitchen, suddenly insubstantial.

'It's all got to go,' Lou said.

'What do you mean?'

Louisa turned to face her from the other side of the kitchen, too old to be in that space. She should be just about to turn sixteen, in her cossies and sulking, hair white-blonde from the sun, not from dye, and straggly, always drying, not shaped around her face in layers. Angry with Phoebe for no reason other than her being a little kid and an easy target. Pointless wanting swelled in her.

'I was thinking,' Lou said, 'maybe you could just gut it, use the structure, but it's a waste of the block. It needs pulling down.'

'Someone will do that, won't they? Heartbreaking.'

'I don't know how it's lasted this long. Dad had big plans for it, you know. It wouldn't have stayed like this.'

'Maybe the new owners will like all this retro stuff. You could hire some mid-century furniture before I take the pics. If it was mine I'd just rip up the carpet and keep everything else.'

'Waste of a killer block.'

Phoebe looked around her at the empty house, imagining the people and furniture, and felt that she was in one of Jack's paintings. If she didn't have to work out how to explain it to Lou she'd take some photos now before that feeling was erased by retro Tupperware and replica Eames dining chairs, and show him them, as a sort of question that would have no answer except that wary look of his, that eye out for trouble even in the midst of a joke or a game.

'Well,' she said, 'you are the makeover queen. I can do the view now if you want, for the board. I might climb onto the roof.'

'It'll cave in and you'll sue me.'

'It never did before.'

'You used to get up on the roof? You were so little, and clumsy.'

'Jack showed me how. It was awesome. You could hear everyone talking. Dad going,' she put on a deep, snappy voice, '"Feeb— where've you gone?"'

'Little bugger.'

Phoebe nodded. She'd made it sound like a regular event, part of the fabric of life, but how long were they all here? She was remembering something that happened twice, maybe three times, and stretching it out across her childhood. 'Come on. We'll do it together. You should, if you never did it before.'

'I don't think so.'

'Come on, Lou. Live a little.'

'Thanks for the tip.'

'Last chance. Can't do it when you're showing people through, can you?'

'I've got white pants on.'

'And I forgot my undies.'

'God, Feeb.'

Phoebe walked back out the front door to the carport, Lou following. There was a narrow gap between the pillar of the carport and the wall and if you didn't mind grazing your knee a bit you could wedge your leg in there as you pulled yourself up to the carport roof and then crawled onto the roof of the house. Her head started hammering again as she stuffed her leg into the gap but it was easier than it used to be, fewer body lengths to traverse, and she was up on the bowing roof of the carport quickly, her head just above street level, looking at the tyres of Lou's car.

'Feeb, you're too heavy now.'

'Nah. Come on. I'll get onto the house while you get on this one.'

She crossed the gap onto the main roof, camera thudding against her chest. It wasn't too hot yet. A line of oleanders on the street shaded this side of the house in the morning and the sun was only just breaking clear. The metal was nicely warm as she crawled up to the peak of the roof and swung her legs around to hang over the other side.

The volume of light pouring into the pale, swelling ocean; even her own view, from the flat, her comfort, her proof that she was home, couldn't touch it. The nearness and noise of the sea, the feeling of suspension. She could hear Lou scrabbling up behind her and turned. Lou's hand slipped from the peak of the roof and Phoebe reached out and grabbed it, felt a tremor. Lou was flushed and serious. Phoebe smiled, let that clumsy moment, even her own minor heroism, pass. 'Come and look, Lou. You'll love this.'

The iron on this side was hot so she tucked her dress under her bum and rested her feet on their soles in her sneakers.

'Oh my God,' Lou said as her hands gripped the roof beside her.

'It's okay. Just move slowly then sit still.'

Sweat was beading on Louisa's smooth forehead. Botox? Probably. Her chest moved in and out like someone on stage, about to speak, or sing. Once she had settled beside her they looked out together over the russet-coloured beach, the sea, aquamarine at the shore, the orange headland and glassy ocean pool beneath. The red and yellow flags were up and a scattering of people spilled all the way down the beach across the rusty band of wet sand, the white and aqua fringes of the ocean. The sound of their calls rose above the rushing sea.

Phoebe lifted her camera and zoomed in on a surfer halfway to his feet in front of a glowing green wave. Surfers were like animals from a dim past or a former life. Familiars, dark bodies against the green light.

'If you came in at street level, this is what you'd see. Bam,' Lou said.

'It's a sweet little shack though. I loved it. It's perfect as it is.'

'I know exactly what I'd do with this.'

Phoebe looked at her sideways. Lou was absorbing it, drawing it towards herself to keep: a glass bowl of light. 'Some lucky buyer, hey?'

Lou said nothing, frowning at the view.

'What did Dad want to build?'

'Oh, he had this insane plan with stairs out over the cliff.'

'No one else has got them. They'd be under water at high tide.'

'Always wondered if he might have got away with it.'

'Nah. Really?'

Lou raised a hand to brush the thought away and slipped slightly, brought it back down again to grip the ridge of the roof.

'I feel like I'm forgetting him,' Phoebe said.

'You were only little.'

'You guys could help, though. We could do something together. You know, go through the pictures. Get Mum to tell us stuff we don't know.'

Lou shook her head, looking out over the sea.

'I can only just remember him now. The way he stood sometimes or the look on his face when he wanted to do something fun, just the two of you. His voice.'

'Don't know, Feeb.'

'Why're you so interested in the house then?'

'I'm just the agent. Thought you might like to see it while I've got the key and there's no one else here.'

'Right.'

'Really.'

'Sitting there drawing plans in your head.'

She turned to look at her. 'Can't help imagining what's supposed to be here. What we should have had. Nothing like the others. Something special. Epic.'

Phoebe felt a stab. This knowledge Lou had that she didn't.

'You got so much more time.'

'Not that much.'

The rock pool was filling up, crawling with kids at the shallow edge under the sandstone cliff, tiny white wakes trailing the free-stylers in the main pool. She made out figures in the shade on the concrete step that lined it, under the treacherous rock of the headland. That cold concrete under your bum. What it was like in the dark, the black water of the pool, the deeper blackness of the sea beyond, the rush of water on the rocks louder, much louder at night, pouring into you.

A look was settling over Lou's face and body that she rec-ognised, the resumption of cool, the gathering of resources. 'I still miss him,' Phoebe said quickly. 'I was so little. You and Jack have all these memories. You could pass a few things on, before they're gone forever. Show some photos, tell some stories?'

Lou shook her head. 'I get you, but it's a terrible idea.'

She was silent, trying not to look like she was sulking.

'Have you ever heard Jack even say his name?' Lou said. 'Mum's not one to rake over the coals, either.'

'Oh, those two. What is it with them anyway? I want to *make* them talk about him. Why can't they give me what they've got?' She laughed at her own brattishness but she knew she wasn't fooling her sister.

Lou shifted her legs around to the back of the roof gingerly, then turned over and crawled backwards on all fours. Even in this movement she kept her dignity. Soon she was standing in the driveway, dusting off her knees and then brushing her hands together. All done, then.

Phoebe turned back to the view. This beach, that bubble of a summer, Lou and Jack as moody teenagers. She closed her eyes and she was back, listening to Dad calling for her in the house, Lou slamming doors, Jack out on the grass, not knowing she was up there behind him, watching him cling to the grass as though a strong gust would blow him right out over the beach and into the ocean.

Then, dizzyingly, she was down there on the concrete terrace by the pool and a woman in a clinging dress was hanging in the air above the water, about to drop, the world blue around her, surf spray crashing through the fence. Caught there in the sky, kids hanging off the railing at the edge of the ocean behind her, the beach colours of this place—russet sand, green-edged ocean.

There was a day, wasn't there? A day when everything had been decided.

BOXING DAY

Jack's skin felt wrong, laid over with an old, grubby moisture. Heat had filled even the usually cool space of the downstairs den and liquid pooled in the creases at the back of his knees where they rubbed against the stiffened velvet of the couch. Beside him Lou stretched her legs and flexed her feet quickly, pushed her arms out in front of her and rotated them, as though movement had built up in her while they had been sitting here watching the movie and had to be released in these weird convulsions.

He looked through the sliding doors; a wind was stirring, flattening the clifftop scrub in impatient gusts. He wasn't really seeing the change in the weather. What he saw was Charlie, hosing the front garden at the old house at dusk. Jack was leaning his bike in the narrow gap between the side of the house and the high hedge, the lorikeets filling the fading sky with their racket, when a peal of laughter, a girl's, made him look towards the street.

There was Charlie, the hose held limply at his side, talking to Monica. The shine of her hair always gave him a feeling in his stomach, a shifting, that made him close his eyes for a moment. He watched his father, his back to him, the way he swelled into his performance, his free hand gesturing. Which of his stories had he unwrapped for this moment? Monica raised a hand to Charlie as she turned away, smiled shyly, as though to apologise for the boldness of that laugh, and crossed the street. He didn't look away from her until she passed through her front door. When he looked back at his father, he saw that he too had followed her passage over the wide street and across her dry lawn, the hose still forgotten at his side.

He blinked the image away. Lou was standing, pointing the remote at the TV. From the look on her face it seemed she'd been sitting there seething. Had he said something? 'Gotta get outside,' he said.

He stepped out into heavy air, a gritty undertow stirring. Down towards the city slate-coloured clouds trailed tentacles across the far hills like huge stingers. How would you paint that, to show how it loomed, as though something that might swallow you whole was coming, right now.

He heard low voices, up on the deck, Mum and Don. Lou appeared next to him, rolling on the balls of her feet, scratching her head through her salty hair. 'They're both having affairs, then?'

'Shhh.'

'Maybe they're all swingers,' she whispered. 'That girl. She kept leaning her tits on his arm with Mum right there.'

'Shut up, Lou.'

'Did she even speak to you once?'

90

'I don't think she really knew we were in the room.' The clouds were spreading out and filling the sky to the south, rain sweeping along the far headlands. 'They're just being . . . drunk.'

'I can't stand it.'

'It's not my idea of fun, that's for sure.'

'He's a weirdo, isn't he?'

'Well, he's weird. That's not news.'

'But you know, is he creepy weird?'

Jack studied her face. She was shifting from one foot to the other, looking out at the surf. He said nothing.

'Come on. Is he weird about girls?'

Sweat trickled from his temples. He looked down at the beach and took three deep breaths. 'I don't think so. Not really. Unless. Is he?'

She shook her head, looking at her feet. She seemed to know what he was asking, thank God, because if he said it aloud or even finished the thought for himself it would stay with him forever.

'Don's chick,' Lou said. 'Mum reckons she's nineteen. Right? He's *forty-seven*.' Their neighbours' party oozed onto their deck, Jimmy Barnes escaping from an open door. 'And he puts on the whole performance. Treating the rest of us like dirt to try and impress her.' She put her hands to her face.

'He's just having one of his days.'

'Well, okay, fabulous. Why do we have to put up with it? Why does Mum just sit there?'

'I sometimes wonder if he just, you know, needs a bit of help.'

The hot breeze blew grit up into Lou's eyes. She wiped them, looking pale and woozy. 'Oh, man . . .'

'How much champagne did you have?'

'Yeah, too much.'

'Someone should be helping him.'

'Someone should be helping Charlie?'

'Yeah.'

'What about someone helping the rest of us? What the fuck was that at lunch? Where did he even go with that . . . I don't know. What shall I call her?'

'I don't think he's slept at all. For days.'

'Sleeping pills then. Is that the help you mean?'

'Well, yeah. A doctor.'

'Like that'll happen.'

'I wish he'd go back to work. Do you think maybe he'll just get bored and start something else?'

'Not while he's busy with his masterpiece. Have you seen his plans?'

He looked at her sideways. 'Not lately.'

She shook her head.

'I was just remembering, before, how he used to be with Monica. Like he was with us. Telling stories. Trying to get her to laugh. He really liked her.' Lou waited for more. 'So maybe it's like if one of us was missing, if *you* were missing, a smaller version of that. It's knocked him about a bit.'

'Why does everything have to be about him? He barely knew her. None of us did, except for you. His feelings. His moods. That's all there's room for. It wears me out.'

What wears me out, he thought, is having to check he's okay every time you enter a room. It's the way the air crackles around him and you don't know whether to keep a lookout or hide. And really, it makes no difference, because whatever's going to happen is going to happen anyway, and the worry makes it worse, like it can be seen, a colour in the room that he seeks out.

Lou glanced behind her, up at the house. 'They've gone inside. Let's go in round the front. See what they're up to.'

He followed her through the narrow gap between the houses. If he could do a headcount, check everyone off, maybe he could just lie down for a few hours, cease to be. He thought for a moment of blackness underground and then came the smell of dirt in some hidden place and he shut the thought away.

Lou opened the door quietly and they crept into the dark corridor, still smoky and hot and smelling of steak and chip fat, and took up positions leaning against opposite walls. If Jack stretched to the edge of the shadows he could see Tricia and Don sitting side by side at the dining table, looking out the doors towards the ocean. Two champagne bottles and glasses sat in front of them, along with crumpled foils, a cigarette packet, a filling ashtray. One of Tricia's hands was on Don's arm, the other was holding a cigarette. They'd closed the sliding doors and her smoke made a screen around them that cleared and filled as she drew on her cigarette and exhaled.

For a moment they said nothing and Jack pressed himself against the wall, afraid to move, keeping back a bubble of hilarity rising in his stomach.

What are they doing? Lou mouthed at him from the opposite wall.

He shook his head.

'She'll come round,' Tricia said.

Don spoke over her, almost. 'She keeps showing everyone the ring, like she's proud, but when we're alone it's like I'm nothing.'

Jack chanced a look at Louisa. She mimed holding a gun to her head and shooting it.

Don went on. 'I'll get a date set, then she backs out. I've had enough. Maybe she's not the girl for me.'

Tricia turned towards him briefly, blowing smoke into his face. 'Young girls get jittery. Then things settle down. That's all it is. You had to pick a young one, didn't you?'

There was a silence Jack didn't like. Don was looking at Tricia, who seemed oblivious, staring out to sea.

Eventually he said, very quietly, 'You shouldn't take that as an insult, you know, Trish.'

'Don.'

'You know if you were free . . .'

'If I were free, what?'

Jack stared at the carpet beneath his feet to avoid looking at them, and Louisa. He could feel her pulling faces, trying to get him to look at her. He wanted nothing more than to escape without detection, but he couldn't stop listening.

His mum again, in an unrecognisable voice: 'Oh, Don.'

Jack looked up. She was rubbing his back, hard. His head hung down, miserable, the circle of shining skin at his crown pointed back at Jack. And yet if you could see his face, what would it show, with her hand on his back like that?

He closed his eyes and heard her voice. 'He's getting bad again.'

Then Don, after a moment: 'You don't have to stay. You've put up with more than anyone could expect.'

'I think about it every day.' She was whispering, as though she knew she was betraying Jack, there, standing in the corridor,

Louisa, Phoebe. 'Just going. Just opening the front door and being done with it.'

'Would you ever do it, though?'

His mother's tone changed. 'When he's starting something new, he's so good. You know, really pouring his energy in. I sometimes wonder if you guys should start something again. It was exciting, wasn't it? In the early days? You love a challenge too.'

'He burned his bridges, Trish. He was lucky to get out unscathed.'

The silence forced Jack to open his eyes. Lou was standing in the shadows with her mouth open, staring at him. He watched his mother crush her cigarette into the ashtray and put her free hand on Don's thigh. He looked back at Louisa. *What?* she was saying. Then his mother spoke again. 'That girl, dressing like that and then making a fuss. Confusing is what it is.'

Jack shook his head and readied himself to cross the corridor into the bedroom. No more. But then there was a thud against the door downstairs, a muffled grunt, a peal of that relentless laughter, heavy steps on the staircase. They fell into the room next to the table, Bree clutching Charlie's arm. 'This girl *is* a knockout!' Charlie announced, as though he were confirming a proposition they'd all made together. They both had wet hair and her dress was clinging, the fabric sticking and rippling across her body. Don was standing up. Tricia stared at them with her arms folded.

And then Lou had broken cover before he could stop her, striding out into the light of the lounge, ready to get in amongst it.

'You should see the look on your face, Louisa Bright,' Charlie said.

'Yeah? How do I look?'

'Like a bloody wet weekend! You've got no spirit, you mob. You're mopers. Take a leaf out of Bree's book. Always laughing, aren't you, doll?'

Lou's voice was as calm as a lake. 'What do you think about that, Tricia? Are we mopers? What about you, Don? You're not looking too chipper either.'

'To be honest with you,' Tricia said, looking out the window, 'I just can't believe anyone would walk across the beach like that in broad daylight.'

Jack wondered what Bree's face looked like. Her hair hid her face at the side. Her shoulders and back were smooth, glistening, and he could see her outrageous undies, red like a warning. She had not stopped leaning on his father since they tumbled into the room, as though she needed help to hold her body upright. 'She caused quite a stir, didn't you, Bree?' Charlie said. 'Don, when are you going to marry this girl? Look sharp or she'll get snapped up, I'm telling you.'

Please, Dad, Jack thought. Give it a rest. There was a pause. The girl wasn't laughing now. They all had their backs to him, Lou standing ready with her hands on her hips, except for Tricia, on the other side of the table. Her profile was pale and fearful. He felt her wooziness transfer to his body. Don said quietly, 'I'll make us all coffee before we drive home. We've probably all had enough for one day.'

Jack couldn't turn away from Tricia's face. It was growing pale, her eyes bulbous. He felt his gorge rising.

'I'll drive you kids in the Mustang,' Charlie said, pulling his keys from his pocket as he set Bree upright. Jack watched his mother.

She might slap the girl, but then still, even now, she might make everyone sandwiches for the trip.

There were more footsteps on the stairs, the galumphing charge of Phoebe, whom no one registered but Lou, holding up a hand to her to prevent her from speaking. There was a look on Phoebe's face that seemed appropriate to the situation. Her mouth was open, ready to ask a question, the same question Jack would like to ask: What are you all *doing*?

'I'm right to drive,' Don said, looking away from Charlie. Tricia stood from her chair. With a hand on the dining table she convulsed twice and threw up on Charlie's bare feet. It hit the floor so hard it splashed onto Bree's legs. 'You're fucking kidding me,' the girl said quietly.

Jack stepped across the shadowy hallway and crept quietly towards his room, breathing quickly. He opened the window and let in the ocean, gulped in that grey air as though oxygen was enough to save him from the people in the house, watched the waves, noted the dark rip forming at the southern end of the beach. He ignored the boom of Charlie's voice in the lounge, hilarious, oblivious, the sounds of the girl in the bathroom behind him, scrubbing insistently; called to mind the tentacles of the clouds from earlier, saw the colours he'd mix, the strokes, the shapes. After a few moments, his breathing slowed and he began to enter the place where no one else could come.

Just as the slipping began the door banging open jolted him out of it, like an ice skid as you began the slide downwards into sleep. His sisters were in the room. As he turned around Lou shut the door behind her and leaned against it, mouth grim. Phoebe was kneeling on the wide bottom bunk beside her, leaning forward on her fists, a cute lion, getting ready to pounce.

'Mum threw up!' she told him. 'Don's cleaning it. Dad's telling jokes!'

He looked at Lou, his chest tightening. She nodded.

'I would never do that for anyone,' Phoebe said. 'Even if I really loved them.'

'Me either,' Lou said.

'He threw her in the pool,' Phoebe carried on breathlessly, still on all fours.

Jack waited for her to elaborate, concentrating on the breeze at his neck drying his sweat.

'That's why Bree's dress is soaked. He just picked her up and chucked her in.'

He watched Lou's face, wishing Phoebe would stop talking. Footsteps pressed on the boards in the corridor and they all looked at each other as though deciding whether to hide. There was a bang at the door behind Lou's head and she flinched, looking as angry as if someone had hit her directly. She stepped forward and Charlie was in the room, radiating joy from his tanned face, his pale eyes, in his proffered fist a long roll of paper. Jack felt old, as though his heart couldn't take much more.

'Look at this,' Charlie said. 'I've got it. The house, wait till you see it.'

Lou stood behind him, hand on a hip. Phoebe was on her feet, ready at Charlie's elbow. 'Show us. Show me my room.'

Jack saw his mother, that movement, shoulders jerking, like a cat that's eaten grass. 'Is Mum okay?'

'Don's got the ladies. Someone had too much champagne. Check this out.'

He unrolled the plans on the crumpled sheet of the bottom bunk. Phoebe leapt back into the bunk and held down one side while Charlie kneeled on the floor and held the other. Lou hovered behind him with her arms folded. Jack took a breath and approached the hot cluster of his family.

He had caught glimpses of Charlie's sketches, laid out in his parents' room, and ignored them, along with the feeling they conveyed, the unwelcome picture of what was inside Charlie's head, the squiggles and confusion, but this was clearer, simpler, inexpertly drawn but enough to imagine. Three square-faced tubes opened towards the ocean in a fan, shading showing glass at the front ends. Jack closed his eyes; he was in the building, saw the view of beach, sea, headland, sky, clouds shifting. They'd be out in the weather, but inside. Then he was on the sand, looking up at this amazing thing, the clouds moving behind its long straight lines, its lovely sharp corners. Those stairs swooping out to the beach as light as a melody, like stairs from a spaceship thrown out towards humanity, trustful, welcoming.

Charlie sat at the other end of the bed and pointed to the tubes. 'Okay, so there's your wing, you kids, our wing on the other side, and this middle one is the living areas, right?' He looked up at Jack, his pale eyes clear and steady, youthful. 'Do you see it?'

Jack nodded, mouth dry.

'This is our bedroom, with a living room behind it, just for us— parents' retreat, don't you know?' Charlie laughed. 'You can fight over who goes at the front of your wing. Or, no. You and Lou can have long thin rooms and a bit of view each.'

'Wait, where am I?' Phoebe said.

'Behind them at first, but they'll bugger off in a few years and you can take your pick. Yours'll have a trapdoor down to the basement, and we'll have to ask if we want to get down there.'

'Will I be the keeper of the key?'

'Absolutely, mate. Then, look, big lounge in the middle, kitchen behind it. Bathrooms, garage, laundry along the back. A roof terrace! What do you kids think about a roof terrace? We'll stand up there, lords of creation.' He projected this last phrase as though he were calling it out over the ocean, the beach, the little people down below.

'Could we really build this?' Jack asked.

'Course we could. I just needed to make it right first. It's got to feel scary but fun. You'll be right out over the edge of the cliff, nothing underneath you when you get to the front here. I'm going to get it put out as far past the cliff as it can go. Imagine that, Jackie. Standing against the glass, looking down. If you push on it really hard, what's going to happen? Except we'll get that bullet-proof glass so you can throw a table at it if you want, just for the hell of it.'

Lou, who had been careful to give the impression she wasn't even looking, spoke at last. 'This is a lot tidier than it was earlier.'

'Had a chat with Don. Genius that bloke. Told me to keep it simple. He said, "Charlie, what's the one idea that's important here?" Gave me a hand with the drawing. That's why I kept him around so long. Clarity. It's gold.'

'So what is the one idea?' Lou asked.

'I didn't know till he said that but then I knew straightaway.' He was looking at Phoebe, who was in that position again, a baby lion, ready, a cub about to jump on a sibling. There was a hilarity rising in Jack. Raaargh! he thought.

'Feebs, you know those fireworks that shoot out in a fan into the sky?'

'I love those,' she sighed.

'That's what this house is. See it, spreading out into the sky. We'll push it out as far as they'll let us. Bit further maybe.' He winked at Jack. 'It'll be like riding a firecracker every day. Like *being* a firecracker.'

Behind Charlie, Louisa's face hovered, disdainful, unconvinced. Oh don't, he thought. She opened the door and slipped out, sounds drifting in from the living room: women's voices, the chink of ice, Don laughing. Phoebe squealed and pressed her face into the quilt below her, round bum in the air, then bounded after her sister, already calling out to the others about the house, her room.

It was just the two of them now. Charlie was rolling up the sheet of paper. 'Jack, I want you to draw this properly for me, right? Before an architect gets his mitts on it, you need to show him what we want. Make it exciting, so he doesn't go off and give us some boring old box.'

'You want me to do it?'

'Well you're the artist in the family. Don's all right but it's a bit basic, isn't it? You'll give it the magic touch.'

A small part of him resisted, reminded him of the disdain his drawing usually encountered in his father, but the bigger part of him was already sitting with his sketchpad, drawing their cliff and the lines of the house shooting out over it, and in the lines there would be defiance of gravity, movement. And then he was onto imagining the house itself, waking every day to a life that felt thrilling, risky, light.

'When do you want it, Dad?'

'Sooner the better, hey? I want to build this thing.' Jack took a step towards him, not knowing his plan, and his father placed a hand on his head and ruffled his hair.

~

Louisa sat on the bonnet of the Land Cruiser, crouched like a locust, hiding in the gloom of the carport as the day dimmed. She could hear them inside, Charlie's voice inescapable. 'Ah Donnie, catching the bus! Getting back to your roots, hey? What an adventure.'

The screen door banged open and Phoebe came out first. 'I want a Magnum. They are so lush.'

Tricia, behind her, 'Do you know how many calories there are in one of those things? That's a day's Weight Watchers' allowance. Easy.'

And then there they all were, a parade of misery, traipsing up the drive in the swirling, gritty wind, the girl in one of Mum's loose hippie dresses. She looked fat in it; it draped off her chest, hiding her thin waist. Well done, Tricia.

Jack was with them, smiling up at Charlie, a sucker to the last.

Charlie turned back as they reached the top of the drive. 'Walking these guys to the bus, Lou-Lou. Want to get ice cream with the kids?'

The others peered into the dark carport, surprised. It's just Dad, she thought, but it took her a moment to be able to speak. 'No thanks.' He waved and they moved off along the street, only Charlie and Phoebe's voices audible. The way he did that, knew where you were, like you were under surveillance.

She launched herself off the front of the car and went inside. A hot breeze blew down the hallway from the lounge room.

She leaned in the doorway of her room and for a moment saw Monica in her uniform, dark but freckly, standing in line in front of her with the year nine girls at the canteen. She had no idea whether it was real, a memory or something else. Part of Lou even now believed that the world was okay, that she would come back, shaken, chastened, in a heap of trouble maybe, but still her.

The ocean's roar was building with the weather. The wind rushed through the cabbage palms in the gully. How long would they be out? If they waited for the bus with the others, it might be hours. She'd stood at that bus stop on the roundabout, dick-heads tooting their horns, for ages. Or they might be back any second. When he reappeared, you never knew until he was there, in front of you, when you turned from a cupboard, or opened the bathroom door. Just there, always.

She picked across the strewn carpet to her drawers under the window and winced at the loudness of the scraping wood as she opened one. She groped under her scattered T-shirts to close her hand on a thin chain, the pendant digging into her palm. The chain was still knotted; she sat on the bottom bunk and patiently unpicked it, teasing out the knots with her thumbnail. She was in no hurry; she was moving towards an inevitable destination and she wanted to avoid it exactly as much as she needed to arrive.

When it was untangled, she looped the chain onto her fore-finger and held it high so the pendant could dangle. It was only now she could see which way the pendant hung that it was clear it was an M rather than a W. She stuffed it into the pocket of her denim shorts, stood quickly and zipped around the house on the thick, quiet carpets, checking, for what she didn't know. Under her parents' bed there was not even dust to be found. Downstairs in the den the ashtrays were clean and the drawers of the bureau were neatly organised. In the lounge the table smelled as though it had been polished and the kitchen looked like it was never used. Still though, for all the work that went into pretending they didn't make messes, for all the cleaning away of the evidence of living that Tricia did from the moment she woke to the moment she closed her eyes, for all the Glen 20 and sea spray, you couldn't quite ignore the whiff of vomit.

The house was tiny; it didn't take long to snoop around it. But there was nothing here, no one, the sea.

~

In the shade of the carport stood the row of vehicles. Tucked against the mossy wall of the driveway was the Land Cruiser. They all got in that most days. Tricia was authorised to drive it to the shops and to tennis. If they went to beaches further afield the boot would be filled with sandy boogie boards, damp towels, rusting beach chairs. Then there was the boat on its trailer. She pictured Charlie's grin when he was hauling it out of the steep drive in some tricky blokish manoeuvre, hand smacking the outside of the driver door, shouting at the kids to get in. Charlie's Mustang, which the rest of them were only allowed in for evenings out, was tucked in between the boat and the bathroom window and covered by an elastic-rimmed tarp, like a huge shower cap.

The wind billowed warm down the deep driveway, snapping the covers on the boat and car. If she uncovered the Mustang it would be coated in orange grit in moments, and if they came back before she finished there'd be no way to hide what she was up to.

She heard his voice: 'What are you doing, Louisa Bright?' There was no credible answer.

She reached under the front bumper for the edge of the tarp and lifted the elastic. It was stronger than she thought and it pinged back, taking a fingernail with it. She shoved her finger into her mouth, sucking away the horrible sensation of her folded nail. She gripped the elastic in two firm fists and peeled it over the burgundy paintwork carefully until it shrank back to a crumpled puddle on the roof. Aftershave and leather smells escaped from the car as she opened the passenger door. Something else, something sweeter, stickier. Hairspray? Every surface was clean.

The last time they'd been in this car with Charlie was a couple of weeks ago, when they'd joined the yacht club on Pittwater, like taking a membership out for this new life. She'd stepped out in a halter-neck dress, full of hope, ready to be a rich guy's lovely daughter, and some piece of offal Charlie knew through a shady land sell-off trailed a finger along her shoulders as he passed at the bar. She'd pressed her nails into her palms and drunk two glasses of champagne quickly. Stood in the carpark, alone, dizzy, holding her hair off her sweaty neck to catch the breeze, hoping that man with his hard round belly pressed against his polo shirt was not lurking among the cars.

She sat in the driver's seat of the Mustang for a moment, smelling hairspray, and shuddered, remembering the trace of his finger.

Lou skimmed her bare feet around the pedals, felt under her bum in the crease between the backrest and the seat, and then climbed into the passenger seat and carried out the same routine. A lightness rose in her as she groped inside the glove box and found nothing but the car manual and a pile of old rego papers.

She climbed into the back and dug her toes under the floor mats, pushed her finger along the crease at the back of the long seat. She felt sweat pooling under her thighs and opened a door to let air in. A gust blew sand inside.

How long would it take her to sweep the car out and brush down the duco? She'd have to leave it how it was, just so long as she got the cover back on before they returned. It wasn't like he could dust it for prints. She heard voices up on the road and shunted quickly out of the car, remembering him at the top of the drive, turning towards her when the others had had no idea she was there.

The voices passed, nothing like her family's, the rhythms of a polite conversation, a man and a woman taking turns to fuss gently about someone, a child, a relative. She wedged herself between the car and the garage wall and took a breath, turned the silver knob to release the boot, stood back as it sprung open. Immaculately vacant. She shut the boot firmly. Was this disappointment in her chest or something else?

She scrabbled to pull the cover back over, dusting grit off the paintwork gently with her hand. Useless; it was whipping up in eddies from the concrete floor, and as soon as she got one end fixed and tried for the other the cover pinged off and she had to start again. Sweat poured down her back and chilled in the cooling wind.

She weighed down the cover on the bonnet and the boot with a brick-like torch and a phone book and tucked the corners under. It was as though a madness had seized her with the shift in the weather and then died down again. Her old man was a genius, wasn't he? As if there would be anything in the car.

~

The line of car roofs reflected bulging clouds. Phoebe sat on the low wall with Jack, struggling with her Magnum, dripping now she'd eased off the chocolate coating with her teeth against his advice. She imagined knowing all these kids being dragged from the shops to the cars as their parents tried to beat the rain. A few glanced at her as they went by, sitting there parentless and unhassled with a huge ice cream, her big brother happy enough to be in her company. She lifted her chin and resumed her hurried licking.

She looked at her fingers. Her hands were covered in it. A puddle was forming near the toe of her sandals. She took it across the footpath to the bin, spots of rain hitting her shoulders and neck, and saw Lou coming around the corner from the street. She walked straight past Phoebe and stole her spot on the wall next to Jack.

Dark clouds tore along the beach across the main road. It had grown cold in the last few minutes and she was only wearing a singlet and shorts. She stood in front of her sister with her arms crossed, ready to stake her claim. But Lou wouldn't look up. She was holding a necklace in front of Jack, her face cross, scrunched. A pendant hung down, a curly letter M. When Lou finally noticed Phoebe there she grabbed the M with her other hand and shoved it in the pocket of her denim shorts.

'You're gonna have to give me a clue,' Jack said.

Lou gave Phoebe a sidelong glance and whispered in Jack's ear. Phoebe couldn't hear what she said over the women calling to each other as they hurried in and out of their cars, the engines starting up, the noisy road. She was covered in sticky stuff and had nothing to wipe her hands with.

Jack was looking at Lou like she'd just said something foul.

'What are you saying?' she said loudly, leaning over them. 'Where did you get that necklace? You've been nicking stuff!'

Louisa looked at her blankly and then back at Jack, waiting for him to say something else. 'You're being nuts,' he said eventually, to Lou.

'What did she say? I *hate* you two when you do this.'

They looked as though they were trying to stare each other out. Good luck, Jackie. 'Let's go home,' she said. 'We're gonna get wet. Come on. Leave her if she's being stupid.'

A presence formed at her back, a gang of boys, laughing, spilling over the low wall next to them. One nodded at Lou. Phoebe expected Lou to ignore him but she looked him up and down, from his thick hair that needed a good cut to his huge bare feet and back again. The group jostled towards the supermarket and disappeared inside. Phoebe felt the air move as one almost staggered into her, caught a whiff of boy smell. Dirty hair, armpits.

'Okay, Feeb. Let's get going,' Jack said.

'I could tell you other things,' Lou whispered to him, like Phoebe couldn't hear, like she'd be *less* interested if she lowered her voice. 'It all fits together if you stop and think.'

Fat drops of rain spattered the path and Phoebe's neck. That boy came back outside with a massive bottle of Coke and pulled his T-shirt up to stretch the back over his head as he stepped into the rain. His ribs were right next to Lou and she stared at them without even looking at his face. He joined the other boys and they all did it, pulled their shirts over their heads to keep the rain off, even though their stomachs would get wet now anyway.

Lou turned back to face Jack, still glaring.

'Don't tell me anything,' he said. 'You don't know anything.'

Phoebe raised a hand and let it fall on her bare thigh like Dad sometimes did to get them to be quiet. Her hand just made a pathetic slap, barely audible over the spattering rain; Dad's made a deep crack that hurt your own leg when you heard it. 'Why are you fighting? Let's go home!'

No one looked at them stuck here in the middle of the comings and goings. Everything was getting noisier; the rain was drumming on the tin roofs of the shops and the canvas awnings. People ran by laughing. 'Fucken soaked already!' a man yelled to his mate on the other side of the road. It was like a completely different day to this morning, to even an hour ago, when everything was bright, steamy. Yesterday, surfing on Christmas Day, felt like weeks ago.

'Thank God!' a woman was saying. 'I thought it would be hot forever.'

You did not! Phoebe thought, but adults came out with this stuff all the time. Anything to have something to say, to talk talk talk at each other. She pulled at Jack's arm. She was wet already. At least it was getting the stickiness off her face and hands.

Then Louisa stood, suddenly, and strode away without a back-wards glance, weaving through the grownups coming out of the shops, running off the way those boys went, towards the beach. Phoebe pulled at Jack, though he was already standing, slowly. 'Come on, or we'll never catch her.'

'She's probably just going home the other way. We'll see her there.' 'Really?'

He stood up. 'Yeah. Better get going. Gonna get a drenching.'

'Why's she got that necklace? She tell you?'

Jack said nothing, just took her sticky hand and pulled her around the corner and under the awning lining the street, the rain so heavy now it splashed their ankles. Cars with headlights on crawled by at walking speed, wipers going madly. There were goose bumps on Phoebe's arms and legs. It was amazing, after how hot it had been, like jumping out of hot sunshine into the rockpool. And then they were running over the crossing with no idea whether the people in the cars had seen them and were going to stop. There was no time to worry about it because it really was like being in the sea, the water driving against them like a wave, and they had to push through it to reach the awning on the far side.

She touched her arm. I'm as cold as a frog, she thought, and giggled.

They ran in their sticking clothes to where the shops ended, just before the school, her new school from next month, its long concrete blocks exciting but also terrifying. How would she find her way around those huge buildings? Who helped you if you got lost?

There was no shelter here on the long stretch past the netball fields and up the hill to the roundabout. Jack stopped and leaned on his knees ahead of her. 'Why are we running? We can't get any wetter.'

They slowed to a walk and she tried to enjoy the rain running down her neck from her hair, tickling. She held up her hands, letting them get washed. 'Bet she won't let us in all wet.'

'Bet you're right. Listen, when we get home let me see what sort of mood he's in, before we tell him Lou's gone off.'

'Why?'

'He's a bit up and down today, and if Lou's not there—'

'You said she would be there.'

'I know, but if she's not . . .'

'Has she run away?'

'No.'

'Then what?'

'She'll be there. And we will be too in five minutes and it will all be fine.'

When they reached the roundabout she couldn't make out the sea below them. Her eyes were filmed with water. Everything was a grey blur. Up on the ridge the rain hurt her legs as it hit but it was a nice kind of hurting, a cold stinging on her skin, hot from running. Jack grabbed her hand and pulled her between the slow cars. An important part of his attention was with her, keeping her safe, at least until they got home and everyone started talking about Lou. If she could keep him with her she could make him tell her what was going on. Then it would be them against Lou.

She felt herself slipping on the wet road in her thongs but Jack pulled her up and kept her moving until they were across and skittering down the steep, short path to the Serpentine. They cut through to the back of the houses using the beach track and out on the ridge the sky was just water—it was hard to see the edge of the cliff even. She scrambled along the muddying track trying to catch up. Jack was holding his arms up like a tightrope walker out at the edge, grey air beyond him, misty charcoal sea. In his own world again.

Phoebe ducked alongside the shrubs until she was level with him, and jumped out in a big star jump with a shriek. Jack balanced for a moment on one tiptoed foot, then let out a noise, a girl-squeak, and tumbled over the curved lip of the escarpment, plunging towards the dune scrub. The world stopped—one, two— as he slipped, before he was caught by a bush. Its flexible branches bent towards air and water, pushed out from the earth by his back and bottom. It looked like there was nothing beneath him, only the ocean swirling below.

Phoebe was still, a rock in the rain. Her brain sped on ahead. If she moved too fast on the muddy track she'd slip too. She dropped to all fours in the mud and stretched a hand towards him. He couldn't reach; she had to crawl closer to the edge. He grabbed her hand and gave it a tug, looking her in the eye, then said, 'Lie on your tummy.' She didn't know from that look if he hated her or was just very frightened.

She laid herself over the curve of the edge and he pulled himself towards her. Her arms ached and her fingers were slippery in his tight squeeze and he didn't seem to be moving forward at all. No, no, no, came her own little voice in her head. Blood pulsed behind her eyes and then he was next to her, reeling her in from the edge, his fingers hard and prodding in her soft stomach.

They staggered up out of the mud on shaking legs, like new foals. Her breath hurt in her chest. The rain, the sea crashing, she couldn't separate any of them. 'Don't tell, Jackie?'

He gave a little shake of his head, blinking slowly. He'd never tell on her, she knew it. She could do anything and he wouldn't tell. He was the same with Lou, and Mum.

''Cause you, you shouldn't have been so close to the edge. What were you doing out there? Mucking around!'

'I said I won't tell.' His chest filled and emptied inside his muddy T-shirt. 'Wait here while I get towels.' He turned and walked across the lawn to the sliding glass doors of the downstairs den, pulling off his shirt and wiping his feet on the mat. Phoebe panted as though she'd run a race, or was mad, madder than she'd ever been. She watched him go, his head bent, but when he stepped inside, the doors reflected darkness and she couldn't see him any more.

AFTERWARDS

Jack stood at the rise of his old driveway on the Plateau, sweating after the climb. He'd only split from Georgie six months before and already it looked as though someone was cooking meth in his old house. Scrappy lawn, a trailer in the corner near the front hedge. Crisping jasmine vines falling off the iron verandah fence and red brick walls. Tiles missing on the front steps.

How long before Indi noticed all this and didn't want her friends over? Maybe he could wait till Georgie was out and do a few jobs around the place. What could she say about it? My husband mowed the lawn and cemented a few tiles back in place. I'm going to need full custody.

He got out of the car and smelled pot, saw smoke drifting out over the railing of the verandah. She was in there on the couch, hidden by the jasmine, had known he was there from the moment he arrived. As he climbed the short flight of stairs he saw her in the deep shade, tiny on the big old corduroy couch. When he reached the top she held the joint up to him, and he took it and sat next to her, his backside almost touching the floor as the couch sank towards it. 'Your hair.'

'Don't say anything. Indi won't let me take it out yet.' The slight rasp of her voice, it killed him.

'Make it rattle.'

'Get fucked.'

'Might give the jasmine a trim.'

'If you like.'

He took a second drag and felt his insides soften. He pulled up his knees and leaned on them, looking at the blue sky above the jasmine tangle as their cubby filled with smoke. He'd rented this house twelve years ago when he came back to Bilgola, having dropped out of art school, overwhelmed by the city and the enforced sociability of the college routine, the constant striving and feedback. It had been such a relief, the reduced pressure of humanity; to pull up in his driveway at night and turn off the motor, the black spaces between the houses rustling, alive with different kinds of life. Then Phoebe introduced him to Georgie one night in the bar and within a month she was living there too, sunbaking on the lawn with a G&T after a shift at the hospital, pulling him under the sprinkler when he got home from work. She'd been on at him to buy it since the moment she twigged that if Lou and Phoebe had trust funds substantial enough to get into property, he must have a pile stashed away somewhere as well.

'What's the story, George?'

'With what?' She sounded like she might lay her head on his lap and go to sleep.

'Could we figure something out? I can't handle it like this. You there the other day waiting for me to trip up. I need to know when I'm going to see her and that just be how it is.'

She took the last couple of centimetres of joint from him. 'How do I know something won't happen?'

'Come on, George.'

'I mean it.'

'I'm her dad. I won't let anything happen.'

She turned to face him; he felt it but kept his eyes on the strip of sky above the railing. He knew what she was talking about. In the last days, when they'd been waiting for one of them to say something so terrible that it had to be the end—boxes had to be packed, access to Indi had to be arranged because there was no going back—she had come home from work to find him lying on the lawn, the mower going, Indi lying on her back in her paddling pool, eyes closed, only her face above the waterline. She'd been eight. She was too big, wasn't she, to drown in that little pool? That was what finished things. Georgie had filled a bucket from the paddling pool and thrown it over him, scooped Indi up, bewildered and shouting. He'd woken to the shock of the water, the grass prickling his cheek, like he was back in his childhood. Except here was the black shape of his wife holding a crying child, blocking out the sky, and a new kind of shame filling him up. She'd locked him outside in the cooling dusk and he'd been sleeping in his mother's shed ever since.

'You're the problem.'

'I take good care of her.'

'You'll have a fit. I'm not saying it'll be your fault.'

'They're not fits.'

She folded her arms.

'I've tried to explain it to you. I think I'm going to faint but I don't, hardly ever.' He'd gone for years with nothing, after he met her and they had Indi, not even a flutter. 'I'm always calm around her. She keeps me calm.' He made himself look at her, at her mouse-ish face, childish and careworn, like a Victorian kid with ten siblings to watch over. 'Listen, I know what you're worried about. I've always got Lou or Feebs with me if we go for a swim, okay? We walk almost everywhere.' She looked down at her lap. 'George, we made a lovely kid. I can't believe we didn't fuck her up, but we didn't. I feel great every second she's with me. That day, I was stressed, about us. I've got all that under control now. I do exercises. I go to the doc's.'

'Yeah, well. You're not gonna be happy unless you have her all the time.'

'I get the deal. I just can't fight with you about it. It's like breaking up over and over again.'

She laid her head back on the couch and stubbed out the joint in the ashtray on the couch arm. 'D'you know she's in the soccer final?'

'No! Why didn't she say?'

'She's waiting to see if she wins. Wants to surprise you.'

'I want to see her win. Or lose, whatever.'

'Yeah. You can come, if she says.'

'Good. Tell me when. I'll make sure I'm free. I really want to go. I promise not to swear at the ref.'

'Doing better than me, then.'

He laughed. 'Georgie—'

'Every minute she's gone, I'm thinking Blondie's gonna figure out a way for your crowd to keep her full-time.'

He closed his eyes. If Lou could do that she would. Joked about getting a bogan AVO. Maybe he'd let her. No, he wouldn't. Indi adored George. She was a fun mum, when she wasn't fighting with him. Loved the things kids loved, making messes in the kitchen, screaming on the rides at Luna Park.

'Indi likes the pool over there, and seeing her cousin. Just trying to make it normal when she comes over. Like life's still good.'

''Cause it's shit here?'

'I don't know what it's like here. I can only look after my bit.'

He didn't have to look at her to know she was crying. He put his arm around her and it felt like it was supposed to, that there was nothing wrong with this. She was bony in her ribs and shoulders, soft elsewhere, her chest, her tummy since Indi; warm, same as ever. She put her hand on his thigh and kissed him. He didn't think anything, just kissed back, pressed the softness of her lips with his own and pulled her up to her feet, her hair rattling. He laughed and she looked at him like he was responsible for her unhappiness and fear and also somehow for this thing she'd done to her hair.

The screen door came towards him. He followed her through it and raised his hand behind him automatically to stop it from slamming. The house was messy, the dishes piled up, clothes lying around, but it was messy in another dimension, far from him. He followed her, thinking of nothing, seeing her brown neck and shoulders under the thin straps of her top. Smells of Indi as he passed through the corridor: bubble bath, disinfectant cream; pictures on the fridge, none of him. He tried not to imagine the moment in which she had stood here, pulling them all down. Into Georgie's room. His room. Messier than he had kept it but mostly unchanged—an ordinary square room made pretty by the light on the floorboards, the forest-green quilt. The thought—who else has been here?—but again the thought far from him, not really his. He fell into it, her bed, into her. Pushed his face against the tanned skin of her neck. Wished, and in the same moment received.

~

Jack crept out of his old home as the heat of late summer was rising, cicadas thrumming with an intensity that felt interior. 'It isn't over, George,' he'd murmured into her neck. She kept her eyes closed, pushed her forehead into his, and he got up quietly, pulled on his clothes. When he was dressed he stood still and looked at her lying there for a few moments, the sun on her face and her dark blonde braids. He kneeled on the bed and kissed her cheek.

She opened her eyes and said quietly, 'Don't know if I believe in fresh starts.'

'We can do anything we want to do,' he replied, and picked up his shoes, carried them out onto the verandah. He opened and closed the screen door with barely a sound, as though he didn't want to startle her back into the hostility that surrounded this hour.

He walked down between the houses and into the reserve. It smelled damp, cool, pleasantly fetid. The birds cawed across the valley. There was no one else in the world.

When they saw each other again, it was likely they would be as they were before, watchful and snappy. But tripping down through the angophora forest, cabbage palm fronds strewn across his path, the light thrown onto the forest floor in warm blankets, he did not feel like his ordinary self. He remembered driving them home from hospital, the string of lights along Manly Beach in the blue night. He felt that dream skin across everything that he must not disturb with words. If he moved carefully in this sunlit world he could keep it.

He let himself think their names, a spell binding them and him in this place. Georgie, Indi, Georgie, Indi, he thought to the rhythm of his steps. Georgie, Indi, Georgie, Indi, till he reached the track to the street, slipping between the houses, past the washing lines and plastic slides, onto his street cast still in morning shade.

By the time he reached the door, something of the feeling had left him. He had started to worry; his old self couldn't be held back entirely. He should have lain on a warm rock in the forest drinking every drop until the shadows lengthened. In the shed he sat on the couch and closed his eyes, thought of the first time they'd taken Indi to the beach since she'd learned to walk. She had charged straight into the foamy wash, her fat legs upended regularly by the pull of the water. They had to take it in turns to follow closely behind and pick her up. She learned nothing, charging on, falling on her face, an adult hand immediately reaching around her chest and setting her on her feet. On she went, laughing.

Eventually he reached for the light. Every wall was covered with pencil drawings of life-sized palm trees, up to the ceiling. When he saw it suddenly like this, it seemed as though the forest outside had burst up through the floor of his shed. Indi loved the pictures, made up stories in which she was a friend of the animals in a secret, magical place. Weird stories. There was always a bossy, troublesome animal who was a stickler for the rules, anti-fun, like a wearying teacher.

He found these grey palms he had made ghostly and comforting at the same time, like stepping through a gauzy membrane into a specially lit version of the real world, appealing and strange. His bits and bobs of furniture, Tricia's cast-offs, huddled in scruffy groups around the room, as though he were just off a ship in some unknown land, the contents of his cabin left in the jungle, about to be strangled by vines, lost in the undergrowth.

Could he really keep living like this? When had everyone else become an adult? Phoebe of all people had bought her place before any of them, as soon as her trust fund matured. She had a proper career too, even if she did do the odd spell of pot washing when it was quiet. There was a deep vein of sense in her that no one had predicted. A selfish sense of what was needed for her own pleasure, an efficient understanding of the wastefulness of worry or self-doubt. She was like Indi, but not as nice.

Through the bedroom door a hibiscus grew out from behind his bedhead. He had painted the flowers deep pink but left the foliage in pencil like the palm trees. All the time he spent alone, kneeling on the bed, his face ten centimetres from the wall, drawing, rubbing out. Kept him off the beer though. All those empty hours.

What was to stop him showing his work, instead of letting it pile up in Mum's roof, giving the odd picture away to friends from college? He imagined standing in a room in an old ware-house, sleek people drifting about bearing slender bubbling flutes, peering straight into his messy interior, turning to each other and commenting.

In his hands were his notebook and pencil. He was drawing a face. Or no, he was drawing half of it, the other in shadow, only its outline visible. On the side that you could see were individual strands of Einstein-like hair, a startled eye with a deep flabby bag underneath, prickles of stubble rupturing grey skin. That face had only appeared for a few seconds on Lou's TV screen and yet here it was, living in his fingers, preserved.

He didn't draw people, that's what he'd told Indi, he didn't make the decision to draw them, anyway. His fingers did what they wanted. Here in his shadowy hut, in Indi's eyes an enchanted place, he sat, slightly stoned, his skin, his nethers, not clean from being with Georgie, and this half-face on his lap casting with its wild eye out into the room where he lived. He tore the sheet from his notebook and took it to the big laundry sink at the end of the room, reached to the shelf above for matches and set it alight, dropped it in the sink. For the duration of the tiny fire the shame was gone.

~

The main house, Tricia's place, was quiet. Though Tricia was not physically present she had left herself behind in the ylang ylang oil burning, the rebellious clutter of dried wildflowers, Polynesian carvings, the jam-making paraphernalia scattered along the wooden bench. Once she had not dared to choose a picture to hang or leave a crumb on a counter. She was never still, before, never sat in her own clutter, allowed the mess of life to gather around her. She had lived in a state of continual readiness, like a soldier whose immaculate kit sat folded at the end of the bed.

In the shower the palm fronds stroked the frosted windows rhythmically, as though they were telling him something, patiently repeating a message he was too slow-witted to understand.

As he stepped out of the bathroom the front door slammed. 'Hey, Mum,' he called.

'Oh good. It's you. Let's have tea.'

She sounded slightly out of breath but pleased with herself. He hid his face while he loaded his clothes into the machine at the back end of the kitchen, making an internal adjustment to her presence. Tried to straighten himself out from the pot earlier. He saw her brilliant short white hair reflected in the door as he closed it, turned and hugged her. She smelled of the candles she burned in her yoga classes, earthy and foreign but at the same time like one of the clothes shops down in the village.

She was taller than him and would always be, unless she began to shrink, which seemed unlikely with all her yoga. As thin as ever, with strong tendons in her arms and neck. He went to her classes, knew she could support her body weight for long periods in contorted positions, like a person transforming herself into the letters of a strange alphabet, one by one. You wouldn't mess with her, when you saw her like that, not just because of her strength but because she appeared to be in possession of a mysterious code that she was writing with her body. She might be performing a hex on you and all it took to release it was you haplessly mirroring her moves. He listened to her voice during the guided meditation at the end of class, *Allow your breath to replenish your body*, and was bewildered by the mystery of her, this calmness she had assumed, as though she were a new person, wiped of their history.

Drinking tea on her deep verandah, they looked out over the iron roof of his shed, glinting amid the cabbage palms. 'I should get out of your hair soon,' he said.

'What? Oh no, done for the day. All I've got in mind is a nap and a spot of weeding when it cools down.'

'I meant generally.'

'You're all right in the studio, aren't you? Just getting your bearings after all that whatchamacallit. Keep the pressure to earn off for now.'

'I've got an idea, though.'

'A business idea? Go on, what is it?'

'Not really. More how to fix things with Georgie and Indi.'

'Hmmm.' She sat back in her cane chair. Her face took on a sulky set in repose, now that it had lost its plumpness.

'Come on, Mum. Better to be together?'

'Sometimes.'

'It'll take cash.'

She nodded, sipping her tea, steam billowing into her face, droplets forming on her tanned brow. Her lips came away dry. He had a shifting feeling, watching her pretend to drink her tea.

'I'll drink this at the shed. Bit behind. Want to get Lou's place done.'

'Oh, she can pay someone to do it.'

'All those meals she makes for us.'

'She can certainly afford them. Anyway, it's Aart who cooks in that house. She's arranged things very nicely.'

'Still.'

They sat quietly for a moment, a magpie making its lovely warble amid the dense greenery. He stood and she brushed the back of his knee with her knuckle. 'Look before you leap.'

He took the stairs as quickly as he could without spilling his tea, or appearing to rush away from her.

~

Louisa sat in her airconditioned car, in a line of traffic on the Bends, the ocean gleaming from down at Bilgola, beyond the gully of cabbage palms. She had been in a hurry but she let her sense of urgency slip away for a moment, sitting here on the ribbon of road hugging its bite of the land, the lush forest crowding all the way to the beach, its cool ripe smell cycling through the vents.

She felt the presence of the house on the Serpentine across the gully, hidden by the shimmering trees. It was small among its neighbours, on a narrower strip of land, and yet it had the best position, closer to the cliff than the others, more dramatically perched above the ocean, more vertiginous and exciting. A helicopter swooped down over the ocean and she imagined a long lens pulling back, seeing her here inside the car, trying to catch a glimpse of her past.

The other day, while Phoebe perched on the roof and took in the view, Lou had sat in her old position at the top of the outside staircase feeling the moisture lift from below, closing her eyes and existing somewhere amid the voices rising from the beach. She was glad that for now no one had replaced the tiny platform, the rotting brown-painted steps. You had to feel that you were on the edge, suspended over that strip that was not quite ocean, not quite land. Charlie had expected the piece of earth he had bought to magically extend itself, for him to own the space around it as well. Sitting there, she had opened her eyes and imagined that for herself, possessing this piece of air.

The day they had left that house Lou had refused to turn back. Tricia had had to drag Phoebe screaming on her heels through the corridor and push her into the Land Cruiser. Lou hugged her on the back seat to hold her out of the way of the slamming door, furious that Phoebe was crowding out the space for grief with her scene-stealing drama. Jack was in the front passenger seat, his head on the dash. Above them, Don loitered on the street with the removalists, the keys to the Mustang in his hand. Tricia looked at him as she reversed out of the drive in the Land Cruiser but said nothing. Mum had left him behind, with the house.

What if, what if, Lou had thought and stood slowly on the rotting stairs.

Inside the house she had placed her hands on the kitchen counter and regarded the layout, made decisions about it. White walls, charcoal cabinets, Tasmanian oak floors. No garden, just terrace, lined with pots of lush and spiky greenery. An amphitheatre to the sea.

By the time she had locked the front door and slipped the string back inside her blouse, she had decided, and with this decision had welled a feeling that if the others knew her plan they would fight her for it. She was the only one who had access to the funds. As if Jack would want it, or Tricia. Still her wanting was laced with competition, an old will to assert her rights. Sitting in her Volvo now, turning away as the traffic began to inch forwards, there was a thread between her and the house, stretching across the gully of gums and cabbage trees. *Mine.*

Ten minutes later, having travelled a hundred metres, she passed the accident, a P-plated Mini crumpled into the rock face, being hauled onto a tow truck, the ambulance gone, a policewoman with her hand to her forehead while another spoke to her with only a few centimetres between their faces.

Death or injury then, that was the delay. They wouldn't be interested in her at least. And surely, if there was anything to worry about, sitting in traffic for the last forty-five minutes had sorted it out. Louisa blinked and calculated the quickest route into the city. By the time she reached the Harbour Bridge half an hour later her heart galloped as though she'd just downed two macchiatos in a row. A parking spot on Macquarie Street opened up for her, a gift. Welcome to town, Louisa Bright. She felt like a tourist, breezy, lightfooted, as she walked down Martin Place towards Aart's office. Felt the grandeur of descending the mall, which she knew would only intensify in Aart's office with its immense windows looking out at the smart shops and people streaming by below. She'd never been able to tell the difference between nerves and excitement, only knew she became restless when she hadn't experienced this rushing of the blood for too long.

When she reached Aart's office doorway, he looked up from his desk, contemplated her face, and closed his laptop. Time for everything in Aart's world. He slipped his wallet in his pocket from his drawer and said, 'I'd like some of that lemon tart they do downstairs.'

'Me too,' she said as he took her hand and led her towards the lift. She would run this evening on the beach.

She still loved to be out with him in public, to be this tall couple, striding through the world. The secretary smiled at her nervously as they passed. She was about fourteen and had those nails and eyelashes they glued to themselves now, and that surprised arch of brow.

Downstairs in the café, she was the only person in view not dressed in a suit. The waitress looked at her for an extra second as she put the two plates in front of them. 'I definitely want it,' she said to Aart before either of them could begin to eat. He looked out the window for a moment, then back at her.

'Is it a good investment? Perhaps you want it too much.'

'That makes no sense. Why make the effort unless it's important to you?' Still, his unruffled surfaces made her feel the need to present a case. 'Yes, of course the house means something, but there's a reason Dad chose it in the first place. The view can't be built out. It's priceless, forever, but the land's completely under-capitalised. I'd want us to live in it—it's completely amazing. But if we don't we'll make a killing anyway.'

'That depends on the price you get it for.'

She watched him fork a small neat wedge of tart into his mouth. 'I'm planning to work her a little bit.'

He raised his eyebrows.

'Nothing illegal. She's just a very confident sort of person.'

'No good for us.'

'No.'

He took a pen and notebook out of his pocket, wrote down a figure. 'Can you do this?' She chewed her lip for a moment, then nodded. 'Okay, then. I'm in.'

She picked up her plate and ate half the tart without stopping. She hadn't noticed her hunger until the smell of lemon and pastry reached her.

Aart smiled at her. 'Aren't you proud of the home you already made? I recall you said to me, "Aarty, this is our forever home."'

'I'd been living in tiny flats in London for years. I was pretty pumped.' She took another bite.

'It's okay. You are not the kind to sit still. So long as Magnus is near his friends and you are happy, I am happy.'

'Five minutes from our street on a bike. Be years till I finish it, anyway.' A dizzying image of a structure rising into the sky above

127

the beach made her look down for a moment, put her hands on her knees.

'You can never go back, you know.'

You can make the past better, finish the job. The grand unveiling. She shook her head. 'Just come and look. You'll fall in love, I guarantee it.'

He laughed. 'You are selling *me* a house?'

'It'll sell itself.'

~

In the shadowed streets between the tall grey buildings, taxis and vans haring by, Louisa shimmered like an alien fish in her aqua top towards the courts on Queen's Square. As she came around the corner she saw them, a blot of reporters with microphones like massive black matchsticks, booms dangling above them on poles, retreating slowly from the court building, hunkered around something caught in the pack. She took in breath sharply. Had expected nothing, somehow, and to be relieved, done with it, even though she had rung the police press office to check the timing.

She ran towards the small crowd, felt the heat of their bodies beneath their suits, caught a glimpse, over the shoulder of a lanky stooping girl with a helmet hairstyle, an elderly couple. He was tall, with a flourish of thick white hair. Middle Eastern. She was little and fat, white, with a soft, tired face. *Them.* Louisa did not hear a word the reporters were shouting. Their faces, the way they looked at these yelling people in suits as though they had dropped from the sky into their private world, their house, while they were eating dinner. It seemed that nothing that had happened in Louisa's life in the past twenty years had really happened. As though this elderly couple, just now, had had their girl taken from them, and this decimation of their faces and bodies was the instant result. This was what happened to people, what would happen to her if Magnus was taken.

The woman, Mrs Kazmi, *Helen*, the name arrived in Louisa's head direct from childhood, opened her mouth. To protest? To make a statement? Louisa for a moment could not look at her; focused on the fabric of the lanky girl's suit jacket in front of her. She knew what she had believed. It was a knowledge she kept tucked away. She would give anything to wipe it from the record of her life, kept in a secret place by her, and surely by Jack and Tricia, perhaps even Phoebe, in the deeply buried fibres of her memory.

The man was speaking. She remembered his voice from the press conference back then, and of course from the old time, before that, when he used to say 'Good morning, Louisa, ready for the Olympics?' if she was leaving the house for swim training as he was about to drive to the university. It was rich and deep, authoritative. He was a chemistry professor. She imagined his students were in awe, of his voice and, for all these years, his bewildering pain.

'May he die the worst death imaginable!'

There was a momentary quiet, broken only by the clicking of cameras. Then a man at the front called, 'Professor Kazmi, will you ever be able to forgive?' And the pack started up again.

'May it be slow,' he said loudly, and they stepped forward, aiming to make a tunnel through the bodies.

Mrs Kazmi, trying for an exit, saw her, knew her straight-away, looked at her without expression for a few seconds. Then something happened to the lower rims of her eyes, a softening, a blurring. They pushed their way through the journalists, walked free.

'Sweet,' one of the men said, slipping his phone into his breast pocket. Louisa separated herself from them and watched the Kazmis, his hand at her elbow, reach the corner and slip from view. She felt as though someone had walked up to her, placed a hand inside her collar and ripped off her clothes with a swift downward pull, here in the middle of a busy street in the CBD, a crowd of reporters standing next to her, about to turn her way.

~

Phoebe made a strong coffee, hair wet from her morning swim, and sat before a milk crate filled with shoeboxes on her dining table. Outside her dark apartment the waves and traffic pressed at the glass. She laid her hand on top of one of the boxes for a moment and it came away coated in dust.

Yesterday Louisa had given her the key to the house on the Serpentine and she had walked around it alone, taking photos. She had tried to ignore the strange mix of exhilaration and heavy-heartedness she felt looking at the rooms. As she was about to leave, she stood in the middle of the empty living room, looking out of the awful screen doors to the far headland, the slick green rectangle of the rock pool below, and sat down on that old carpet and cried. Just a few brief sobs, a quick release, and then as she stood up, leaned on the Formica kitchen counter to steady herself, a memory resurfaced. In the depths of the shiny green bench her reflection hovered, deciding.

Up on the street, she took one last look out over the tin roof to the Pacific, checked Tricia's yoga studio timetable on her phone. She kicked up the stand of her scooter and motored away around the headland, remembering Tricia's roof-space last time she'd been up there, fishing out her tennis racquet. She held an image of the crate she needed, tucked under the eaves among Jack's canvases.

In the hilly backstreets of Avalon the trees cast cool shade across her neck and the cicadas thrummed over the buzz of her scooter. She had a clear run up the steep driveway; no cars, no Tricia to tell her she should have left it down near Jack's shed to avoid the hairy descent. The hairy descent of the mad driveway was the best thing about this house, with its cream walls and camellia bushes, its cosy, hippie grandmother atmosphere.

Up in the roof she dragged out from amid a pile of boxes the crate of shoeboxes she'd spotted last time. Under the small window she took the lids off, sweating under the hot eaves, listening for the cars. When she eased herself backwards down the ladder with the entire crate she felt like someone in a TV show, riffling through secret files, stealing classified information, but these photographs were hers. Tricia had never told her she had them. She was just taking them back. Still, she occy-strapped the milk crate to her luggage rack on her scooter with fumbling fingers, hurtled down the driveway recklessly fast, the extra weight pulling her around on the gravel. A relief to hit the flat open road towards the village, away from the gloomy crowding of trees, a feeling that what she had tied to the back of her bike was some kind of currency.

There had been diversionary tactics before she had felt ready to tackle the shoeboxes—drinks at the bar, a joint before bed, a morning swim. Now, blinds closed against the present, she began to open up photo wallets at random, flicking through, the colours working their way through the packs: orange beach, green carpet, brown deck. Odd close-ups of shells, a spider in a gutter, Barbies. Jack and Lou with their dark tans and white eyes, Mum like a model, not even forty, Dad always gripping someone hard around the neck, or clowning. God, he looked like Jack. Their wild sandy hair, those pale green eyes. Or Jack looked like him, with his crow's feet from his outdoor work and surfing, their ages converging. In all the world of people they were so closely connected, these two, she felt it as a kind of pain, like coming up against a high, smooth wall with no opening. And yet it was true what Lou had said; she had never heard Jack mention him. If Phoebe did, in her family's presence, there was a quick flick of her mother's eyes towards him. Very occasionally she brought him up deliberately to watch for that reaction, and there it was, that lizard swivel, every time.

In the dark flat she scanned the first clear image she found in the pack of Charlie, sitting on the beach with the dark cliff behind him, his face, his smile lit against it. She blew up his face on her laptop: the lines around his eyes, the smudge of sand on his cheek. She could see individual grains, as though her face were right next to his, could feel the roughness of the sand, his stubble against her cheek. Then, like being whacked in the chest by a surfboard, came the feeling of after he had gone, hers alone, so far as she could tell. When she woke as a child her first thought was to find him, to engage him in some game or story, to drag him outside on some mission before he went off with Jack or Lou. Where's Dad? she would wonder, and the inventing would begin. Afterwards, as long as they stayed in that house, for those weeks, she waited for him to come home. That exhausting alertness, hearing the front door from the bedroom, the bleakness inside when she heard her mother's voice, or Lou's or Jack's.

When they moved, she had to begin again, remaking herself one tiny piece at a time. She started her new school at the end of that summer and she walked into her classroom, Tricia holding her hand, and then there was cold air where her hand had been. She had been less than nothing, not surprised when no one spoke to her, sensing when they stared that all they saw was a ghost, a shadow move through the room, not solid enough to make any difference to anything. The colours and shapes of the kids, their smelly, lurching presence, existed in another world. As she had begun to feel better, grew older and away from the hole in her life, she had watched Lou and Jack harden into themselves, Lou striding along that shining road, collecting prizes, Jack watching the world for what it was about to do to him.

Not for her, thank you.

She began to scan the better photos, tidying up a few details as she went, sorting them into folders. After a while it settled, the sense of being knocked off balance that came with seeing Charlie's face—and something else emerged. She had once rebuilt herself friend by friend. Every time a kid spoke to her or laughed at something she'd said, she became more real. Regained her substantial self, the nugget of dark, treacly laughter at her centre. Evidence was revealed of her own existence. There was something of that here, in this work on the photos, the removal of flecks, the lightening of shadow on a face. It did happen, he was here with us.

So many of them were just the blur of childhood, the glimpse of movement poorly captured, familiar colours. She made a pile of these, then pulled one from an envelope and thought: *Oh.*

Down at the rock pool. The girl. *That* girl in the air above the still-smooth water, foam crashing over the wall at the edge, everything about to break open. Except for a protruding leg at the edge of the shot, it was perfectly framed to catch her frozen above the pool and the photo had in it the sure knowledge of what came next, the shriek and the plume, the displacement of water and swimmers. Brief chaos. She could hear them screaming, the wave crashing over the wall.

I'll crop out that stray leg, she thought, but then looked closer. Pale orange shorts, short tanned legs with golden hairs. Dad.

She recalled the feeling that came to her on the roof of the house the other day, of that coolness on the steps by the pool, out of the glare of an intensely hot day. It was the girl at lunch that Lou hated. Mum wasn't nice to her either. Dad. Dad threw her in and then she walked back to the house in her wet clothes. She zoomed in on what could be seen of the girl's face, her neck and arms. She was smooth and plump in the face and chest and hips: a child, not a child.

The rock pool at Bilgola, she never swam there. She realised that for years, for most of her life, she had thought of it as a place you didn't go, that in spite of the work of the waves and the light and the rain, the continually altering shape of the sand, it was a place not yet cleansed of its past.

~

In the tangled loop of a dream came a knock at the door and a hard buzz from her phone on the table next to her head. The sun was high beyond the blinds. She picked up her phone. *It's your mother at the door. Are you there?* And then another appeared: *Yes you are, I heard your phone.*

Then her voice, out on the landing. 'Phoebe?'

She put the milk crate on a chair, scooped the loose photos into it, carried it through to her wardrobe and shoved it on top of her shoes. At the door Tricia gave her a suggestion of a smile and stepped inside. Its nerviness brought flickers of her old self, before the reinvention. She wore very long earrings, made more prominent by her short white hair and deep tan. For a moment Phoebe wanted to pull one to get her to look at her properly instead of that sly smile, that brisk movement on to the next object of interest.

'Hey, Mum.'

'Hello, darling.' She dropped her bag on the arm of the sofa and fell into the cushions, arms spread.

'What's up?'

'Nothing at all. What are you up to?'

'I fell asleep, working.'

'Did you know that sleep deprivation is as dangerous as smoking?' That conspiratorial way she had of telling you things you didn't want to know, as though she knew you did really. 'They've done studies on shift workers.'

Phoebe pressed her teeth together to keep the words in until she'd woken up properly.

'Let's open the blinds, get a bit of air, shall we?' Tricia said.

Phoebe pulled up the metal venetians with a sharp clatter, shoved back the sliding door. In it all rushed, the rumbling of the traffic at the lights, the beeping pedestrian crossing, the salt air. Her mother in the sudden daylight looked fabulous—lean, well dressed in pale-coloured floaty silk and cotton, her cropped hair glowing against her tanned skin—but also exhausted, when you looked closer. A hollowness under the eyes, hidden by her tan. It occurred to her that Tricia was old enough now to get sick in serious ways. She thought of her stepping out into the bright blue space between Phoebe and nothing, dropping from sight, and sent the thought back down.

'What are you working on?'

'Not much. Bit of work for Lou.'

'Don't you go giving her mates rates, dear. You're an asset to that business.'

Phoebe put the kettle on and groped about in the cupboard for a peppermint teabag for her mother. Tricia hadn't always sounded like one of those women in the boutiques, looking for a swish scarf to wear to book club. She had grown up at the far end of the Blue Mountains in a tiny cottage. Her dad and granddad had been miners, her mother had shot through early on. This was all recent news, shoehorned out of her by Indi for a family tree for school. Phoebe remembered her doing strange new things when they moved to the house in Avalon. Taking up yoga. Enunciating more carefully. Burning oils. There had come a point beyond which you never saw her smoking, or angry, or cleaning, beyond the bare minimum. Before she turned from the kettle with the cups though, Phoebe remembered her mother in the green kitchen in the house on the beach, giving Charlie an enraged sideways glance, a knife in her hand above the cutting board.

'Actually, I did want to get something off my chest,' her mother said, mustering herself.

'Go on then. What's up?'

'I need to talk to you about Jack, actually.'

Phoebe was on alert. 'Really?'

'Everything's okay. There's no need to worry.' Tricia, angular and stylish on the worn sofa, looked out at the hazy sky above the beach.

'What's happened, Mum?'

'You know, the money I borrowed from him. He didn't seem in too much of a rush to get it back. Muddles along, doesn't he?' She examined her long old fingers. Phoebe wondered as always where her own fleshy juiciness came from. Some fat great aunt she'd never been introduced to, whose genes her sister had either skipped or kept under military control. 'He sounds like he wants to buy a house, though.'

'Good on him. About time.'

'I used quite a bit of the money. He said he didn't care what I did with it, he had no plans.'

'Whoa.'

'The thing is he'd need quite a big mortgage and you know with his income . . .'

'Mum. How could that happen?' she said quietly.

'Well, the studio's never been a money spinner. I was doing okay with my super until the crash.'

'And he doesn't *know* this?'

She bit her lip and shook her head, was looking anywhere but Phoebe's face. 'Look, I was making a killing on the market, everyone was. And then as soon as he wanted his money I was going to be ready with it, with a nice bonus on top. I know it sounds bad now, but it felt like I was doing the right thing.'

'But why not just ask him first?'

'I just . . . He didn't want it. You can't even talk to him about it.'

'You're going to have to move, or get a normal job or something.'

'Who's going to want me at my age?'

'Sell the business then.'

'I'd get nothing for it until it's got some profit on the books.'

Tricia's thinness seemed like frailty in the big couch. 'What then? What are you going to do?'

'I'll be back to square one in another year or so, then it will all be fine. No one's going to be rich but we'll be back to where we started. It's not the right time for him to buy. The market's so insane. *You* know, Phoebe, you've made a packet on this place already.' She was talking so fast she was breathless. 'And really, I worry that he's pinning everything on a reunion with Georgina. That can't be a good idea—'

'You need to be straight with him. Work out an arrangement. Your house has got plenty of room if they need a proper base.' She found her face heating up. Christ, her mother would rather do anything than face up to a difficult conversation.

The mug wobbled in Tricia's hand. Her bony chest rose and fell. 'The easiest thing on everybody would be for Jack to just slow down, take stock. It's not going to suddenly be all sweetness and light just because he buys a place.'

'You have to tell him.'

'Phoebe, I can't bear to. I can't bear to let him down.'

Phoebe looked out the window and shook her head. 'The damage is done, Mum. You need to cop to it or you'll make it worse.'

'You're good mates, you two. You were sweet to him when she kicked him out.'

'She didn't kick him out.'

'Phoebe.'

'Okay, but he stayed away so they wouldn't be fighting around Indi all the time. He wasn't well.'

Tricia seemed to have come to the end of her nerve. She looked into her tea as though there was something worrying in it. She was going to have to say it, whatever it was she wanted Phoebe to do. She watched her mother do a bit of yoga breathing and waited. It was a sort of dark power moving in her, a liquid thread unspooling.

Tricia stood, unfolding herself to her full height, still managing to look vulnerable. It was rare this, surprising, at odds with her slightly snooty yoga serenity. 'What about if you had a chat with him? He's best off where he is for now, where I can keep an eye on him. Don't you think?'

Phoebe let out the breath she had been holding and laughed.

'I'm glad you find it amusing, sweetheart.'

'I don't. I just can't believe it. Jack, of all people.' Then quietly, 'If it was me or Lou, that would be one thing . . .'

An expression passed across Tricia's face, a current, so brief it seemed imaginary. What was that? But already Tricia was raking her fingers quickly through her white hair, adjusting her scarf and leaning forward magisterially to kiss Phoebe on the cheek. Peppermint. Cinnamon. Ginger.

At the door Phoebe said, 'If you want to get your money sorted out, seriously, talk to Lou. Or Aart. They're machines. They'll turn you into a machine. It's painful but you just have to submit.'

'Oh, well . . .'

'It's like being sent to the principal's office, a really smug principal. Worth it though.'

'I don't know, love. It's all such a lot of fuss, isn't it?'

Tricia floated into the stairwell in her flowing silk, pulling her garments about her, re-camouflaging like a moth melting into a tree branch. She raised a hand behind her without looking back.

Phoebe watched her glamorous form vanish, her scent lingering in the scruffy stairwell. What had that look been on her mother's face, running along behind her features, before she'd sent it back again? A kind of exasperated knowledge, an expression that said: You wouldn't understand.

~

On the bed, Phoebe scooped out the top layer of photos from the crate and dumped them on the sheets. Beach and blue, glimpses of green cupboards and carpet, flesh-coloured shapes, blurred patterns. Thumbs, clothes, nothing. She brought one close to her face, frowned and squinted. A hand with black hairs along the side of the thumb ball in a sharp edged mat. Hibiscus fabric. Her mother's dress but not Charlie's hand, with that dark hair.

She was on the stairs in the old house again, down to the den, that itch to be a part of things she was being excluded from, taking pictures so that she could understand later what she was seeing now.

The house was stifling and everyone was sulking and prickly. Don and that girl he brought with him that day. Her stomach shifted. Mum's dress. Don's hand. Here she was, her future self, trying to decode the messages she had sent herself, still locked out of the world of her own childhood, her own life.

This particular envelope had several photos of Dad but mostly glimpses, just his shorts in the frame, like in the picture of the girl, mid-air. One of him with his arm around Lou's neck, elbow height, going to bite her, her face half hidden by her white-blonde swimmer's hair. What you could see of her expression showed something about her that they all knew but never said. She was turning away from him, pretending to be pissed off, but there was a smile suppressed in the set of her jaw. Golden one.

Next door a man shouted at a toddler. The little girl was always trying to get out onto the balcony and climb the railing. Phoebe hoped they moved before something happened.

She looked at Charlie, looking out at the future in that sidelong glance from his daughter's hair. A youngish man glimpsed in motion, in fragments, by her clumsy first attempts at photography. She wished she had been better. He was almost gone from the world, wiped not by the slow erasure of time but by sustained effort. The others emitted a strange energy that prevented you from saying his name. As long as she had been aware of anything she was aware of this. Leave it alone, Feeb.

If she wanted to know something, or just to speak, just to remember, one of them would steer her gently and then gruffly away, as though she were a child drawn repeatedly to the dark path, where the den lies, with its needles and its scraps of clothing.

BOXING DAY

Jack's muddy shirt sucked at his chest and he held it away from him, revolted, as he opened the downstairs doors. His breathing was still hard. The messy grey water had surged over the fallen rocks as his weight bent the branches of the shrubs on the cliff. There was no time to be scared until afterwards, until he was pulling Phoebe back, his fingers prodding her stomach, the sea foaming below.

Her plump dejected figure lingered on the lawn; he couldn't look at her. A couple of damp beach towels hung on a hook in the laundry behind the den; he grabbed them and went back out to her. She didn't turn at the sound of the sliding door. A gap between fronts cast the beach and sea in strange colours, the wet orange sand a deeper shade than usual, like the dirt out at Broken Hill. The water was a murky pale green. Rain spread in a slick across his face.

Lou's face, down at the shops, as she held up that necklace. See? Proof.

He felt as though he were being forced to run in the dark, plunging forwards without any idea of what was around him, under him. He grasped hold of a habit: think the worst thing. Take it, throw it out to sea.

He approached Phoebe's hunched back, his bare feet sliding in the mud, could see how bad she felt and wanted to show her that he forgave her, that as bad as it felt, he knew that something so scary couldn't come from anything she had meant to do. He wasn't quite ready yet though; he needed to think through this other thing first.

Let's say it's true, he thought, this disgusting notion that Charlie had something to do with Monica never coming home, that he was, as Lou said, weird about girls. Just for a minute he would try to see it. Memories of Charlie leaning over Louisa's friends, flirting with waitresses, were stored safely in his brain, as many as he could possibly require, ready for vivid recall. What had Mum been saying to Don about him? And talking to Monica out on the lawn. How many times? Plenty of times. As she left for school, as she came home from hockey matches on weekends with her long socks and her brutal-looking stick.

No one would ever go near her, would they, if she had that stick with her? It gave her a fierceness, backed by heavy wood, designed to be wielded. He hoped she had had it, at the same time as he knew it made no difference now what he hoped, that there was something skewed about his logic, wanting now to give her a weapon when that moment had already passed and what was done was already done.

Phoebe seemed to be standing at an odd angle, the beach rising up to meet her. It was on him, the feeling, faster than ever, no time to sort out his breathing, have a word with himself, focus on the horizon. A surging in his head and no air coming into his body at all. He gasped for it but just took in rain. He managed to touch Phoebe's arm on the way down and crumpled in the mud behind her.

She was down now, staring into his eyes, saying something. The rain was like thunder, the sea so loud it was coming over the cliff to swallow the lawn and the house behind them. 'Breathe with me,' she was saying, as though from underwater. 'In.' She made a fish mouth, like she was talking to a kindergarten class. 'Out.' She mimed relief, her chest and shoulders sinking. 'In.'

He watched her mouth, grappling for the moment in which his breathing might meet hers. The mud was wrapping him up, pulling him down. Phoebe sat in the slime in front of him, rain streaking down her face, laid a hand on his shoulder, formally, as though anointing him. 'Out.' Fish mouth. Chest collapsing. 'In.' He nodded, mud in his ear. Took a breath. She nodded. 'Out.' After three breaths there was a panicky flutter in his lungs but he kept his eyes on hers, gold like a special creature's, and followed her. The rain was gentle on his face, helping. He closed his eyes. She was rubbing his shoulder with her small plump hand. He took hold of her wrist so that she wouldn't take it away. 'Don't tell them.'

She didn't reply and he felt something in her silence, smelled something familiar, tangy sweat, oil. He opened his eyes and Charlie's face was there above Phoebe's shoulder. He was looking at the sky, as though to gather strength. 'Come on, Jack. Not now.'

Jack looked down at the blades of grass, the sound of his breath like the sea in a cave. There was a bindi patch a few centimetres from his face. He sat up slowly and looked past Charlie and Phoebe at the dull beach. Charlie was standing now, hands on his hips, rain and wind flattening his hair.

Phoebe was looking up at the balcony. 'Why's there a policeman up there, Dad?'

Jack waited for his father's answer, knowing his mouth was open.

'Your sister's missing.' No she's not, Jack thought. And then, Is that all? 'Get changed and go see your mother.'

Phoebe lingered, watching Jack.

'Something not clear to you, Phoebe?' She bolted. To Jack, who was looking up at the woman in uniform on the stairs, he said, 'Out of the mud, for pity's sake.'

Jack stood slowly, made himself speak, voice hoarse. 'I just saw her. Why do you think she's missing?'

'She left a note.'

He turned and Jack stood in the rain for a moment, taking in cold wet air, listening to Charlie squelch through the mud behind him. After a few more breaths he passed into the stuffy den, and the smell of smoke, the voices of adults. He readied himself at the base of the stairs. Tricia's bright upmarket tone, brought out for strangers who intimidated her, blustered bravely on as Phoebe tried to talk over her. 'We're going to pull it down, of course. The site is really wasted as it is . . .'

He climbed the stairs to find two police officers sitting at the dining table with Phoebe and Tricia: a square-shouldered Islander man, and a woman with short hair and brown arms, emitting capability like a sports teacher. They were of a different scale to anyone who lived in the house, massive and orderly. 'Sister run off, hey?' the woman said after staring at his muddy clothes for a moment.

Jack studied his mother's expression. Two bright spots glowed high on her cheekbones. 'She'll be back any minute, head in the fridge,' she said. 'You don't want to spend your Christmas bothering about this.'

'We're working anyway,' the woman said. 'If it's not this it'll be some clown splitting his mate's head for looking at him funny.'

'Idiots. Jeez, I love Christmas,' the man said in a Kiwi accent and laughed. He looked Jack up and down, still stranded on the top stair. 'We might have a word?' A chilly breeze gusted into the house when he opened the door to go out to the platform, catching the curtains so that they billowed across the table and swept back over its surface.

Jack followed him out, wondering what Phoebe had already told him. Where had Charlie gone?

'You people are about to fall into the ocean,' the policeman said, peering down at the cliff edge. 'Worried about your sis?'

They had to stand very close on the platform, the man taking up most of it with his pumped-up chest and arms. The rain had eased but it was cold. Jack looked out over the bay, goose flesh on his skin. A girl was running along backwards in the water's white fringe, her hair streaking across her face horizontally towards the boy that followed, hands in his pockets. No one else was on the beach.

'I've just seen her. Like, twenty minutes ago.'

The man waited for more.

'Crossing the road to the beach, at Avalon. We were down at the shops.'

'We'll go check it out. I've got to say, your dad sounded real worried on the phone.'

'He's having a funny day.'

'Funny?'

'He's sometimes a bit . . . edgy.'

The man gave a single slow nod. 'You think he's jumped the gun?'

Here were the grownups, the people to put things back in order. There are times when he doesn't sleep, he might say, and everything starts lurching about. He's being odd about Monica Kazmi. We knew her. *I* knew her.

He saw the M twisting on its chain from Louisa's hand. This guy would tell him how stupid that all was. The relief that would be, or the opposite, a quickening of attention, the retrieval of a notebook from his chest pocket.

'She won't be far. Lou's got a temper, but she gets over it real quick.'

Even now he was scanning the grey waves and the dark, flat pool, though she'd already swum today. If he could get rid of these two he'd go out and look, back down at the shops. His money was on her being tucked out of the rain in a playground cubby with the boy with the hair.

'Your dad's gone out searching.'

'He won't find her.'

'You don't reckon?'

'Not if she doesn't want him to.'

'They don't get on?' The big police officer turned towards him and he felt his attention radiate in the small space.

'Sometimes they get on great. He thinks she's amazing.'

'Not today?'

She's not being amazing in the exact way he's picked out for her, no. Jack concentrated on the murky swell and waited for the man to leave. The dizziness lingered. This guy had already seen him pass out once; he wasn't mentioning it but it was there in his eyes, a sidelong doubt.

'We'll do a bit of a reccy but most times it turns out to just be a bit of a sulk. Especially at Christmas. Think of any other places we should look? Friends she might visit?'

'We've only just moved here. We don't know anyone yet. What did the note say?'

'It said she didn't want to live here any more, in this creepy house. What's that about, d'you reckon? Seems like a top spot to me. Your folks are nice people.'

Jack shook his head, counted out his breaths silently. The man laid a heavy hand on his shoulder and gripped it. He'd give anything to be able to just curl up somewhere where there was no possibility of being spoken to for hours. 'She'll be back soon enough, giving you the shits.' The rain was increasing again. He stepped back inside and Jack was forced to follow him to take shelter.

Tricia followed the officers to the front door, leaving the room empty but for Jack and Phoebe. They looked at each other without saying anything. Charlie's voice could be heard out on the drive, his voice calm, slightly out of breath. 'I don't want to waste too much of your time, officers.' At the sound of Charlie's voice he wanted to hide, but there was nowhere to go in this tiny house.

Charlie had been running. He couldn't have gone far but even a few minutes worked magic on him, like swimming for Lou. Sometimes, when one of them was batting around the house like a moth, Jack thought: Oh God, please just go and burn it off.

'Did you see her?' the man asked him.

'No, but she's a wanderer. Flighty. You got girls?'

The woman answered: 'Oh yes.'

'Gets a bit feral when her old man doesn't pay her enough attention. I've got this feeling she's all right, just trying to teach me a lesson.'

'Well, good,' the man said. 'We'll have a drive around. We've got a pic from your missus. Call us if she turns up.'

'She'll be back,' Charlie said. 'Tail between her legs.'

Then he was stepping into the room wearing only his running shorts, his skin shining from rain and sweat. He was smiling, his body relaxed. Tricia was behind him, chest held high, as though holding her breath.

Jack studied his father's face, but he couldn't see what he was looking for, some sign of what was next.

'Nice guys,' Charlie said.

Tricia shook her head. 'Embarrassing.'

They were standing over near the corridor, heads leaned towards each other, as though nothing that had happened today had happened, like a couple at a bar.

'What's embarrassing is my fourteen-year-old son curled up on the lawn crying like a girl. I couldn't believe that. What timing.' Charlie didn't look at him. It was as though he wasn't there.

Phoebe stared at Jack's face. He closed his eyes and ducked his head.

Charlie continued to Tricia, 'They know how dads worry.'

'Oh it's just hormones. I could slap her.'

'My tax bill's going to pay their wages till next Christmas. They can earn it for once. Get that girl in line.'

Tricia approached the table and let her spine collapse into a dining chair. Jack slipped quietly down to the den, lay on the couch and closed his eyes. Upstairs, Charlie put on his *Crooners'* *Christmas* CD. Jack pulled a blanket over himself while Bing dreamed of a white Christmas. He imagined snow falling above the beach, so thick and fast it coated the waves. The weight of the blanket warmed him through, sleep pulling him away from the world, the air outside turning white.

~

Louisa took shelter from the rain on the cold slab under the surf club balcony, her legs protruding onto the dark sticky sand. She watched the waves curling in a line along the shore, their edges messily crumbling. At the far end of the terrace some guys goofed around, shoving each other, laughing too loudly, their boards lined up against the wall behind them. She knew it was them; she'd seen them at Bilgola, she knew that guy outside the shops as soon as she saw him, like she'd always known him. She couldn't look up long enough to check that he was there without it being obvious, and then she thought, Fuck it, I'll look if I want. If looking makes something happen, then good. The boys whooped, pushing each other off the edge of the covered slab and into the rain, her frank stare making them push harder, jump further out.

One of them separated from the cluster, him, walking towards her, no mistaking his intention. He'd changed into his wetsuit. It hung from his hips, sleeves slapping his legs as he approached. She could do nothing but watch. He held her eye, not smiling. So sexy not to smile. She took up the challenge, didn't smile either. Then he was standing over her and she knew from the dip in noise, audible even beyond the drumming rain, that the rest were watching.

'What you doing sitting on your own?' He was as tanned as a boy living in an island hut, cheekbones running from the corners of his mouth up into his dark blond hair.

'I don't know anyone here.'

'You new, are you? Going to our school?' He gestured towards the other end of the beach where the local high school sat behind the dunes. His voice wasn't what she expected, not as deep, friendlier.

She nodded.

'Come and say hi now. Then you'll know people on your first day.'

She looked for a trick, an angle, sneaked a glance at the others, five or six of them, quiet now and waiting, as though something important was about to happen. The rain was louder now, muffling the sea. They were in a tent with watery walls, no world outside.

She stood slowly and held out her hand. He shook it, holding it too long, looking pleased with himself. 'Ruben.'

'Lou.' He finally released her hand and they walked side by side towards the others. One of the boys let out a rising cheer and another smacked him in the ribs.

'Fellas, this is Lou. Coming to school after the holidays.'

They introduced themselves, asked her questions—'Where you from?' 'You surf?' 'Got sisters?'—all at once; friendly, goofy boys, a couple of them tiny but then one even taller than Ruben, big knock knees, spindly thighs. This one reached down into his sports bag, gaping at their feet, and drew out a two-litre bottle of Coke. He passed it to her, head on one side. There was silence. She took a swig, carefully, wiped her mouth. 'How much Bundy did you put in that?' she said and chucked back some more. They laughed and a heavy silent kid next to her elbowed her gently to pass it on.

'Come here a sec,' Ruben said, and took her hand, pulled her out from the shelter of the balcony overhead and onto the sticky wet beach.

'Gonna get pretty wet.'

'Do you care?' he said, pulling her over the ridge of sand.

She was feeling the Bundy already; she wasn't sure the champagne at lunch had worn off. The wet sand under her feet felt good, cold; and the rain on her eyelashes, the heat in her chest.

He pulled her down against the steep dune, out of sight of the others at the surf club. She laughed, soaked, covered in sticky sand. 'Hey, Lou. You're quite the cutie. Give us a hug?'

She smiled and extended her arms, looking him in the eye. Fuck you, Charlie. Fuck you, Dean. He wrapped himself around her, held her firmly, to his ribs. His body was like a wall hot from the sun: hard, flat, radiant. What now? The beautiful grey surf rolled in. His finger drew a line down her neck to the fabric of her T-shirt, plastered to her. She could have stayed like this for hours in the cold rain, her body protected by his, his goofy friends out of sight, their calls drifting from the club. Tucked in, private, warm.

He let go and she lay back against the wall of sand behind her. He grinned at her.

'What?'

'Oh, nothing.'

She tried to resist the warm tide of booze and his body to think things through. It was not hard to figure out that this guy, Ruben, was some kind of trophy. He knew it; it was what she liked about him. She wanted him to still be talking to her when she started school or she'd be over before she began.

Just as his hand alighted on her bare wet thigh she laid a flat palm on his chest. 'Ruben, was it?'

He laughed.

'I've got to go.'

'No, don't. In a minute.' His voice had an odd edge—growly. She almost laughed herself.

Tucking her feet under her bum, she stood up into the rain, her hair sticking to her face and neck. She smoothed out her wet shirt where his hand had crumpled it at her waist. Her bra must be showing through. He looked her up and down, almost discreetly.

'I've really got to go. See you at school? What year are you guys in?' She nodded towards the club where one of the boys was doing a somersault backwards onto the sand.

'Year eleven, when we go back. How about you?'

'Ten.'

'Whoo-ee. What have I got myself into here?' But he was smiling, and he took her hand to pull him up, then draped his arm across her shoulder as they climbed the dune.

'Can I call you?'

'Not unless you want to speak to my father.'

'Er—no?'

'He always answers the phone and talks to whoever it is for ages.'

'Oh my God, girl.'

'Seriously.'

'He goes to work though, right?'

'Not any more.'

He faced her, hands on his hips, puzzling this. 'How do you, like, talk to people?'

'I guess they come and see me. Or we, you know, meet.'

'Original. Where d'you live, anyway?' he said as they passed the surf club, ignoring the other guys, and stepped into the empty carpark. A bus went by, spraying up a huge puddle. They stepped backwards in tandem, as though performing a dance move.

She gave the address. 'On the cliff above Bilgola. You can get to it along the cliff track. It's the nasty peach one that looks like it's falling in. Middle room upstairs, if you want to chuck a stone at it.'

'Ha. Cool. Well—'

A police car pulled up right next to them. The driver stuck her head and a beefy shoulder out the window. There was no one else here, in the rain. Louisa's face grew hot.

'Louisa Bright?'

'Yeah?'

'Your olds are worrying about you, love.' The woman gave Ruben a good long stare.

Fury rushed up in her, like lava. She felt him looking at her, couldn't look back. 'They send the cops out after you?'

She turned to him, grabbed the wet cloth of his T-shirt, kissed him long on his soft mouth. *Tell them that.* She released him and he took a step back. As she turned towards the cop car he melted away, that chunk of air taken up by his solid hot slab of boy flesh empty except for the rain.

The man in the passenger seat was getting out. Louisa started to shiver. He walked around the car and opened the back door for her. 'In you get.'

'Do I have to?'

'Reckon you do.'

Once she was in, dripping water on their leather seat, and they were pulling out onto Barrenjoey Road, her new world—the rainy beach, those shoving boys—sliding away, the woman laid an arm along the back of the passenger seat and turned towards her. 'Anything you want to tell us before you get home?'

She turned the M over in her jeans shorts pocket, folded her arms and felt on her mouth that hot kiss in the cold rain. He was so gone, there would be no stone chink on the window or scratch at the door, nothing, until she saw him in the yard at school and slipped her armour of coolness over her shoulders, looked right through him before he got the chance to laugh at her.

'What made you run off, love?' the woman tried again. 'What was that note about?'

'I was upset.'

'Why?'

'You met my father, right?' She felt dizzy as the car took the bends. I'm a bit drunk, she thought.

'Yeah, okay,' the man said, handing her a card. 'Take this. We can help, if there's something worrying you.'

She shoved it in her pocket and the officers exchanged a glance, looked around at the beach houses and palm trees, sank into their seats. 'Wouldn't mind a place down here,' the woman said to her partner.

'Back of beyond,' the man replied. He thrust his arm into the back again. 'Have a mint.' Could they smell the Bundy on her? She took one from the packet, surreptitiously holding her other hand in front of her face and breathed, put it in her mouth.

They turned off onto the Serpentine and she looked out the rainy window, the curve of Avalon stretched out below. A group ran from the surf club to the water, one of them doing jumps—backflips?—down the sandbank. She felt her exile, up here, in a patrol car, and understood the message. There she was with a boy, and boom, a cop car arrived from nowhere to pull her back in, like Charlie was a god.

The heat of the kiss with Ruben dissipated and there was Charlie, one night last week, in the tight space of the corridor when she came out of the bathroom, her hair wet. He leaned over her, hand on her neck, and said, 'Louisa Bright . . . you are the loveliest girl I have ever seen. You even leave your mother for dead.'

She had gone into her room feeling *pleased* with herself. Caught her bright-haired reflection in the black window, smiling.

~

Hidden beneath the quilt in Jack's top bunk, Phoebe held her palm close to her face. In it Lou's M pendant gleamed dully. She stroked it with her forefinger, wondering where it had come from. It was so pretty, she would have liked to keep it, but it would be strange to wear someone else's initial. And she'd never asked for a necklace like this because when she had a pencil case with a big P on it, the other kids had teased her.

Why did Lou have this? And why did she dangle it in Jack's face like that? She shouldn't bully Jack. He'd just faint, and no one knew how to get him breathing properly again but her. What if she wasn't there one day and he just lay there flapping like a fish on the floor of the boat. She hated that moment, always wanted Dad to hurry up and bash its head with the handle of his knife to make it stop.

When she had come in here a little while ago the rain had stopped but the bellies of the clouds outside were turning a deep sullen blue. Phoebe had kneeled under the window, plunging her hand into Lou's wet denim shorts, just lying there on the floor, encrusted with sand. She fished out a lovely orange twenty-dollar note. She gave it a rub and put it back and her finger nudged the necklace. She wasn't a thief. She just wanted to look, to see if there was a clue here to the fuss.

Beyond her outstretched arm her fingertips propped the quilt a couple of centimetres above the mattress to give her a breathing hole. A small circle of her room was visible between the bunk railings. She practised blinking, loved the way the circle opened and closed. The door hit the bunk next to her head and she jolted, dropping the quilt. Lou's breathing was here in the room. Phoebe's hand swallowed the necklace and she twisted her foot so it held the quilt up a tiny sliver at the foot of the bed. Lou stood at the window, watching the rain lash against it, shaking out her arms like someone on TV about to run a race.

'Well?' Mum's voice was right beside Phoebe's head. She tried not to flinch, to give herself away, breathed as slowly as she could, pushed back a nervous fart.

'Well what?' Lou said in a tight voice.

'Running off? Getting the police called out after you, on Boxing Day?'

They were speaking in furious whispers, so Dad wouldn't hear them fighting, probably.

'Which idiot called them anyway? It's the middle of the afternoon.'

'Honestly! It was you who left that stupid note. You seem determined to get him going.'

Phoebe's breath was hot around her face and sweat puddled at the base of her spine. She couldn't see Lou now. In the little gap past her foot all she could see was the window.

'What are you doing?' Tricia said.

Lou's head reappeared, she had stood up after crouching down. 'I had a necklace, a pendant. From your wardrobe. Someone's taken it.'

Phoebe stiffened, applied all her will to making herself small and still.

'What about it?'

'It's an M.'

There was a long silence. Eventually Lou let out one of her world-beating sighs, as Mum called them. It made Phoebe start just enough to lose her spy hole. 'M, right? *Monica?*'

Another long pause.

'You *silly* girl,' Mum said with that edge in her voice that told you you'd just said something shamefully stupid. Then the floor-boards creaked at Lou's end of the room. 'Are you joking?'

'Do I look like I'm joking?'

'Why on earth would you think there was a necklace in our wardrobe that belonged to Monica?'

'He's insane and creepy. He used to talk to her all the time. Jack noticed it too.'

'Don't say things you can't unsay.'

'Just listen, would you? He goes all show-offy with every girl he meets. What about Don's girlfriend? She's only just older than me.'

'Being a flirt is not a crime.'

'It's disgusting. He's married to you.'

'Oh, he's old-school, Louisa. All men were like that when I was a girl. You notice it when it stops, I can tell you that for nothing.'

'I should have given it to the cops,' Louisa said quietly. 'Then we'd be having a different conversation.'

Phoebe's hand clamped down harder on it, on the thing they were talking about. Its sharp corners dug into her palm. She wanted to be rid of it, to send it flying to the middle of the ocean.

'They would have laughed at you, love.'

'They're already laughing at us. They would have done a DNA test on it, though.'

'Louisa,' Mum said in an urgent whisper. 'I want you to stop and think about that necklace. Really think about it.'

'You can't just put me off because you don't want to hear it.'

'What else does M stand for?'

There was a silence, then Lou spoke very quietly. 'Who gave you that?'

'You, Louisa. When you were little. And sweet.'

Phoebe waited in the silence, thinking, Oh!

'Oh God, Mum. I'm so embarrassed.'

'Look, it'll be okay. Just stay out of his way, say please and thank you, sorry for being a pain, can I get you a drink, Dad? We'll step very carefully till bedtime. Your dad will sleep for eight hours and be normal tomorrow. Right, Louisa?'

'Normal.'

'As good as. Yes?'

She didn't hear Lou say anything but she must have nodded because Phoebe felt the air beside her shift as her mother closed the door next to her. Then there was the bang of the sash window being shoved up in its frame, a gust of cold air. Lou had most of her body out of the room. 'Oh my fucking God,' she said into the wind. Then the door opened, the wind rolling a pen off the shelves, and she was gone too.

Phoebe pushed back the quilt from her face and took in a gulp of cold air, sweat on her face in the gloomy room. She pushed the pendant into her pocket, rubbed her arms quickly and climbed down the ladder. Lou's pile of clothes, the denim shorts, were still on the floor, stiffening.

Closing the door quietly behind her, she went quickly to the pile. She pulled the M out of her own shorts and considered it for a moment, lying there in her palm, the chain spooling down onto her knee as she sat on the carpet.

Trying to keep the shorts exactly as they were, she gathered up the chain ready to put the necklace back where she found it. Chilly air moved at her back and she closed her hand on the chain, shoulders hunched, waiting for Louisa to go bananas. It was Dad's voice, though. 'What's that you've got there?'

She opened up her hand again, without turning, and he crouched next to her, his familiar heat and the smell of his soap from a recent shower spreading into the air around him. He took the pendant out of her open palm and let the M dangle in front of him. 'Where did you get it?'

'I found it.'

'Where though? Phoebe? It doesn't belong to you, does it?'

She looked into his eyes and thought she would try something. 'I think it means Monica.'

It worked; all of his attention was with her. 'How could that be?'

'That's what Lou thought, anyway.'

He took it from her gently. 'Where did it come from?'

'Lou had it. Maybe, maybe Monica gave it to her.' Lou's voice, in her head: Little liar!

He rubbed her head, stood slowly, the necklace still cradled in his hand. 'There's a reason we've got this.'

'Really? What is it?'

'I don't know. Let me think.'

She had a feeling as he left the room with the delicate chain spooling from his fist; it was like when she had begged Tricia for ten solid minutes to go on a rollercoaster with Jack and Lou at Dreamworld, and then, as she climbed into the cart, a churning had started up in her stomach, intensifying as the cart began to rumble and move beneath her. There was the same queasy certainty things were coming that she would now much rather avoid, but that there was no use in complaining, having brought it on herself.

AFTERWARDS

In the windows of Lou's shopfront were wooden shelves lined with randomly angled framed pictures, all by Phoebe, of jetties, boats, kids playing in a treehouse, a teenage girl surfing, a long table in a dappled garden, colourful with food. The only glimpses of actual houses were a blurred patch of grey weatherboard behind a tree or beach, a sunlit stretch of deck with a dog asleep on it.

What if you just took some of this? Jack thought. What if you said, Ah bugger it, and gave yourself permission?

He stepped out of the sunny street and into the cool office that felt not like a real estate office but a gorgeously lit café. Imagine Charlie, standing here, vibrating with glee at the way things had gone for Lou, the life she'd made. Jack was so used to having these thoughts flicker through him that he barely noticed the brief jab that followed them. Someone leaning towards you at school and spiking the back of your hand with a compass then looking away like it had never happened.

The sight of Lou's head agent Nik, whose suit and hair emitted a soft sheen, almost made him walk back out of the door. At the far end of the office, chatting at a table with the shockingly pretty office assistant, he saw him and stood up, smiled like Jack was a long-lost brother. He walked the length of the room between the trestles, a couple of clusters of women eyeing him, and shook Jack's hand, looking into his eyes. 'Coffee? Or is it strictly business? Connie can see what jobs have come in for you.'

'Not here about the gardens today. Wanted a quick word with Lou.'

'She's doing a viewing but she'll be back in a tick. Can I help you with anything?'

'I suppose I was wondering what you had on the books.'

Nik rubbed his hands together theatrically. 'A punter! Step this way.' He raised his forefinger at Connie, who was managing to make typing look like playing concert piano. 'Connie, two macchiatos please.' Jack smiled at her and she smiled back disarmingly. A chink was opening, a portal into another world. All he had to do was step through.

Nik guided him into an orange chair that supported his back gently as though it were sentient and slid a brochure towards him across rough grey wood. On the cover were the kids in the treehouse from the front window. Looking closer, he saw that they were the children of friends of Louisa. He opened the brochure to more traditional real estate pictures: beach and Pittwater views, intimidating kitchens, a surprising number of pizza ovens. In one, a mini-movie theatre with rows of reclining seats. He looked at Nik. 'Don't know that I'm in the market for one of those.'

'Belongs to a sci-fi freak. Holds *Star Wars* cosplay parties.'

'Got anything . . . cosier?'

'Let me get a picture of you as a buyer, Jack. Any must-haves?'

'A roof and walls. Nothing fancy.'

'In the affordable range?'

'I suppose. Although affordable's a funny word, when you stop and think about it, isn't it?'

Nik laid a hand on his shoulder and gave him a sympathetic look. How did Lou spend her days with people like this? He turned the page to a house that was pretty and modest, a big version of his shed really, a timber house perched in the trees, a sloping lawn in front, wooden steps from the street to the house. 'That looks nice.' He knew it was one of Phoebe's pictures, the way she made you want things, the way she used light to do that. The last of the sun on a roof. Kitchen lights in a dark house, a kid sitting on a counter.

'Helps to know your budget.'

Jack looked at the pictures, imagined. A shady deck with a table and chairs, some small images of the rooms, light and simple, with skylights, wooden floors. Palms outside the bedroom windows. 'Be plenty by now. Enough for this.'

'Want to see it? I'll ring the owner. If it's free maybe Lou can take you.'

Jack nodded, not trusting his voice for a moment.

~

Outside the kitchen window Lou faced away from him on the sloping lawn, laughing into her phone. Jack sat down on the pine bench at the dining table and imagined Indi in the garden, calling to her little mates, kicking a soccer ball around.

He didn't notice that Lou had appeared at the door. She leaned on the frame smiling, waiting for him to speak.

'It's a lovely house,' he said.

It was, steep and shady, like Tricia's block, only a street away, the house itself bright and spartan, with painted wooden furniture and old-fashioned patchwork quilts in the small clean rooms. This 1970s kitchen with colourful checked tiles above the old wooden bench. He'd be happy to keep everything exactly as it was. Although, in another month the chill in the rooms would be stronger, and the price was eye-watering by any sane measure.

'I can see you in it.' She gave him the sad sort of smile you give to people you don't believe will make good on their talk and wandered back outside to make another call.

There were three small bedrooms, enough for everyone, with a room spare to paint in. He stood in the little boy's narrow room, with its blue Thomas-the-Tank doona and boxes of Lego and trucks. Outside the window was a frangipani, its bony shape as lovely as something invented.

He should not have set foot across the threshold. This sort of wanting could be the end of you.

~

Lou tooted her horn lightly at a couple of women who had stopped their tanks on the crossing to chat out of their windows, cut her way through the lawless crossroads of the shopping village. 'Come on, dickheads,' she said amiably.

I'm going to spend the money, Jack thought, watching the people on the pavement, the flirting boho teenagers, the glossy mums. It won't bring disaster. It will just be . . . gone.

They pulled into a spot a couple of doors down from the office at a slightly skewiff angle. Been at the turps, sis? A brief thought, barely registered, the shadow of a bird.

As they re-entered the gentle hubbub of her office he wondered about the ripple that spread across her staff, the smiles that lingered slightly too long, the suggestion of a look one of the girls gave a colleague. He imagined she could be a bit of a bitch to work for, if you weren't her brother. Queenly, anyway. Not short on confidence.

Lou beckoned him into her office and slumped in her chair on the other side of the desk, arms open, palms facing upwards. 'So?'

He grinned shyly and looked away at the digital photo frame on the wall, constantly rotating Phoebe's photos of houses, gardens, beaches. She'd been on at him forever. It was her faith, owning land. Nothing bad could happen to you if you had that. Here amid the coloured chairs and lovely long tables, that seemed pretty convincing. It was the one thing his sister and his wife had in common. Georgie had just wanted a home. He could see that from the outside it seemed hopelessly impractical, stubborn, to hold out.

A mad idea came—what if he surprised her? He imagined taking her there in the car, blindfolding her . . . but he couldn't take another step in that sequence without imagining how that would feel, to have your vision blacked out and be driven around, your body forced through unknown space while you tried to control the panic. It was the worst thing he could imagine doing to anyone.

'Really going to do it, finally?'

'I don't know. I liked that house. But Lou . . .' He leaned forward on the desk. 'It was a million bucks!'

She laughed.

'It's got fibro walls! It will kill me if I hang a picture!'

'We can get all that checked out. As long as you know what you're dealing with and don't start knocking holes in it yourself.'

'Listen to you. You'll pick my pocket if I'm not careful.'

'It is a nice house. Not a bad price either, believe it or not.'

'A million bucks! There's no garage!'

'Worried about your lovely car?'

'I'm just saying.'

An uncharacteristically shy look came over her. 'Might be buying something myself.'

He said nothing, and she smiled. Understanding transferred itself through the table, into his fingertips.

'Tell me you're joking.'

'What?'

She coloured, looked through the glass wall behind him into the open office.

'Why would you?'

'We didn't know what we were sitting on. We should never have sold it. I never will again, I tell you.'

'You can't buy it,' he found himself saying. 'I'll never visit you again.'

Lou laughed. 'What?'

He felt as though he'd taken mind-altering drugs and was only now regaining his sanity. He was on his feet. She looked lost, briefly, looking up at him. Blurry around the edges. 'Come on, Jack. Sit down.'

'I don't want that place.'

'Jesus, Jack. Spend some money for once in your life.'

'It's not my money to spend.'

'He gave it to you. Whose else is it? Come on, sit down.'

He folded himself into the chair and counted his breaths.

'You hated him. Well, okay. You're an adult now. Take the money and live your life. Stop telling other people how to live theirs.' Then she was looking beyond him, towards the door. 'Get my brother some water, would you?' she murmured to a minion.

The water appeared in front of him. Jack had his breathing under control but didn't have words that Lou would understand. He wanted to make a deal. *If I can live without my own place forever, you can live without that one, okay?*

'I didn't hate him,' he managed to say, without looking at her. It was a long walk past the huge tables, feeling Nik and the women watch him go, without saying anything, without seeming to lift their heads, the whispering at a level beneath human hearing.

~

Louisa reached for Jack's untouched glass of water, watching her fingers tremble. Sudden raging hunger. Letting meals go made up for the calories in vodka and champagne but it could backfire. She pushed a couple of buttons on her phone and Connie out in the main office turned around and looked at her, raised a thumb with just enough enthusiasm for Lou to detect sarcasm, hurried out the door.

Through the windows she saw Jack crossing the road, barely bothering to look up at the gleaming utes and mum tanks bearing down on him. She continued arguing with him in her head. Why is Charlie's money okay for the rest of us, but not for you? What makes you so fucking pure and the rest of us so grubby?

She unlocked her drawer, extracted two minibar vodkas and turned the high back of her swivel chair towards the office. Downed the bottles, one straight after the other. She held out her hand; it was no longer shaking.

The house on the Serpentine had crouched on the cliff for all these years, waiting for her to return to it, to be ready to make it what it should be. She saw it, as it was, ugly, decrepit, and as she would build it: sleek, pale and low from the street amid the greenery; from the beach enviable and commanding. And Jack, she had no doubt, would sit on her terrace like everyone else, would drink her champagne and eat Aart's food without complaint.

She thought of Magnus as a young man, standing at a large window, looking out at the view, bringing his friends home to lounge around between swims, to hog the kitchen bench, to crowd the terrace in uni holidays, later with young families, her house the centre of operations until she died.

When they had bought the house they had now, she had sat at her desk in the real estate office in Chatswood, dreaming of her baby as a toddler and a rampantly physical boy, throwing himself into the pool she would put in, shouting and eating sausage sandwiches with his little mates. He wasn't that kind of boy at all, but she hadn't known that then, when he was a long, thoughtful baby. She had believed in some part of herself that he was recovering from the awful birth, the tangle in the umbilical, having to be cut free after hours of trauma for both of them. But that was just how he was, thoughtful and private, like Aart. She wanted him to always be like Aart, to have that life of calm and ease, immense windows, delicious food, scouring swims that filled you with air and light.

The night before the auction for their house, Louisa and Aart had stayed in a serviced apartment at the beach, near where Phoebe lived now. The noise of the sea was constant, the briny smell rushing in through the open windows, filling the white curtains like ghosts. Sleeping this close to the sea, after years in an Islington flat with buses swooshing by on rainy nights, had thrust Louisa back into that time at the end of childhood before she strode away from her family without a backward glance.

Aart slept under the billowing curtains, untroubled by nerves. She remembered the way he was, when he came into her London office on a cool blue April day and bought the Islington flat after one viewing. It was almost a flirtation. She said it was a bargain and so he slipped his chequebook from his inner jacket pocket, smiling. And now he trusted her to make good choices, and he would be in the city most of the time anyway, at the bank, sleeping in their Potts Point place. His skin was the dusty brown that fair-haired Europeans often seemed to go, his arm a beautiful dark shape on the white sheet in the light from the streetlamp. When she watched him sleep, she could not imagine a more perfect husband. None of that wobble of faith she got sometimes, that daylight sense that if she let the cover slip she would be revealed to be a rust bucket, a fool's investment, and he'd vanish without regret.

She did not sleep, running through the strategy she wanted to stick to at the auction, then simplifying it so that when she laid it out for him she would sound in control rather than obsessive and panicky. In the morning she rose calmly, made jokes as they ate breakfast in the village amid the fit blonde mothers with their casually perfect ponytails and beach dresses, discussed their plan of attack. They agreed that he would do the bidding, that it was important to buy at the right price, and she took a sip of her coffee to hide her face. He felt that if you really wanted something you should let someone else do the deal. For most people, their wanting showed in their voice, in the movements of their body and face. A bratty voice inside was saying: but *I* want to win! The part of her that lived in the world though, among other people, was as relaxed as the old blokes out on the pavement patting each other's dogs.

They walked along the beach towards the house, carrying their shoes, swerving down to the edge of the ocean at the flags to avoid the camps of towels and umbrellas spread across the beach. Cold water rushed over Louisa's ankles. The sand at this end of Sydney never came off once you got your feet wet. It made toddlers look like crumbed cutlets as their parents held them under the beach shower at the end of the day.

At the north end of the beach they climbed the path up to the carpark and washed their feet under the tap. The house was only fifty metres along the street. Just before they reached it, Louisa turned back towards the beach. The climbing sun threw a buttery light on the sandstone headland at the south end, the long bay of orangey sand, green sea, blue sky between. This wide street, the surfers running to the sea, boards under their arms, the bright, spongy lawns. Rain was forecast; a bank of clouds was building in the east. She imagined clicking her fingers at the sky and doom-laden clouds billowing in across the sea, reducing the crowd at the auction, easing the excitement that would lead to a frenzy.

As they passed along the side of the house a shadow fell across half the crowd. The house, in this dulled light, the auctioneer perched in the doorway at the top of the stairs, spruiking away, looked like what it was, an eyesore with a lot of greedy, competitive people clogging up its patchy lawn.

Lou whispered to Aart, 'I'm going to go, you do as we planned.' She felt the eyes of the auctioneer and the agent on her as she moved through the crowd. She could not watch Aart do it. Outside the house she ran to the beach carpark and felt the breeze sweep the sweat from her skin. Down on the sand, the clouds had cleared away many of the families and the beach was lonely, moody. She walked along the shore line, reclaiming this place of her youth, wet to her calves, rain beginning to patter on her skin, opening her body to the breeze. Around the headland growing larger before her was the old beach, from that old summer. The only reason to ever go back and do something again was to give yourself the chance to get it right.

Her phone beeped in her pocket and as she pulled it out dots of rain and sea mist appeared on the screen over a message from Aart. *It's ours.* Good, she thought, *excellent*, but knew instantly from the tugging in her gut that there was a loss intermingled with this win, because she had allowed Aart to do it for her.

Louisa sat in her office recalling her real wins, her true victories. Swimming had given her that feeling for a while in childhood, but then it had worn off as the others got better and she became more ordinary in comparison. And then there had been the opening of her own office, all those deals. She wanted that feeling again; it was what life was for. Those days when you could not be stopped, when all the air above the ocean rushed into you and you were light, fast, out ahead.

She looked out over her office, at her well-turned-out staff moving gracefully and purposefully between the long, clean tables with their folders and coffees, and thought: do it, Lou. Get the thing done.

The phone rang for so long she entertained a fantasy that Mrs Beringer had died, out there in her awful retirement villa, that a significant obstacle between Louisa and the house had been removed, just like that. She would sleep and wake in it for a month before she did a thing, alone, seeing, imagining, feeling where the walls would rise from the ground and the windows frame the ocean. The structure was solid by the time the ringing stopped: sandstone retaining walls held back the crumbling cliff and voltaic glass panels soaked up the sunlight, but Mrs Beringer's voice dissolved the world she'd built. 'What is it?' Sleepy, confused, querulous.

Time to begin the grinding down.

'Louisa dear?'

'Hi, yes. It's me.' She cleared her throat.

'All set?'

'It's a nice property, Mrs Beringer.'

'Not a bad view, is it?'

'No, it's very good.'

She watched the women in the office, Nik standing on the pavement with Connie, shaking his head at her parking. She let the silence swell.

'Something worrying you?'

'No, of course not. It's a beautiful home. I can absolutely sell it. You weren't kidding about the view. We've taken the most beautiful pictures. You won't believe them.'

'Okay, dear. Out with it.'

She ran a finger along the sharp edge of her desk. 'Well, you must have thought about the subsidence issue.'

'The what?'

'The front of the block. The instability.'

'We never had the least trouble. There are beautiful homes all along there.'

'It's very slow, the process, until there's a major storm, along with a big tide. Although I think we can take some of that climate change gloom and doom with a pinch of salt, can't we?'

'We had surveys done when we bought the land. It is absolutely sound.'

'How long ago did you say that was, Mrs Beringer?'

'I'm beginning to wonder whose side you're on, dear.'

Lou closed her eyes and imagined Mrs Beringer sitting up against a beige bedhead, that enormous chest sheathed in an old-fashioned dusky pink nightie with quilting across the bust. 'An agent's supposed to give you nothing but good news, right? But you know all the good news already. It's an amazing position you've got there. A great weekender if the buyer doesn't want to rebuild.'

'Why would they rebuild? It's a perfectly serviceable house.'

'Exactly. It's lovely as it is. People go overboard, don't they? I just want everything on the table at the beginning. You'll get a great price in any case. But buyers these days think of themselves as professionals. They'll get a survey, just like you did.'

'Of course, and all will be well. I hesitate to tell you your job, Ms Bright, but have you seen the prices on that street in the last year? I certainly have no cause to worry.'

Lou could see her free hand trembling on her knee. She waited, rehearsed her next sentence, then spoke it. 'I can get you the best price it is possible to get. That's what I do.'

Here came her sandwich in a brown paper carrier bag. In Connie's other hand was a long black. Perhaps her whole future would be different if she'd eaten her lunch at a sensible time. 'I'm sending through the first pictures now. You'll see how they accentuate its unique position.'

'It's the only house on that cliff slipping into the ocean?'

'I meant the closeness to the edge that gives you that view. It's extraordinary.'

There was a long silence. 'I'll take a look at them. We'll talk again soon.'

Lou swivelled her chair so its high back was facing the office and devoured her sandwich. She felt as though she'd just closed the door behind her on an interview room in which she'd enthusiastically displayed her own stupidity to a panel of stony faces. She calculated the price you could get for that house, if no one was wearing you down, if your agent was on your side. She imagined presenting such a figure to Aart and shook her head.

~

On the narrow balcony, Phoebe released smoke from her mouth and closed her eyes. The cloud of sea noise, the revving of motors at the traffic lights, a young man calling out something filthy, a brief eruption of male laughter absorbed by sea and traffic. It was distant from her and yet deep inside, as though she had swallowed the world and it reverberated in there. Then, a familiar voice, a child. 'Phoebe, you're not allowed to smoke!'

She opened her eyes and peered over the balcony. Jack and Indi, holding hands, peering up at her, Indi slightly cross.

'Sorry, Indi. Giving up.' She put out the joint in her ashtray. 'Look! Finished! No more!' She held up her hands so they could see them.

'Want to come for a walk?' Indi asked, all forgiven.

'Sure. Wait there.'

She looked out over the beach, trying to get it together. It was a misty dream, the sparse figures on it hovering, blurred. The paleness of early evening cast a flat sheen on the water.

'Come on, Feebs,' Jack called. 'Or shall we come up?'

'All good, I'm coming.'

She couldn't let them into the unit. She'd been working on her old photos; they were strewn across her dining table and kitchen bench. A plan was taking shape, but even in her current state she knew it was vulnerable to Jack's resistance. She brushed her teeth and changed her top, attempted a smile in the mirror, caught her wonky grin, her shining eyes. A walk was probably a good idea.

When she came down the air was grainy, the beach, the pines soft-edged. Jack and Indi had disappeared, but she could hear their voices over at the playground. She crossed the street slowly, walking through the evening as though she were easing her way blissfully through dry ice and dancing bodies.

She thought about her plan, a last indulgence before she was with Jack and needed to put it aside. One way or another she would get the family together and project the photos onto the walls of the old house on the Serpentine, while they had access to it. The ocean roaring through the back doors, the house still smelling how it did, walking about amid the ghosts of themselves projected onto their faces and bodies.

She settled into the swing next to Indi and grinned at her, struck her feet against the ground to set herself going. Indi laughed and began to tip herself forward and back to race her into the sky but was too little to find the momentum. Jack gave Indi several huge pushes and for a swing or two they matched, flying towards the sky and beach with their heads back, laughing.

Back on the ground she was unsteady but Indi took her hand and they all walked over to the beach in the last of the light. At the lip of the sand Indi turned to her formally and said, 'Mum says to say hello to you, Aunty Phoebe.'

She glanced at Jack. 'Tell her hello back. Tell her to drop round. Your mum and me are mates.'

Indi nodded solemnly. She glanced at Jack again and he gave her a shy smile.

'You guys don't normally hang out mid-week, do you? Is this extra?' Phoebe said.

He nodded.

'Things going all right, then?'

'Yeah. Not bad.' He looked down at Indi's head in a deliberate way to tell her to leave it there, so she did, though she had questions.

On the sand, Indi played at the edge of the water, and they sat on the slope of the beach, Jack laughing at his daughter showing off. 'Remember when you learned cartwheels? You forgot how to walk.'

Phoebe laughed but watched him surreptitiously. Unlike him to say remember anything. She caught the scent of him, lawns, petrol, breathed it in.

'Seen Lou?' she said. 'What's she up to?'

'Yeah. You know, moving and shaking.' He was looking out beyond Indi at the darkening waves.

'What? You two had a fight?'

'Nah.'

'Come on. What?'

'I looked at a house.'

'Really? Which one? Did I do the pics?'

'On Hilltop. With the cute old kitchen.'

'Oh God, that is a gorgeous house.' Him and Indi in that place. 'Can you afford it?'

'I'm not gonna do it.'

'No?'

'It's not my money.'

'What do you mean?'

He shook his head. Indi was wandering along the edge of the waves, pointing her toes and dipping like a gymnast on a beam, doing smart turns and retracing her steps.

'Because you gave it to Tricia?'

Jack was watchful but said nothing.

'She came round, worrying you wanted to buy a house.'

'Why is she worried?'

What was the point of him going about thinking he had money he didn't and Tricia letting him look at cute little houses and dream of the future. 'I don't think she's got it all, Jack. I don't think she can give you it right now.'

'Well, that's that settled then.'

'Jesus, Jack! Don't be so accepting! Make her borrow some. What is it with you?'

He wouldn't look at her but she watched his face and a look of impatience appeared briefly, a quick sigh. He got up and went over to Indi, turned his back to her so she could jump up for a carry. She looked at their shapes against the pewter waves—the way they were together, gentle and playful, Indi as much as him, tender with her father—and realised that of all the people moving about in the world it was these two who were her favourites.

She closed her eyes, allowing the joint she'd smoked on the balcony to send its wispy tendrils through her. That look of Jack's, irritated by her lack of understanding, just for a moment, that's what Mum had looked like too, before she'd left Phoebe's place. A series of images came, like a little movie. After the funeral, the weird quiet service in a chapel with no one but them and Don, no coffin, no readings, just some guy with a mustard jumper and a dog collar addressing their small group solemnly and impersonally, they had traipsed out into the blinding heat of the cemetery, she and Lou too stunned to cry, to do anything except blink into the glare. She remembered the traffic roaring by somewhere out of sight and turning back towards the chapel to see Mum and Jack in the shadow of the building. Jack was hitting the wall. A brick wall, rough bricks. It must have made his hand bleed but she couldn't remember seeing that, then or later. What she remembered was Mum grabbing hold of his arm and holding a finger in his face, giving him a talking-to. He was shouting at her, and she didn't know now why she couldn't hear that in her memory. Perhaps they were further away than the image she retained suggested.

Perhaps she had forgotten what he was saying. She didn't think so. She thought that she had never known. That she had always actually wanted to know. Because then he leaned on her shoulder and cried and she held him away, said something to him. 'Okay?' Phoebe thought she said. More than once. 'Okay?' And he had nodded, and then finally Mum had let him lean on her, had hugged him, and turned away from Phoebe and Lou and into the shadows.

These memories, like a piece of glass on a thread around her neck that she forgot about it until it shifted and cut the skin.

On the beach it was growing dark. Jack and Indi were standing in front of her, watching her quizzically, as though she had been acting strangely, and it was true that she had been somewhere else and had to refocus on the reality of this world, now. Indi leaned forward and rubbed her cheek. 'Morning, sunshine,' she said.

Phoebe hauled herself up out of the sand. 'I love you guys,' she said. Indi hugged her solemnly, as though she needed comforting.

'You really do have to stop smoking, Feebs,' Jack said, but he looked queasy, as though he could see the pictures inside her head.

BOXING DAY

When Jack painted he did not have to remind himself how to breathe. He sat under the window in the cool draft rushing in off the beach with his watercolours and his sketchbook and painted the trailing tentacles of the sky. The skin on his face, cool and damp, tingled.

Charlie's voice ran on steadily out in the lounge, but the movement of Jack's brush, the long sweep of those tentacles, blurred the edges of his words. One kept breaking through: three syllables, rising and falling, impossible to confuse with any other: Mon-i-ca.

Tricia's voice, finally, clearly, in response. 'Oh, please leave it alone. It's none of our business, is it, in the end?' A cupboard door banged, twice.

He left his sketchpad open to dry on top of the cabinet, out of reach of the weather, and leaned into the gap between the window and the sill, immersed in the sounds of sea and rain. The curtain of water brushed his face. When Jack was the age Phoebe was now, when he still had a gang of little mates and played with them on the street—tip, footy, catapults—Charlie would turn the corner of the street in his bricky orange Volvo, headlights on in the dusk. If it was winter, Jack would sit on the front steps in the dark after dinner and wait. Charlie would eat on the couch, glassy-eyed, and Jack would sit in close. Charlie ate one-handed, his other arm clenched around Jack's chest, squeezing hard. Jack never said it hurt. Charlie would let go soon enough, too soon, to go into the dark office beneath the house and work some more.

There were eruptions, sometimes, squalls, Charlie's mood building and breaking and building again over several days like summer weather. If some well-meaning adult had asked, What is it he does? Jack would have found it difficult to explain. He had never hit anyone, even shouting was rare. He developed grudges and watched you so carefully you felt you couldn't cross the room without it drawing comment. He had names for you that you couldn't get out of your head. For Jack: Wuss, Princess, Useless. For Phoebe: Chubber, Baby Elephant, Clod. And subjects he wouldn't leave alone. Whether they were eating properly. Was Tricia putting on weight, letting herself go? Were his business partners out to get him? Odd obsessions with the news—the nuclear capabilities of Russia, teenage gangs in the suburbs. Most disconcerting were the eruptions of playfulness, seeing who could jump the furthest off the boat, racing them along footpaths filled with shoppers, Tricia unable to watch, Jack left panting and trembling.

The squalls passed and you could still be hopeful in the long blue stretches in between. You could believe that everything would be all right because life was good, most of the time. Jack might still be everything Charlie wanted him to be. Phoebe just had puppy fat, her squishy arms and legs no different to other little kids. She rode on Charlie's leg as he walked down the stairs to his office. Tricia cooked and cleaned and played tennis, never ever losing. Her legs in her whites were deeply tanned and scissored across the court, part of a relentless machine made for winning. Jack used to go with her when he was little and draw on the court with a stone, glancing up every now and then to indulge his secret pride in his mother beating one of his friend's mothers, again. And then, because she was the club coach, they had to put up with her giving them pointers. When Phoebe was big enough to come he drew her hopscotch squares and noughts and crosses grids and let her win. At home Louisa's hair flashed through the dark house as she ran through the corridor and up and down the stairs and Charlie followed her; for her there was just enough left over from his work.

Jack took a breath and wiped the rain off his face with his sleeve. Charlie had always had spells; they'd been a part of Jack's childhood in a way he absorbed when he was younger. As Jack grew older he saw the pattern, read the signs, became sensitive to drops in temperature, distant tremors. And then Tricia kept everyone moving, at tennis, swimming, his art lessons, until they passed, like a southerly, leaving a few chairs upturned but a freshness in the air.

Charlie needed work, great tidal surges of it, swamping him daily, keeping him tired enough only to talk about the deal he had made today, the builder he ground down, the old lady he finally convinced to give up the last house preventing him from whacking up a block of units. To tell them again how he alone had had the grit to survive the recession without a single quarter of loss.

But there had been whispers of something else, of taking things too far, pushing the boundaries. What Don had said to Tricia when they thought they were alone—that he burned his bridges—wasn't a surprise, not entirely.

Jack tried not to think about the days unspooling ahead of him in which he would be prey to Charlie's moods and comments, the way he sought you out, this tightness in his chest ready to clamp down at any moment. When things were difficult and Charlie left for work, the atmosphere changed in the house, the light even. Tricia made jokes. Phoebe took a break from showing off, was just funny and sweet. Breathing was easier. Perhaps Tricia could talk him into starting another business. Building a house was all very well but then he would never actually *leave* the house.

He pulled his head back into the room and was re-immersed in the sounds from the kitchen, Phoebe singing, pots clattering. He wanted to resist it, he knew this was his problem, but he needed to just ... check. Out in the lounge the awful green carpet had dulled to the colour of mould in the overcast weather. Tricia was kneeling on the floor in the kitchen with her head in a cupboard, passing back to Phoebe a cheese grater, an egg whisk, a pile of cooking pots. Phoebe was piling them all on the kitchen bench. Tricia's hand thrust towards her and Phoebe passed a cleaning cloth. Then Phoebe tapped the metal items with a knife to the rhythm of a Bryan Adams song she just would not leave alone, singing it under her breath. Jack watched this activity for several seconds rather than look at Charlie, hunched over the dining table, cutting sections out of the newspaper.

Phoebe finally noticed Jack. 'How come he doesn't have to help?'

Tricia carried on, inside the cupboard, spraying and scrubbing. Charlie laid down his scissors and turned towards him. 'Oh good. I do need your help, outside.'

'It's raining.'

'It's just water.' He stood up and moved towards Jack, passing him in the corridor. 'Come on, Jack. I need you to hold the ladder.'

Charlie brushed past him, smelling more strongly of sweat than usual, the freshness of it tipped into sourness, eyes pink. Jack pressed back against the wall to let him by, but followed him out the door into the rain. 'Dad?' he called after him, but he didn't hear. Water was gushing down the driveway. It ran over his feet, cool, distracting. Charlie was squeezing between the cars to the back of the carport, shifting the ladder from one corner to the other, leaning it against the high shelves in the corner behind his Mustang. 'Come and hold it off the car.'

Jack moved slowly into the carport, into the smell of dust, oil, damp.

'Dad, are you okay?' he said as he took hold of the ladder.

Charlie didn't answer, began to climb, pulling boxes out from the shelves, peering inside.

'Are you sleeping all right? Sea's noisy, isn't it?'

'Do you remember those flying lanterns we set off on that beach?'

'In Koh Samui?'

'I've got a whole packet of them. I saw them when we moved.'

'They won't work in the rain, will they?'

'It won't rain forever.'

Jack looked up at his father's strong, short legs, his shiny back. What was in his head? How did one thought lead to the next?

He imagined the workings of Charlie's brain like a school of fish, responding to some unknown force, flicking sideways, surging forwards in a new direction and formation.

Charlie laughed sadly as he rummaged on the top shelf. 'Remember Feeb? Running along the beach after them, crying?'

'I had to catch her.'

'Pretty quick for a little chubber, wasn't she? Not as fast as you, thank Christ.'

The velvety darkness of the tropical night had swallowed her in seconds. He only knew which way she was going because of the shrinking beacon in the sky and her bereft sobs, louder than the warm sea lapping his ankles as he ran. He ran with his hands forward to catch her, found a soft shoulder, picked her up and let her cry snottily on his bare shoulder.

'What happened to your running, Jack? You were like lightning.'

Those race days, Dad on the sidelines, screaming. He ran in secret now, when Charlie was out, in bursts on the beach, on the track behind the old house, giving in to a once simple pleasure that had become illicit and complicated. 'I didn't know you brought any back.'

'Promised Feeb. She marched me to the shops. I didn't know the words. Had to act it all out. Glad I did now. They'll be perfect.'

He chucked something down behind him and Jack let go of the ladder, a panicky flutter moving through him as he caught it, a plastic bag filled with flattened paper lanterns on wire frames. He replaced a hand on the ladder as Charlie climbed down.

'Are you allowed to do these here?'

'Oh, Jack,' he sounded so weary that Jack felt sympathy for him for a moment. 'Grow a set, would you?'

Jack shook his head minutely and returned to the front door. Charlie trotted after him. He took hold of his arm gently and turned him around. 'Hey, Jack, would you like me to call those coppers back? Get a permit?'

'Oh,' he said, the two of them standing close in the entrance. 'Can you—do that?'

'Don't be such a goose.' He walked back to the carport, laughing. Jack watched him for a moment, imagined running up behind him and pushing him onto his car, getting him on the ground, putting a knee in his face.

Inside, Tricia was plunging the clean pots from the bench into the sink, almost overflowing with foam. Phoebe was drying up, singing loudly, theatrically.

'Mum!' Jack said sharply, wanting an answer before Charlie came back in.

She paused and looked sideways at him.

'Why does he want those lanterns?'

'Apparently he's planning a ceremony.'

He looked at her for a few seconds. She was telling him something with her expression—*leave it alone*—and then she continued to wash pots that had already been washed. The clock above her head said six-fifteen. If he went to bed when Phoebe did, offered to read her a story, this day could be over in less than three hours. He couldn't imagine this thumping of his heart, the heat at the base of his neck, ever receding. The rain drummed heavily on the roof. He just needed to keep away from Charlie. Frightening urges welled, to do something to him, break his nose, or an arm, hear something splinter, make something, finally, crack.

~

The rectangle of water, a glossy green film this morning, was roiling charcoal lava now. The sky, the rock platform were different shades of slate. Even the crumbly orange cliff was dull: old, wet honeycomb. Louisa dived in and salt water shot into her nostrils. She pushed forward and the fatigue from her previous swim, the churn in the water, made it feel as though she were dragging her body through honey.

For three exhausting laps she was a body not a mind. She rested her elbows and head on the concrete lip of the pool, lifted her goggles and looked at the little house perched up there on the rock at the far end of the rainy beach. Surf crashed over the corner of the pool, pulling her legs towards the beach and away, swirling softly.

She turned towards the pool, looked out over the dark rock platforms towards the next blunt headland and wished she could erase the last two hours, or erase Jack and Tricia's memory of them. She shivered with the expulsion from her body of the crazy belief she'd dared to put into the world. He was the one who'd gone off with that girl and called the cops on her. Still, Louisa, her own voice sounded in her head. *Still.* Yeah. Okay. The last of her fury and the last of her shame ebbed with the movement of the swirling water, leaving her body free and clean.

She kicked along on her back, away from the beach and the house, looking at the messy sky. A thought arrived: I'm done with swimming. I'm not doing maths tutoring either. I'm not going to Sydney Uni. Simple as that, off it all went, into the clouds, other people's ambitions leaving her body. She'd get a job, save up. One day, her own business. In the meantime, going off to work in a tight dark suit and a shining white blouse with just enough buttons open. Swimming after, in the little pool at Avalon that was pointless for proper laps. Maybe Dad could build it into his designs that her room would be like its own apartment, with a separate entrance and a shower. Her own couch. Her own place, till she was ready to get out there on her own for real. By the end of the lap it was her future, life changed in a few strokes. She just needed to step out onto that shining path.

Sensing she was nearing the wall she turned her head to see that Jack was sitting on it, his feet dangling into the water. She could stand up at this end. She folded her arms to keep warm and waited for him to speak. A shaft of light found him, he was bright against the dark cliffs and sea.

'He's planning some sort of ceremony.'

'What?'

'For Monica.'

She looked at him. 'I don't know what you mean.'

'He got me to help him find some lanterns in the carport, like those ones we set off in Thailand.'

'And?'

'Mum says it's a ceremony.'

She caught his look. 'Being weird's not a crime, is it?'

'You've changed your tune.' Jack shook his head and looked at the surface of the grey water. The skin on his thighs was deep brown in the dull light, raindrops quivering, blond hairs magnified beneath.

'Forget I said anything. It's just a necklace.'

'How did it get in his cupboard?'

She shrugged, looked out over the dark ocean.

'Sometimes I feel like if I have to spend another day with him it's going to kill me.'

'I figure he's Mum's problem. We just inherited him. Guess what, though?'

He looked at her fearfully.

'I'm dropping out of school, after this year.'

'Lou.'

'I'm gonna get a job. Uni's just more school. I want to go to work. I want to make my own money. Heaps of it. And travel. Do everything.'

'You'd really go?'

'World's a big place.'

'Oh God. Wait till I'm at college would you?' Poor old Jack. He looked like someone had told him they had six months to live. 'What job would you get without your HSC?'

'Real estate.'

'Really?'

'I'd love it. All those houses. Having the keys. Pretending they're yours.'

'Yeah?'

'Yeah,' she said, smiling.

Jack started looking a bit more relaxed. 'You're really shivering.'

'I've got to get back in properly or get out.'

Jack slid off the concrete and into the water next to her. 'Let's swim for a bit. Show me how to do a tumble turn.'

Louisa sank slowly, suspended in water thick like setting jelly. It held her, shifting her gently. She streamed along beneath the surface, molecules of something alive entering her nostrils, weeds stroking her ankles. She surfaced behind him, his shoulders shaking. 'Do it here where you won't bump your head. Be happy to show you where you're going wrong.'

He smiled at her and ducked beneath the surface, fell into a messy half tumble, kept at it long past the point of clear failure. She watched him twisting like a lame tornado through her goggles. She nudged him in the back with her toe and up he came, gasping and smiling, raised two thumbs.

She smiled back at him. 'That was shocking. The ugliest thing I've ever seen.'

~

Mum was scrubbing the backs of the cupboards, a tub of Gumption on the floor beside her knees, but Phoebe must have helped enough by now. They'd been doing this for ages and it wasn't dirty to begin with. Dad was in the shower.

'Hey, Mum,' she said. 'Want to smash me at Monopoly?'

She didn't turn around, didn't even stop scrubbing. 'There's still so much to do.'

'You must be super bored by now.'

Tricia withdrew her head from the cupboard and looked at her for a minute, a tiny smile behind her lips. 'You don't have to help any more, but I'm going to keep going. Thank you, Phoebe.'

'Tell you what. I'll set up the board on the bench and throw the dice for you. You can just tell me if you want to buy stuff.'

'Okay. I'd like to land on Mayfair and Park Lane early on while I've still got the cash.'

'I'll see what can be arranged.'

It was a phrase she'd learned from Dad. It was how he answered all her requests. You never knew whether it meant yes or no. Usually no, but he liked to surprise you, so when he said it a bolt of excitement went through her.

She went over to the bureau near the table to find the game. At the same time she was fitting songs to the rhythm of Mum's scrubbing. The newspaper was on the other side of the table, the writing upside down. Dad had been cutting out sections of it and stacking them in a neat pile next to the paper. She tested herself to see if she could read the top one, but she had to stop singing in her head to concentrate. One thing at a time, for you, Phoebe Bright, her P.E. teacher Mr Drummond had said to her after watching her try hurdles. You run, or you jump, right, Feeb?

Mon-ic-a Kaz-mi . . . She looked sideways at her mother, whose shoulders were still clenched and knotty as she worked away. What was she scrubbing at? It was like the time Phoebe had upended tomato sauce on the carpet at the old house and Mum wanted to get it clean before Dad came home. She stood up quietly and shuffled across the thick carpet around to the pile of clippings to read them the right way up. She went to the sentence with that name in it.

The bag of missing schoolgirl, Monica Kazmi, was found in bushland behind her school, The Bush High. She has been missing since 20 September 1994. No other traces of the missing sixteen year old have so far been discovered at the site.

The Bush High was Jack and Lou's school. Or it was. Why had Lou thought the necklace was hers? Were they friends? She looked at the picture and tried to remember her. But Lou didn't have any girlfriends, she realised, without ever having thought about it before. That was strange. Who did she talk to at school in break?

She read some more. Monica Kazmi went to school one day, went to all her classes, and was never seen again. Phoebe tried to imagine it, except it was Louisa, waving to some kids at the gate, wandering along the sunny bushland path behind the school where all the big kids cut through to the back of the suburb, and disintegrating in the sunlight. Scrub, scrub, scrub went Tricia's steel wool like a small creature in the wall. The breeze from the window dried the sweat on Phoebe's neck. She had heard the name before today. She had seen the face of the girl in the photograph. She came to life suddenly, walking past Phoebe's old yard out the front, waving at her on her way to school. 'Say hi to your brother,' the girl said and carried on. Phoebe liked her; she was a bit plump, like her, and really pretty, with her long dark hair and brown skin. She instantly liked pretty girls who were a bit fat; it offered extra evidence of something that she already knew but was glad to have confirmed.

Jack and Lou were walking across the yard from the path in their togs, dripping wet. How come they were allowed to swim in the rain? They were looking at each other and laughing, Lou making a twisting move with her arm like an elephant's trunk. Phoebe opened the sliding doors and threw herself down the wooden stairs, not caring about splinters in her bare feet.

She stood in front of them and opened her mouth to speak but could not form the question she wanted. 'Monica . . .' They scowled down at her. Louisa looked up at the house and then carried on up the stairs. Phoebe wrapped her arms around her brother's wet body and buried her head against his skinny chest, closed her eyes and saw the girl's black hair and white teeth, saw her smiling face clearly for a moment. She wanted to ask questions but she could not form the words. She had a little cry against Jack's chest but even in this could not tell exactly what she was crying for. 'Come on, Feebs,' Jack said quietly. Perhaps he had forgiven her now. She wiped her face with her forearm and he took her inside.

AFTERWARDS

Jack drove down the hill, sky fading above the dense trees. Indi was coming to stay for four days from tomorrow, the knowledge lit everything. Down he went towards the ocean, past a truck and a queue of utes and Beemers on a street corner: a *Home and Away* spotting. For an instant as he slowed to negotiate the narrowed street the cluster of camera operators and other crew cleared and there was a glimpse in the garden of a starlet's hair reflecting the last fall of evening sun. Her hair was long and black, like an Iranian girl, like a girl from the past.

Phoebe had announced a surprise. When his phone lit up on the passenger seat he thought about pretending he hadn't seen it. He could live without Phoebe's surprises. Sometimes she had something to get off her chest, like the time every single one of them forgot her birthday and she threw a maudlin party at her unit, got smashed and shouted at Tricia. 'You're a cold fish!

You never put me first!' She had a friend with her, Annaliese, who kept stroking her arm and flirted persistently with absolutely everybody until Lou had instructed her to leave. They all ducked around the idea of their own birthdays, but for Phoebe no family event could be allowed to slip by uncelebrated. You'd think you'd gotten away with it and then she'd turn up on your doorstep at some odd hour with a strange cake, grinning.

Sometimes it was a dramatic unveiling of her latest pictures. He hoped for that, the jolt of light and energy they gave you. She saw the light in waves and in people, offered proof that the world was miraculous, and for the time he spent looking at her photos of the ocean and the people in it, so unlike his paintings of abandoned places, he could see through that special window to light and life and colour.

The crickets thrummed over the car engine and in that pulsing was a sense that life was not quite real. It was like the feeling in airports, that he was set loose from the world. Down in the gladed streets the air was heavy with humidity and the sea rushed along behind the racket of insects. He thought about the house he'd seen, the sun in a warm puddle on the floorboards, the sound of the kids in the schoolyard drifting up the hill, distantly raucous like kookaburras calling across the valley.

Not for the first time he imagined living somewhere else, somewhere much, much cheaper, something he could properly afford, for himself, if he worked hard and saved. A distant slice of coast. Another bit of green. Mountains maybe. Somewhere without hordes of rich people building up into the sky to annexe off a bit more view. He thought about removing Indi from Phoebe, from her cousin Magnus. No longer lying by the pool on one of

Lou's loungers while the kids shoved each other in, eyes closed for just a moment, cold beer nudging his arm and Louisa saying, 'Coldie, Jack?'

As he pulled into her street, having to slow down to wait for a couple of kids on bikes to get out of the way, he knew that round here, this place to which Dad had brought them on a lavish whim, was where he was happy. That he was often happy enough, in spite of his gloomy thoughts and unsettling paintings. His version of a good life, more than he could have expected. Engine off, the ocean was loud. Look where I get to spend my time, he thought, stepping onto the bright nature strip, its green springiness one of the many small undeserved gifts of his daily existence.

As he walked down the side of the house he could hear Phoebe shouting happily in the pool, Magnus shrieking and laughing. Beyond the side wall he saw them, his sister and his nephew, pushing water at each other violently, helpless with laughter. Magnus was not usually so animated. He tended to wander around regarding his family with affectionate bafflement. Where did he come from, Lou's quiet, loose-limbed son? He was like an old fellow in an American movie who dispensed occasional wisdom from behind the counter of a shop in a small town, except that he was thirteen and had no experience of life or difficulty. None that Jack knew of anyway.

Jack leaned on the wall in the shadows and watched Magnus playing, a row of elegant palms at his back, plumes of water obscuring him in the misty dusk, and thought what a beautiful boy he was, even though he'd never heard even Lou call him handsome. He considered the blessing in this boy's life of a determined, brave mother, a calm and generous father, wondered whether when it came down to it everyone's parents were a mystery to them.

He crossed the lawn and leaned against the glass pool fence, peering over the top. 'Oh hey, Jack,' Magnus said and gave him a gentle smile.

'Jackie!' Phoebe called and got a face full of water. She blinked and shook her head. 'Are you all right?'

He smiled. Yes, he was, Indi was coming to stay. The texts from Georgia to make the arrangements were friendly. There had been extra access, an easing of rules. Indi's brilliant game-winning goal, George hugging him while she jumped up and down. Perfect joy for maybe five seconds. He lifted a hand and carried on up to the shaded deck, where Aart was lying on a lounger with his laptop on his stomach. Jack sat on the one next to him and touched his arm briefly, waited for him to finish what he was typing. He should have brought something. Here he was, expecting to be fed, his hands rudely empty.

'Hello, Jack. No Indi?'

'Tomorrow.'

'Louisa said you looked at a house the other day.'

He wondered what else she had said. Not much, he suspected. She was a cool customer around her husband.

'I can't come at the money. Reckon I missed the boat with property.'

Aart laid his laptop on the decking. 'Sometimes it just needs thinking through. Louisa knows what is a good price, though. If you decide you want it.'

'I know that kind of money passes through your fingers in a second every day. Stresses me out just thinking about it.'

'Other people's money is a different thing to your own. Not really made of anything.'

Jack felt strangely grateful that Aart took his fear seriously. He had never felt very close to him, partly because of this thing about money, his ease with it.

Louisa crossed the invisible threshold from her house onto her deck with a couple of sweating beers. 'Thought I heard your voice.' She handed him one and took a swig of the other, winked at him, their argument done, for now. Magnus stood at the edge of the pool with a towel around his shoulders. Phoebe threatened to splash him. He made a graceful gesture towards his dry towel, calling on her better nature. She grabbed his ankle and pulled him in.

'More wet towels,' Louisa said.

'They dry,' Aart said, and Louisa sighed.

'Tricia's inside,' Louisa told Jack, tipping her head at the house.

'Right.'

'Have you talked to her?'

'What about?'

'Giving you your money,' she said quietly.

'Phoebe's been talking to you too, then?'

'She can find it. Aart will help her sort herself out. Just stick up for yourself.'

'I told you I don't want the house.'

'You do, though. And you should. If not that one then another. An apartment even. Something.'

He took a drink.

'You can't hedge with Mum, you know. You've got to hold up a sign saying *Give me the money*. Carry a piece for good measure.'

'Right.'

'I'm serious. Hum and ha about it and she'll happily let you miss out if it makes less hassle for her.'

'Nah.'

'I'll do it if you like.'

'No thank you, but thank you for asking.'

She drank her beer, keeping her eye on him.

Phoebe and Magnus came dripping and laughing onto the deck. Louisa went inside for towels. Jack wished Indi were here already. She granted him a kind of immunity. People left him alone with this stuff when he was busy with her, knew their time was precious.

'She's right, you know,' Aart said. 'People who are too shy to talk about money get ripped off all the time.'

Okay, he thought. Our mother, not yours. And then there she was in the wide open doorway, her height always a surprise, dressed from head to toe in silk of an indeterminate silvery colour. How much did that cost? he thought before he could stop himself.

'Hello, love.' Her glance quickly slipped over him to Phoebe and Magnus, who took a couple of steps towards her in his dripping shorts, arms outstretched. 'Oh, keep back, you little devil,' but she allowed him to embrace her gently, leaving dark prints on her pale blouse, and closed her eyes as he did.

'Hey, Tricia,' Phoebe said, a sharpness in her voice that made Jack look at her face. The laughter of a moment before might never have happened. Even Magnus looked at her sideways. Jack set his beer carefully down on the deck, passed through the gate and stepped quietly into the pool, clothes lifting around him, the water filling his ears and nose, the world eliminated for a watery moment free of other people.

~

He sat on the edge of the deck dripping, cool in the last of the light, legs swinging and fidgeting like a kid's, Tricia next to him, the others busy inside, except for Aart, slowly skimming the far side of the pool for leaves and bugs in his expensively draped pale shirt. He was like a Buddhist monk in the way he performed his duties, in his slow, contented purpose.

'Looked at a house, Mum. Wondering if it might be time.'

'Lou mentioned it. They're getting shockingly expensive, aren't they? Do you think we're in a bubble?'

'She reckons it's a good price.'

'And what do you think?' He heard the evasive lightness in her voice, recognised his own methods of avoidance.

'I kind of thought it would be nice to have my own place for Indi to be in. But you know. Never wanted to touch the money.'

'It's not like he stole it, love. He meant it for you.'

He sat quietly.

She put her hand on his knee. 'Money's just money, love.'

Everything was too close to the surface for him, brimming. He took a breath. 'What do you think Phoebe's got in store for us?'

'I do appreciate her talents but I'm not sure I can look at any more of her surfers. They'll regret those ponytails and beards down the line, I can tell you.'

Jack laughed dutifully as Aart propped the net against the pool fence and wandered towards the house, picking a beetle from his shirt and placing it on a palm frond sweeping the lawn.

'Listen,' she said, hesitant enough for him to turn towards her, 'about the money. I'm going to need a bit of warning. It's not just sitting in the bank.'

Tears filmed her eyes. This was how money talk went as far as he was concerned. Hard-edged and brutal, confirming the wrongness of letting yourself want things. She really didn't have it, this money he'd been spending in his head. It just wasn't there, whatever his feelings about it. He wanted to say, Don't worry, Mum. Forget it ever came up. Something in him said, Wait though. Let's just see what she has to say.

'What if . . .' he felt her pause, kept his eyes on the surface of the pool, still quivering where Aart's net had last touched it. 'What if you helped me extend the shed a little bit, made it self-contained, for me to live in? You could have the house, have the others there, if it all worked out the way you want it to.'

That possibility opened up, Tricia's shady rooms, in which he had spent his last years of childhood, sheltering Indi too as she grew into a young woman, and closed again. He turned and looked at her.

'What? I mean it. It's a big block. Plenty of space for everyone.'

'You and Georgie.'

'Well, not under the same roof.'

'I don't think so, Mum.'

'I can be very well behaved.'

'I wouldn't actually want you to be, every minute, forever. It'd be a prison sentence.'

For me, he added silently. He felt himself waking up to the feeling that actually, he needed to get off that bit of land owned by his mother. He needed some days, weeks, when he didn't see her and all she brought with her. He waited, feeling other options hanging in the air.

'Okay, well, I suppose that's not the only thing I can do. I've got money, of course I have, in the house. I'd just have to do some reorganising to raise it, get a partner in the business, maybe. And a mortgage. I think perhaps I should talk to Aart and Lou about a plan. Word has it they can be very helpful.'

She was making a joke but he found himself unable to respond to it. Words formed. He could not believe he would say them, still wanted to let her off the hook, but then he did. 'Let me know what they say.' He had to look at her now. Her head was bowed, her hands gripping the edge of the deck gently beside her. 'It's okay, Mum. You've always looked after me.'

'Not as well as I should have.'

'In all the ways that matter. I just need to know what's possible. Get over myself, maybe.'

'I've let you down.'

'Life's messy. We're okay.' He put his hand on her back, thin and muscular beneath the silk, looked out over the world Lou had made, the sun setting on it tastefully. 'There's something else.' He didn't know where he was finding this flint, except that it suddenly felt like it would take more out of him not to say these things. 'Don't be a snob about Georgie, Mum. It doesn't help.'

He felt her take a breath beside him. 'I know, love. I'm sorry. I've got some bad habits.'

The deck boards pressed down behind him. 'Uncle Jack? Nanna?' It was Magnus at the back door. 'Aunty Phoebe wants you to come in now.'

Jack stood and stretched, catching the last of the sun slipping beyond the neighbour's fence. He took out his phone, saw a message from Georgie at the end of a thread about Indi's visit tomorrow. *Hey J, miss you.*

He held his hand out to his mother, although he could not imagine a time when she would ever need assistance to get herself to her feet. She gave him a shy smile as she took it and he felt the elements of his life lift up and swirl around, giving no sign of how they would settle.

~

Louisa stared at the huge radius made by her broken glass on the kitchen tiles, a blokey cheer rising from the lounge room. The large pale tiles shocked her with their beauty every time she entered the kitchen. Gorgeous, but unforgiving. I'm a bit hammered, she thought as she reached for the larger pieces. Thankfully no one came to help her. She cleaned up and poured another glass of semillon.

In the lounge they were all arranged, waiting on the couches while Phoebe, crouching on the rug, fiddled with her iPad and the remote. 'Right!' she said, joining Louisa. She hit the iPad, and the TV screen lit up with a blurry picture of the beach at Bilgola, that deep, wide cup, the sea pouring in, a view from the front edge of their old block. Music started up at the same time. Classical music. She knew it, something Dad had liked. Something very sweet, with delicate violins. *The Lark Ascending.* Louisa felt suddenly winded by desire and pressed down the thought of her clumsy phone call to Mrs Beringer, the silence in response to her email.

Another picture, from the bottom of the goat track, looking across the northern end of the beach towards the cliff. That track was a proper path now with metal stairs congested in early mornings

with middle-aged men and new mums driven up and down relent-
lessly by bossy personal trainers. But this was before. The colours
and image quality suggested age. And there it was, the house, the
closest to the cliff, up on the small deck a dark figure with pale hair.
'Good God,' Tricia said. 'Is that me?'

'I reckon it's me,' Louisa said. 'Look, I'm in cossies. You wouldn't
have stood out there without a dress and full makeup.'

Jack stood up. 'Better get going. Early start.'

'Ah, Jackie,' Phoebe said. 'Been working for ages on this. Need
you to tell me where some of the shots were taken.'

The picture disintegrated into another; this time it was definitely Louisa, standing at the edge of the ocean pool, ready to dive
in. 'I don't remember that,' she said. She was surprised to find her
voice break. She looked invincible, heedless, so ready to immerse
herself in that world of blues and greys.

'Your legs were like a Russian shot-putter's when you did all
that swimming. It's good you gave it away before it was too late.'

'Thanks, Tricia.'

Jack had sat down but was teetering on the front edge of the
couch, ready to spring.

Bluebottles on the shoreline in a mucky fringe, super close up,
glistening indigo balloons, long stingers submerged under ridges
of sand in which you could see individual grains. 'That is great,
Feeb,' Jack said quietly. Lou watched him, wondering whether he
would succumb to this plan of Phoebe's to reminisce, to find some
memories he could be happy about, to give some up.

'You know what would be cool?' Phoebe said, raising a finger in
the air as though she'd just had the thought. 'We could pick up my
projector and put it on the wall in the house.'

With my key I suppose, Louisa thought. But then, wouldn't that be amazing? Before the old cow takes it off me. I'll get one cut, she thought drunkenly. And never use it, just keep it in a drawer, to look at now and again.

An image appeared of a woman at the moment of contact with the water of the ocean pool, an eruption of water just beginning to plume. A curvy woman whose glamorous hair was inflated by her movement downwards, the disturbed water a tight circle around her about to spread. The violins swelled as though she were something glorious.

'That's . . .' Jack started.

'That little piece Don inflicted on us.'

'Whoa, Mum,' Phoebe said. 'She was Don's girlfriend, right? She was okay, wasn't she?' She was looking at Louisa.

'She did put out a slutty vibe, as I recall.'

Magnus looked at the picture carefully. For all anyone knew he was assessing its artistic merits.

'Amazing pic though,' Jack said. 'How old were you?'

Before Phoebe could answer, there was a picture of Dad, sitting on his boat surrounded by the blue of Pittwater, angophora-covered shores, boatsheds, hauling up a large shining fish on his line and laughing.

Jack stood up. 'Thanks for the drink, Lou.' He went out to the kitchen. Louisa followed him. The music stopped.

'Carry on,' Louisa shouted back.

'I'm saving it. We'll wait!' Phoebe called out after them.

'Jack,' Lou said quietly. 'Don't sulk. Maybe it's time we did this.'

'Is there going to be a round of applause at the end?'

'You love Phoebe's pictures.'

'They're great. She's always been talented. I can live without sitting through a tribute to Charlie, though.'

'He's only been in one.'

'I can see the way it's going. The pictures of us were just the warm-up.'

'Don't you just miss him? Why must he be the great unmentionable?' She fudged the pile up of syllables in her final word and Jack frowned.

'Do you? Still, now?'

'When I set up the business I thought: Ta-dah! Check this out, Charlie. When the pool was finished and it looked just like I imagined it would. Magnus being such a brilliant boy. I look at Aart and I think, Dad would like you.'

'You still want him to be proud of you.'

'He was my dad.'

'To say, "That's my golden girl."'

'If you like, Jack. Yeah.'

'If he appeared in front of us now he'd take one look at me and shake his head.'

A silence fell between them in the low light of the kitchen. Tricia was telling Aart about Bree and the way she had dumped Don—'my husband's business partner'—for a regional TV producer. She'd seen her pop up on the weather on holiday in Noosa once and choked on her Pina Colada. Is that all Don was to you, Mum? Lou thought.

'I've got to get some sleep,' he said. 'Indi's coming tomorrow.'

'You're a sweet guy and a great dad. That's what people see.'

'Okay. Anyway.' He lifted a hand and went out the back door, visible for a moment as he passed by the window, a brief apparition, looking so very much like their dad.

~

Phoebe watched Lou's face as she returned from the kitchen, without Jack. Her cream chiffon top sat unevenly at her neck and her hair was roughed up around one ear. What's the story? she thought. What is going on with you? It was odd to see her look anything but composed. Phoebe's means of access to Lou was to remember: Lou in the car to school crying with rage at their mother, after the move. Better, Lou sitting on her in their old den and farting, helpless with giggling; further back, teaching her to do cartwheels in the yard of their first house until Phoebe could move down the entire street wheeling smoothly like an unwinding mechanism. Lou jumped in the air when Phoebe nailed it. Then Phoebe would wait for Dad's car and start her slow roll towards him, arriving at the drive as he opened his door.

None of this helped; in this present moment she could not fathom her.

'Do you really want to do it at the old place?' Lou asked.

'You game?'

Lou allowed herself a little smile.

'Where's Jack?'

'Not his thing.'

She wouldn't let him spoil it; she'd take it round tomorrow and he could look at it on the iPad. And she would ask him questions and watch his face for clues.

She took a breath. 'Mum?'

Tricia took a moment to decide, gave a small nod. 'Wouldn't mind giving it one last look.'

Aart touched Lou's arm and turned towards her, said something quietly.

She shook him off. 'It'll be fine!' Phoebe watched this move with interest; Lou was not looking at her husband's face as she spoke. It seemed childish, or drunk and bratty.

'It's not like we need to break in,' Phoebe said to Aart, smiling. 'Lou's got the key. Once in a lifetime opportunity. Meant to be.'

Lou reached inside her shirt and dangled the key from its string. She turned towards the kitchen and took her car keys from the hook by the door. Aart stood between Louisa and the door, again whispered something in her ear, to which she once more shook her head. Phoebe hovered by the couch with her gear, head cocked, hand on her mouth. Aart and Louisa leaned towards each other. Something in the way he spoke urgently, and she would not look at him, echoed her memories of her parents together.

'I can drive,' Tricia said. Yes, Mum. He couldn't argue with that. Tricia didn't drink.

Louisa gave him the car keys and stepped around him. The three of them were silent in the dark as they walked through the passageway to the street, the air warm and scented, cockroaches scuttling before their feet. Phoebe let out a giggle as they reached Tricia's Golf on the street and Lou did too, as though Phoebe laughing was a button, a trigger.

'I did used to love hearing the ocean at night,' Tricia said.

'You can hear it from your place,' Louisa said.

'Not like this. Like it's going to go right over you. That house was a shocker though. Just awful.'

Phoebe folded herself into the back of Tricia's car, shaking her head. Lou had already assumed the right to the front passenger seat, as though their age difference was as significant now as it had always been. What could she say without proving the point?

Anyway, they were going. She felt on the brink of something, like standing in a bar and knowing there was a pair of eyes on you. That certainty in your blood.

The ocean boomed as she stepped out of the car on her street. She ran up the stairs at the back of the block. Was Lou going to buy the house? Phoebe could spend the next year photographing it properly, finding the little corners of her memory, under the den where she used to listen, or sitting on the roof. A year, or however long Louisa lasted before she tore it down, made a big crater in the hill where their childhood lay.

By the time she emerged back onto the street with her projector bag they were bibbing the horn like kids. She laughed and ran across the street, her bags bumping her hips. Her skin felt brushed by an electric fabric but it was just the sea, the night.

They were silent as they drove up the hill and turned off down the Serpentine, headed out to the point and sharply back towards Bilgola. Tricia parked on the street a few houses down. They stepped quietly down the dark driveway, not speaking, and Louisa turned to them at the front door. 'Ready?'

Phoebe reached inside her bag and touched the cool metal of her projector. She imagined being on the other side of the door, walking among the flickering light of her family as they were when she was a child. 'Come on, Lou,' she whispered. 'Open up.'

BOXING DAY

Jack peered out of the front door in the damp grey dusk, the Land Cruiser shivering under the carport like a wet dog. The headlights came on, illuminating the rain. In the car, Charlie leaned forward over the steering wheel.

Tricia, hovering behind Jack in the hallway, whispered, as though Charlie could hear over the engine and the rain on the roofs. 'You need to go with him, Jack.'

'No way.'

'He won't actually go. You just need to distract him before he gets there. Get him to buy takeaway or something. Go on. We need some dinner and I'm not cooking again.' She gave him a little push in the small of his back.

'I'll talk to him, but I'm not going with him.' He stepped out into the rain and walked around to the driver's window, bare feet grinding wet dirt. 'What are you doing, Dad?'

210

'Can you imagine what those people are going through?'

Jack felt a pain under his ribs like a stitch. 'Are we talking about the Kazmis?'

Charlie turned to him. 'No one's stopped to think how they must be feeling.'

Some of us have, Dad. 'Are you sure they'd want visitors?'

'They'll be having a time of it, with her bag turning up, let me tell you.'

Charlie was still, his eyes on the driveway ahead. Jack accidentally brushed his arm with his own as he leaned forwards. Charlie's skin was warm in the cool wet night. Jack shrank away from it.

'Let's go tomorrow, hey? It's a horrible night.'

He looked Jack in the eye. 'Are we going to let a bit of rain stop us doing the right thing? We need to show them it's not just them having a hard time. They're not alone in this business.'

'Hang on. Let me get my shoes.' In the rain between the carport and Tricia still hovering in the doorway, he concentrated on the funnels of water trickling between his shoulder blades, the incredible sound of the rain on the roof.

Tricia was eyeing Charlie with her thumbnail between her teeth.

'Can't you go, Mum?'

'I've put up with enough today, haven't I?'

'Let's just let him go.'

'We can't. God knows what he'll say to them, the mood he's in. And we won't know what's happened till they call me and I have to make excuses for him.' He pushed past her to retrieve his tennis shoes from the corridor. Behind him the car was rolling out into the rain. 'Go on, quick,' she said, 'before he goes without you.'

Climbing up into the passenger seat, Charlie rolling the car up the slope in the drumming rain, Jack half longed for a faint to take him out the other side of whatever this was, waking up to a sunny morning, freshened by the southerly, the rainy night.

He looked up out of the window at the sky to prevent himself from being sick as the car slid around the Bends. Mist rose from the cabbage palm gully; he saw only treetops and the lights of isolated houses tucked high into the bush escarpment. A woman was doing the dishes at a window and he wished he could be part of the life he was seeing, of quiet chores and boredom. A holiday in someone else's life. He made the same wish as he spied into the unit blocks of Newport and Mona Vale, until they were climbing through the low clouds clinging to the hill and up into the sandstone cut-through towards the bush and paddocks of Ingleside.

Once, last summer, Jack had returned from a bike ride on a long slow dusk and as he jumped down from his bike had caught a flash of red moving across the street among the soft greying colours of evening. It was Monica, on her lawn, her dad taking a picture of her. When he saw her, he remembered it was the night of the school social, and wished for the first time that he was going, although it had not occurred to him before. He stood at the edge of his path as she waited for Mr Kazmi to take the pictures. He was not close enough to see her face but he could tell from her body that she was smiling. A moment later they were walking towards him. Her dad, in a suit, tall, gentle, proud, was walking her around the corner to the school gym. They waved at Jack from the other side of the street. She held her father's arm and smiled at herself, walking in heels along their suburban street in the evening. They looked perfect, but he wished he'd asked her, that it was Jack walking her down the street as she laughed quietly at herself. He never would have had the courage, but still.

In the car, now, with Charlie, he still wished. Tiny things could change the future, if you were brave enough to make things happen instead of watching your life unfold helplessly, peering at it from between your fingers.

Here were his streets, the streets of his whole life until a month ago. The shops went by: the Chinese, the newsagency, the vet and the corner shop. The Chinese was open and the convenience store's lights were on too. If you went in, you'd see the man who was always there, reading his newspaper but ready to fold it snappily and rise to his feet to greet you.

'Hey Dad,' he tried at last. 'The takeaway's open. Maybe we should get something nice for dinner while we're here.'

Charlie said nothing, but carried on along the winding road to the back of the suburb, past the school. Jack watched the dark concrete science block slide by, his chest tightening with the memory of all those dissections of eyes and hearts, the tubs of dead frogs, piled high, the lunch containers of bulls' eyes. For some people there would be nothing to worry about, your dad visiting a former neighbour in trouble to offer help. He felt hot and ill and could not think how to stop him.

As they pulled onto their old street he thrust his face towards the open gap at the top of his window, feeling the wet air, then Charlie was pulling up the handbrake and they were opening their doors and slamming them, muffled by the rain. Their old house was throbbing with light and music. If it were a cartoon the house would be inflating with the line of bass. A housewarming, for the new people?

No time to feel the strangeness of that. Charlie was already on the Kazmis' property. Don't, please, Jack thought, but they were walking along the path past the square-edged lawn towards the front door where a light shone faintly in the glass panel above it. Then the light above the porch came on and they were fully lit, unable to turn back. 'Dad,' he squeaked nevertheless as they stepped under the porch roof and Charlie lifted his hand to the doorbell. Footsteps ran along the corridor and then the door opened quickly and Mrs Kazmi appeared, small, open-mouthed, expectant. 'Oh,' it took her a moment to speak, 'Jack. Charlie. Oh.'

She was out of breath. She looked as she always did, wearing neat dark jeans and an ironed blouse, subtle lipstick, clean hair. She was like a teacher, or librarian. Absolutely respectable and tidy, kind. Except they had made her run to the door, hoping for news, and in spite of her careful clothes and hair she was hollowed out beneath the eyes, and somewhere deep in her too. Jack wanted to dissolve into the rain.

Charlie held his hand out to take hers, studied her face, his head tipped.

'Thank you, Charlie,' she said eventually, as though he had given her something. 'Thank you for your thoughts, but everything is going to be all right.'

'We're praying for you,' Charlie said.

Jack couldn't look at him. It must be clear to her, surely, that they did not pray, that Charlie in fact called churchgoers God-botherers, holy rollers, Jesus freaks.

'Thank you,' Mrs Kazmi answered. She reached a hand up to the door, to pull it closed, and Charlie caught hold of it.

'Helen,' he sounded excitable. 'We're going to do something special for your daughter. Where we live, it's just perfect. We're letting off sky lanterns. You know how people light candles? This is better. You make a wish and let it go.'

Jack swallowed, watching Mrs Kazmi's face. She was squinting slightly.

'The idea is, you give us something of hers, right? Something very small, and we send it up with the lanterns.'

'Lanterns?' Her voice broke a little.

There were footsteps in the corridor behind her and well above her own head the face of Mr Kazmi appeared. His thick dark hair and beard were neatly trimmed. His pale shirt was ironed.

Jack fixed upon his face as though it were up to him to sort this all out before it became any stranger. A proper adult, that was all he wanted.

'Mr Bright? What can we do for you? You know that we have some family trouble.'

Mrs Kazmi turned her face up to her husband's. 'They're praying for her. With . . . lanterns?'

Mr Kazmi's face was lined and handsome, the night falling in the deep crevices in his forehead, across the flat planes of his cheeks. 'What do you mean?' he said to Charlie.

Jack wanted to tug at his father's hand like a small boy, draw him away.

'We have beautiful lanterns, you send them into the sky and you make a wish. It's really powerful stuff. You should see them. We're going to set some off for Monica.'

Mrs Kazmi gasped quietly at the sound of her daughter's name. Now Jack did pull gently on Charlie's arm.

Mrs Kazmi looked up at her husband. 'Charlie wants something of hers, to—tie to the lantern?'

'You've got it. I've got her necklace . . .' What? Jack thought. 'But there are three lanterns to set off, so anything else you've got would be good.'

He addressed this request to Mrs Kazmi, as though she had already agreed to it, and they were just hammering out the details. Mr Kazmi stepped forward into the porch light. He was a tall man, and his long face seemed to point down at Charlie's like a microscope. He spoke gently though. 'You have something that belongs to my daughter?'

'Oh no, not with me. It's at our place on the beach, with the lanterns. Be honoured to have you both down there, anytime.'

Jack pulled on his arm. 'We have to go,' he said quietly. Mrs Kazmi had begun to weep silently, with her mouth slightly open. He did not want to watch, it seemed very private. This is the worst thing, of all the things he's done. This is it. I hate him, now and forever.

'Explain to me how you have something that belongs to my daughter.'

'Now, don't get upset. Louisa had it. Girls give each other things, don't they? What can you do?'

Mr Kazmi looked at his wife, and at Jack, and seemed to decide something. 'Charlie,' he said quietly. 'I don't understand why you are here, or what you are saying to me. Perhaps you are not feeling very well. Please go now. Take your boy home.'

'I'd be upset too. I'd be beside myself. You're both holding together really well.'

'This is a private matter.'

Bubbling out of Jack came words, bright, squeaky. 'Sorry to bother you, we're going now. Good luck!'

Oh, he thought as he pulled Charlie away. I could absolutely *die*. His skin burned as they climbed into the car. He was barely aware of his old house across the street, pulsing with the party.

'We can still get something,' Charlie said, tapping the dashboard.

Jack shrank inside himself. There was no help anywhere. They passed from his street and he swore he would never, ever return to it. His cheeks burned with shame. Then, at the school, Charlie slowed, turned into the carpark, sliding a little in the mud. He came to a halt at the edge of the football field, glowing faintly next to the dark of the bush beyond. 'Can we just go home?' Jack said.

'Won't be a second,' Charlie said and reached across him to the glove box, withdrawing a long heavy torch.

'Please, Dad. Now!' But Charlie was jumping down into the noisy mud, his footsteps receding. His torch swung at waist height over at the start of the bush track. It disappeared into the trees, flickering, disappearing, a tiny flash, then nothing.

Jack opened the window and tried to enter the noise of the rain and the insects, become part of that universe of sound. But he was here, human, alone in the night, while his father ran willingly into a bad, dark place. He should go after him, push him down, lie on him in the mud to stop him from doing anything else at all, or get out of the car and run in the opposite direction into the night. Impossible to stay here, in this cold metal box that smelled of Charlie, fear coming for him. He had his hand on the door, ready to jump down and let his feet decide. Then the torch-light swung out onto the bush path, juddering and growing larger.

He dipped his head, watching until the shape of a man grew out of the darkness.

Charlie's footsteps splashed up to the door quickly and it was open, his panting filling the car. His brick torch hit the passenger door hard and the car was moving instantly, backing out of the carpark at speed, rolling out onto the smooth tarmac of the road. 'What, Dad? What's up?'

'Police tape was still up. Didn't realise I'd gone past it till I came back.' He turned to face him, his eyes wide. 'Hooley dooley!'

Jack leaned his head against the window and twisted his head away from him, tears standing in his eyes. He watched the street-lights and glimpses of roofs unspool, dark gaps between them where the trees were thick and the bush spilled through to the empty pavements. Beyond these houses and gardens the Kazmis stood in their clean dark kitchen, holding each other, crying. Perhaps he was shouting about this insensitive man, their foolish neighbour. Or she was sitting in the lounge, looking at her hands on the ironed denim of her jeans, while he stood, tall and righteous in the hallway, calling the police.

~

From the shelter of the carport Louisa watched Jack hose down the car on the driveway in the dim light from the other houses. He directed the high pressure nozzle into the gaps around the headlamps and turned it on the tyres, squirting the treads. He had already washed the roo bar, the duco and the windows.

Behind her, in the hall, the light was on in her parents' bedroom. She saw through the crack that Tricia was lying on the bed in a short nightie, reading a magazine, her long limbs tanned against the smooth white bedspread. Lou went in and sat down on the bed. Tricia didn't look up. It was one of her interiors magazines, the vast deck of a glass beach house on the front. Louisa sat on the white quilt, feeling grubby. Tricia eventually laid her magazine on her lap and looked her up and down. 'What's up now?'

'Mum . . .' she said quietly.

'What?'

'Dad went up to the Kazmis. Jack said it was awful.'

'Oh no. Jack was supposed to put him off.'

'Then he went up where they found her bag, behind our school.' She leaned forwards, whispered. 'Jesus. Why?'

'I don't know. Well, Jack said he wanted something from up there for his thing with the lanterns.' She felt her voice rising. 'Dad's covered in mud.'

'So they're back? Nothing's happened?'

'He crossed the police tape, in the reserve. Mum, he told the Kazmis he had Monica's necklace. How does he even know about that?'

Tricia made a face that said she had no idea, smoothed her palms across the magazine spread, the sharp façades, the deep blue of the pool. 'What's he doing now?'

'Watching TV with Feeb. He's trying to catch a weather report.'

'What about Jack?'

'Washing the mud off the car.'

'Get Dad's clothes.' Tricia stood from the bed, shooing Louisa off it at the same time. 'Come on, quick. Tell him I'm doing a wash now.'

'You're going to clean up? That's it?'

'Just get his clothes, Louisa!'

Louisa felt like she did before a race, stepping up onto the starting block, checking the surface of the water: this is really happening. What though, what was really happening? She went slowly down the stairs into the den, trying to be quiet. Charlie was leaning forwards, elbows on his knees, watching the news. Phoebe was gabbing away about something, but she might as well not be there.

'Dad?'

He didn't look up.

'Dad, Mum wants your clothes to wash.'

'Now?' he said, eyes still fixed on the business news.

'You're getting mud everywhere.'

He stood up in his shirt and shorts, caked in mud. He looked like he'd been rolling in shit. He pulled his clothes off without looking at her, standing in his undies, keeping an eye on the TV. He chucked the shirt and shorts towards Lou and Phoebe took her T-shirt and shorts off too and handed them to her like she was used to maids. Whatever, Feebs, Lou thought, and ran upstairs to the laundry where Tricia was waiting, shoved it all into the machine while her mother poured about a litre of detergent into the drawer. Tricia slammed the door shut and pressed the button. The machine thunked and water began to pour in and Tricia was off out the door. Why are we in such a hurry? Louisa thought. What do we think is going to happen? She followed Tricia outside, watched her shoo Jack back from the car and climb up into the driver's seat. Jack stood next to her, the hose dribbling at his feet.

The car moved forwards into the rain and Tricia jumped out, ran back under the carport, her glowing white nightie sticking to her, and disappeared into the dark behind the boat. Then she emerged with something in her hand, the Dustbuster, and pulled herself back up into the car. Louisa couldn't hear the machine above the downpour on the iron roof of the carport but her mother's shape in white glowed as it moved vigorously about the dark cabin.

Jack turned off the hose and chucked it on the ground, went inside without speaking. Louisa stepped out into the rain to climb into the back seat. Tricia was in the front, jabbing the Dustbuster into the footwells, pale hair trembling. 'Mum,' Lou shouted over the vacuum and the rain hammering on the roof. 'Stop it! This is mad!'

She looked up briefly, leaving the vacuum on. 'I'm fixing this mess. You're all driving me spare.'

'How is it our fault?'

Tricia gave her a look, but switched the machine off and sat down in the passenger seat in front of her.

'We barely knew her, Mum.'

'He takes things personally when he's like this. Has to be in the thick of his own drama.'

'Jack said Mrs Kazmi was crying and Dad didn't even notice. Mr Kazmi wanted to know how we had something of Monica's.'

Tricia gave a shake of her head and turned the Dustbuster back on, climbing into the back next to her, jabbing at the floors from all fours on the seat. She smacked Louisa's knees to move her out of the way and did that part of the seat too.

Finally Tricia turned off the vacuum and leaned back next to her, her breath heavy, her perfume citrusy, light, as though she were a free spirit, a child of nature. They sat, the two of them, side by side, not looking at each other, rain drumming on the roof. 'Be nothing left out there now. All washed away.'

'Should we call someone? Explain how he's been?' Louisa said. She was beginning to shiver in her wet clothes.

'It'll be fine now. Lucky with the rain. We can explain about the necklace if we need to. I'm sure I've got photos of me wearing it. Jesus.'

'What if he doesn't sleep tonight?' Louisa's eyes and throat were sore. 'What if there's more of this tomorrow?'

'Sometimes I put something in his drink when he hasn't slept for a while.'

'Like what?'

'Just a pill.'

'He's got medication?'

'No, I have. How do you think I put up with all this malarkey?'

'Shouldn't he talk to a doctor, Mum?'

'Oh God. Never in a month of Sundays. He needs to sleep. Tomorrow we'll send him off to join the golf club, all right? And I'll get Don to find an architect. Your dad should *never* be left idle. I should have seen it coming.'

'D'you reckon it will be okay, Mum?'

Tricia gave her a small nod, pressing her lips together.

'All right,' Lou said, 'if you say so,' and felt little, childlike, as she jumped down into the driveway, into the downpour, turned back to see Tricia wiping down the seat behind her. She crept back to the top of the stairs above the den and the glow in the dark of the TV screen below. A great storm cell was passing over the coast and out to sea. In the flicker of the screen Charlie nodded quietly, his arm around Phoebe, his other hand on his knee, ready for action.

～

Phoebe swelled with news, she couldn't keep it in, but there was no one in the living room, and Dad was tying up his shoelaces down at the den door. Jack came in, soaking wet, as she was about to head back down the stairs. 'We're setting off lanterns for that girl!'

'And why are you doing that?' His voice was quiet, weird.

'So we can make a wish!'

'Good luck in this weather.'

'It's going to be clear all night. Dad made sure.'

He raised a hand. 'Well, have fun.'

'Why are you mad at me? I haven't done anything to you.'

'I know, Feeb,' he said, still sounding angry. 'I'm not.'

'Just come with us. You can't miss lanterns.'

'I can watch from up here.'

'Won't be the same if you don't get to let them go yourself.'

The door slid across downstairs and she feared Dad would go without her if she didn't hurry. She left Jack there with his sour face in the gloomy room next to the dying Christmas tree and ran downstairs after her father, who was stepping out into the darkness, a cloth bag over one arm and the packet of lanterns in the other.

The air outside was soft and cool, but it wasn't raining any more. Phoebe caught up with Charlie on the muddy track and he took her hand to steady her, but then he slid for a second in the mud and she planted herself, feet apart, until he was okay. Inside the houses above bright screens shimmered—in the dark there must be people sitting around them you couldn't see. At the end of the ridge she heard TV laughter over the last of the rain dripping between the layers of leaves. When they reached the junction of the steep track at the base of the figs and palms, the damp, rotting smell was even stronger than usual. It was black here at night and she wanted to hear a voice, even if it was her own. 'Can we swim, after, Dad?'

He didn't answer and she worried that she'd broken the spell, woken him up, and they'd have to turn around and traipse back to the house for showers and teeth and bed, the lovely lanterns still in their packets, the night as dull and dark as before. Then he stopped in the dark and squeezed her hand too hard. 'My little mate.' His voice was slow, like he'd been drinking whiskey. She squeezed back and tugged him forwards down the track towards the sound of the sea.

They stepped carefully through the dark over jagged fallen fronds and came out halfway down the hill, the shape of the headland visible in the light from the blurry moon. 'I love it at night, Dad.' A bat swooped across the path in front of them, cutting a shape out of the sea.

The beach was narrow, the tide swallowing the sand that had been crowded with people earlier today. They let go of one another's hands and trudged over the ridge of remaining sand to the shore where it was easier to walk. There could be no more perfect way to end the day, about to set off all the lanterns. Doing something good for that girl, releasing the magic that would draw her home. Dad all to herself.

They reached the concrete platform surrounding the pool, the surface swirling and sucking, and Charlie sat down on the long step. He placed something cold and heavy in her hand. 'Turn that on, Feeb. Hold it steady.'

She felt for the button and pointed the torch at his hands, which were pulling objects from his bag: matches, a gum leaf, a reel of cotton, a piece of bark, then finally, in a little pool in the scoop of his palm, the necklace, the M.

The thought pressed on her: It isn't hers really, Dad, but there was a solemnity to the occasion, the waves roaring against the pool wall, the circle of light on his hands in the massive dark, that could not be broken. He unspooled the cotton, the other things in his lap, and bit off a length. He picked up the packet of lanterns from the bench beside him and opened it, pulled one out. She dared not speak as she watched him tie the thread around the stalk of the gum leaf and then to the frame at the base of the lantern. He passed Phoebe the matches, set everything else aside and stood, gripping the lantern by its base, its tall white shape massive and eerie against his body. 'Hold this while I light the match.'

'Do we have to say anything?'

'Just wish as you let it go, remember?'

'Are you gonna wish?'

'I'll do one in a sec.'

She took hold of the lantern, a breath seeming to pass over her skin. A stronger gust of wind caught at the fabric and she held tight while he sheltered the match flame with his hand and nursed it towards her. He lit the reservoir and she held the lantern away from her in outstretched arms. It glowed like magic, like she remembered, and she felt the wind wanting to take it. What is my wish? she suddenly thought.

'Let go.'

'Wait!'

'Now, before it burns you.'

She opened her fingers and a gust took it over the choppy pool, several blurry dots of light sailing across the water towards the ocean. The lantern itself was miraculous as it rose into the sky, buffeted, wobbly, but climbing. Her wish as she watched it climb in the night was inarticulate but fierce. She remembered it afterwards as a wanting, something in her body rather than a wish made of words. Something to do with Charlie and her family and her own place in it: love and intensity, desire to be at the centre, the heart, always.

But I'm supposed to wish something for Monica, she thought as the lantern grew small over the oily ocean. Next wish. Next wish is for that girl with the long dark hair who used to smile at Jack, for her to turn up on her own doorstep right now, and her mum to open the door. Shouting then hugs that squeezed the air out of her.

She would not stop watching the tiny light until it disappeared. Behind her Charlie held out another lit lantern, with the scrap of bark attached to it. He passed it to her and she received it solemnly, turned towards the sea. In her head she made a formal statement: Monica, see this light and return to your family, and released the lantern with a little flourish, like a magician letting go a dove or a cloud of butterflies. She remembered, a dream from early childhood, the whole beach in Thailand setting off their lanterns and feeling that she was underwater, among jellyfish, swimming among them.

'Last one,' Charlie said, holding it up, the necklace trailing beneath, glinting in the light. 'I'll do this one.'

He closed his eyes, his face brown and tired, glowing in the light, and opened them, let go. It began all right, the pillow of light drifting upwards and out towards the corner of the pool, but then it stuttered sideways and dipped dangerously close to the water. Charlie darted along the edge of the pool and leaned over, patting the lantern upwards with his hand. Fear for the lantern made Phoebe step towards him, but it had worked: it drifted up again, out over the rock platform, staying low. Charlie ran along next to it, gave it another pat, but it would only go forwards, not up.

Phoebe's hands were scrunched into fists. *Come on, Dad*. The dark had swallowed him but he had managed to set the lantern rising steadily and the shrinking window of light in the blackness set out over the edge of the ocean beyond the platform. People would see it from their houses at the next beach along and wonder what it was. She watched it superstitiously, afraid to take her eyes off it until the very last moment. It was there—tiny, tinier—and then it was not. Her heart closed over the absence. The sky was dark and she heard her own breathing over the waves against the pool wall, rushing over the rocks.

She waited for a minute in the dark, the edge of the pool just visible in the moonlight, and edged towards the bench to find the torch. Her hand ran over the cool concrete, until she knocked it, set it rolling. She managed to catch it before it fell and turned it on, walked the length of the pool towards the rock platform along the shining wet concrete. Somehow she was unable to call out into the vast dark.

At the far end of the pool she pointed her torch out over the rock platform. The shelves and dark pools glinted under the looming headland. The surf club at Newport shone across the black water, the red and yellow strings of car lights passing each other behind it.

'Dad!' she said, weakly at first, her voice lost in the waves and the wind, and then deeply, strongly, as though she were playing softball and her base was still free, threatened. 'Dad! Dad!'

It was so dark out on the slippery rocks. She edged forward, as quickly as she dared. Her heart was too big for her, breath was difficult, like she was Jack, panicking. She slipped onto her bum and her feet were in warm water, a rockpool. She pulled them back quickly and scrambled to all fours, gripping the torch hard against the rock. She lifted it out into the darkness and swept it across the platform one way and the other like a lighthouse. 'Dad!' she called, but there was no reply, and only the sea there in the dark. No people anywhere. She turned back towards their beach, looking for the house on the cliff, and thought it might be the small black space near the middle, a hole in the row of big houses blazing with light. It seemed tiny and far.

A response came from behind her, not Dad: Jack. 'Where's Dad, Feeb?'

And then before she could answer there he was too, the shape of a man in the night coming up onto the concrete platform. She directed the torch at him. Something flailed behind her ribs at this, the man in the dark, her fear before at losing him. The words on her lips had been: He's gone, into the dark, into the water. But now she did not have to say them.

'Didn't think that last one was going to catch.' He was out of breath. 'Ah, Jackie. You missed the lanterns. We're all out.'

'I didn't want to set them off anyway.' His voice came out tightly, like air squealing from a balloon. Now that Dad was okay, and all the lanterns were gone, she wanted to run across the cool sand in the breeze left over from the storm and climb into her warm bed, under her doona. If Lou was sleeping already she could get away with laying a leg, an arm, alongside hers, feeling the lovely heat of skin as she fell asleep. Maybe she could have some ice cream before bed. Sometimes when everyone had gone to bed she sat on her own in the den, secretly licking the spoon in the dark with an enormous grin on her face.

Dad and Jack were looking at each other; she could see them only dimly but she could feel it. Jack said, 'You think you can do whatever you want.' She knew he wasn't talking to her but it was very strange that he would speak to Dad like this, and she wanted to be away now.

Her feet began skipping across the wet concrete. She touched Jack's hand and off she went. No one stopped her. No one called out. She kept running, alongside the pool, listening to her feet slap and her breath in the dark, the roar of the sea, nothing behind her. She misjudged the line of the tide as she came off the path and landed thigh-deep in surging water, almost slipped. But then she righted herself and heaved her legs up beyond the waterline, found the high ridge of dry sand and ran for home, up through the jungle towards the road, exhilarated, not knowing she could do this, finding that she loved it. This aloneness in the dark, this daring of the smell and slipperiness that she could not see.

AFTERWARDS

The house on the Serpentine was unlit as Jack walked down the driveway. That old smell: mossy dampness, the sea and some sweet plant. It was a mix that existed in this exact recipe here and nowhere else. For twenty years this place in the world had smelled the same while he and his sisters and his mother had grown older, changed. Not changed.

He pushed open the door and heard a naughty gasp, an outbreak of giggles: kids, sprung. He wished sometimes he could move among his family as a formless, unnoticed being, close but causing no reaction, allowing them to live their lives without his interference. Nearness, that would do him. As he moved down the short corridor, the place he hovered as a boy, avoiding his family yet needing to observe them, shadows flickered from the lounge. There was silence now. 'It's just me.'

'Knew you couldn't resist,' said Phoebe's voice.

He touched the wall at the corner and held onto his breathing. He had changed his mind on the way home, had come here to keep them out of trouble, not to be rescued. He tried to recall the feeling he'd had earlier, driving to Lou's as the evening came, that Indi was coming tomorrow, that the world was lit with it, but the rooms of his past were taking over his body. There never was any air in this house.

On the wall of the living room was a photograph of all of them on the jetty at Palm Beach, the shed at the end behind them. They were huddled together more tightly than they needed to be for the photographer's frame and smiling. Pittwater glittered behind and around them; they were elevated on a path out into a shining nothing. They looked surprised, as though good fortune had befallen them.

Jack sat down with the girls on the floor, something loosening inside. Lou put her arm around him. 'It's okay, Jackie.'

Charlie's face, his pale green eyes, his happy surprise. He was a small man, little and strong, like Jack. He had always thought of him as large, towering. His voice, his movements. Still though, at the sight of him, a current ran through Jack, an exhausting alertness.

'That's the day we first saw the house,' Tricia said. 'Do you remember? When Lou cut herself on the oysters and then flirted with that boy who fixed her up?'

'I did not.'

'You did. You flirted with everybody. It was incredible to watch.'

Phoebe laughed. 'I will never take shit for that from you again, Lou.'

'Fair enough. Although you are thirty years old.'

Jack looked around in the light from the picture. 'God, nothing's changed, has it?'

'Good,' Tricia said. 'I'm glad to see it like this one last time.'

'How long are you going to stay for?' Jack said. 'I'm just going to sit on the back stairs for a while.'

'We're not going yet,' Lou said.

'I came to get you out of here before something happens.'

'Ah, Jackie. We're all big girls now.'

He stood up from the cluster of his family on the old carpet that he knew was green though he couldn't see it, and slid the door open. It stuck in the same spot as it always did and he gave it the necessary joggle without having to think about it, the memories of all his comings and goings as a kid lodged inside him. Outside the sea roared up at him, filling him, and he sat on the top step and looked at the dark shapes of the land, the edge of the ocean, as though he were looking into a tunnel inside him that sucked him backwards.

For a moment he thought he saw it again, a dot of light rising into the black from the massive bluff above the rockpool, and then it disappeared. It was a different kind of night tonight, balmy and sweet, gentle. That evening he had stepped out into the chilly air brought by the southerly and closed his eyes, had heard the door downstairs open and felt Phoebe and Dad pass beneath him and cross the lawn. Just go away. I could sleep, I could sleep. But his heart raced as though he'd taken a drug.

He had opened his eyes and heard Phoebe ask Charlie a question, down the path, towards the undergrowth. I've done enough, being there with him at the Kazmis', cleaning the car. Too much. I can't keep watch all the time.

How much time had passed between then and the lanterns floating out to sea? Ten minutes perhaps. The first two had set off as though they had small motors and steering equipment attached— straight out from the pool at a regular angle.

How long had he stayed there, counting his breaths? Behind him in the house Mum was lying in her room with black night-shades on and earplugs in. Lou was in her bunk with her Walkman. 'Stop worrying, Jack,' she had said before she put her headphones on. 'Tricia gave him a pill. He'll be out like a light in no time.'

But it was not worry that had drawn him down these steps, these very planks of rotting timber, or not only worry. Jack, an adult now, supposedly, a father himself, childhood far behind him, was back there, rage like a gas filling his lungs, running down the path and across the wild night-time beach towards the pool as the third lantern set off low and juddery before it too got loose and sailed out into the sky. I will get him home and then I am *done*.

He made himself walk carefully along the wet concrete beside the pool in the night, saw no one. Could he have passed by them on the dark beach? They couldn't be out on the rock platform with the sea like this. A flickering light shot out from behind the headland and he found Phoebe coming off the rocks alone, bewilderment on her face, and then a few seconds behind, Dad too, stepping out of the dark. The moon appeared in a gap in the clouds and Charlie came towards him slowly, more slowly than seemed natural.

What if he hadn't said it? He sat here in his own future and let it in, that wish he'd always held at bay. He wished he hadn't said it, he wished he'd stayed on these stairs, left everyone to do whatever they were going to do, had not infected their lives with his feelings.

'You think you can do whatever you want,' he'd said, and Dad had seemed tired, confused. Phoebe looked at him for a moment, seemed to make a decision, and passed by Jack, stroked his hand on her way past as though performing some kind of relay, and ran into the night, leaving him to say what he was going to say.

Charlie stepped up from the rock platform onto the poolside concrete, his figure clear in the moonlight, and put his hand on Jack's elbow.

'Today's gone on forever,' his father said, and tried to walk him along towards the beach. 'Time to hit the hay.'

Jack shook him off. 'You've put us all in danger.'

'I don't follow you.'

'Going into a crime scene. Bothering the Kazmis. It looks weird.'

'They're upset. They'll see I meant well.'

They walked towards the beach. Jack couldn't look at him. His body was shaking in the cold breeze but it was seeing his hand quiver, rather than feeling it, that made him notice this. 'And now I've cleaned the car. Got all the mud off, so it's like you never went there.'

He could feel Charlie staring at him. 'Why did you do that?'

They reached the end of the pool where the path led up to the surf club and Jack stopped. 'Why are you so interested in her? Did you do something?'

His father put both his hands heavily on Jack's shoulders and leaned forward, looking into Jack's eyes. 'Jack?'

Charlie was an inch or two taller than him, although before long they would have been about the same. Jack pushed his hands off. 'You haven't shut up about her. All. Day. You used to talk to her. I saw you.'

Charlie bit his lip and frowned slightly. If Jack saw that look on someone's face now he knew what it signified: a slowness, a lack of comprehension that came with alcohol or drugs, some kind of confusion. Then, he had thought, It's true, isn't it, Dad?

'Now you're collecting things, setting off lanterns, like she's already dead.' He was having trouble speaking and yet at the same time he could not have kept the words back. 'You know what happened to her.' Behind his father white foam crashed against the wall of the pool, sizzling on the concrete as it receded. 'Dad, if there was an accident,' he choked, 'it's got to be better if you just tell someone.'

And then Charlie reached forward, placed a hand over Jack's mouth and shook his head. There was no violence in it; he had just decided, it seemed, that Jack must not be allowed to say another word. He remembered it now, his father's warm hand, smelling of dirt as well as the usual mechanical smells he gave off, his fingers hot and dry, laying themselves gently across the bottom half of his face, the other hand gripping his shoulder. The look on his face too, something breaking through the fog to make him see what Jack was saying.

That look, Jack caught glimpses of it in the mirror now he seemed to have taken on his father's form, and always turned away, pressing down the panic.

Charlie stood very close and Jack smelled sweat and oil. He wanted air, all that air above the ocean that lay beyond his father's body. Standing on the lip of the pool with his father's hand across his mouth and that look on his face, Jack felt a force rushing up through him and he pushed as hard as he could, everything pulsing through him and out through his hands, into his father's body, falling backwards into the black sky. He was here, present, too present, his skin against his mouth making it difficult to breathe, and then not here, just Jack and the dark and the surging white sea.

Oh, he thought, and stood frozen for a moment. It was shallow over the back of the pool, and it wasn't far to fall. You could bump your head though, falling into a metre of water, and be in trouble. Oh God, even now he had to look out for him. He ran a few steps forward and peered into the water. He couldn't see him in the little peaks and troughs sloshing against the wall, so he dropped down into the waves and was instantly knocked off his feet and pulled outwards away from the beach, his ears, nose and eyes filled with water. He swam strongly, not knowing his direction, spreading his arms and legs as widely as possible to feel for his father, for them to grab hold of one another, find their feet and get clear, onto the sand. Three strokes and his head was above water, but he was a frightening distance from the beach already, his feet cycling and finding nothing, heading past the pool and headland towards Newport in the southern rip. *Dad*, he thought, and breathed in and out quickly, treading the glutinous water, allowing himself to be taken towards the far end of the pool. Then he took a great gulp of air in the dark and went down, kicked himself sideways from the surge and towards the dark headland, bracing for collision with the rocks. Now he was stranded by the rip he had some control, bobbing up and down on the breaking foam, the top side of his foot sweeping across a smooth surface. He reached forward, found a rock, lost his grip on the smoothness and a wave pushed him back against the shelf. He grabbed hold and scrabbled, sat on the dark platform, his breath tearing his chest, trying to listen over the sound of himself for his father's voice.

One version of Jack had stood on the wet rocks, the surge pulling at his legs, calling out for his father in the dark beneath the cliffs, before running back to the house across the dark beach, standing over his sleeping mother, dripping water onto her floor, waiting for the moment he was able to speak.

The other was with Charlie, in him, under the waves, hair floating above his face, sinking down and away into the cold, black water, then and always.

~

Lou's phone had buzzed in her pocket as she stood on the front step of their old house with her mother and her sister. She was lifting her key from inside her shirt and she'd had a feeling what that electronic poke in her thigh would turn out to be. She pushed the key into the lock anyway and in they went, Tricia saying, 'Oh, my word' as Phoebe shone the torch from her phone into the bedrooms and down the corridor to the lounge.

As Phoebe set up her gear, she leaned on the cool laminate bench in the kitchen and pulled out her phone. The first line of an email showed on her lockscreen. Mrs Beringer. No deal, unless she wanted to bid in an open market like any other punter.

She stood in the dark while Phoebe sat on the floor, fiddling with the projector, Tricia holding a light steady on her hands, and felt a loosening of her grip, like earlier, when she had dropped the glass on her kitchen tiles. She had watched it slide through her hands and fall towards the floor so slowly it seemed she had meant it to happen, had watched with slow curiosity at the moment of impact, the radiation across the pale tiles.

Aart had said to her, back at the house, that he had seen vodka bottles in the recycling, bottles he had not seen in the drinks cupboard. 'You are hiding how much you are drinking, Louisa.' She had needed to stop him talking, had shaken him off and run away. I know, Aart, she thought now. I know.

She remembered the Boxing Day lunch in this house, the bubbles of the champagne going to her head, swigging Bundy from a Coke bottle with those boys down at the beach. She knew that boy; he was an electrician with a fleet of vans. She smiled when she saw them and looked for but rarely saw him. There was always a trace of something, a drop of grief in a vat of experience, as the van passed by.

She imagined standing in her beautiful kitchen at dusk with a sweating crystal balloon of white wine in her hand; the quiet mornings, everybody gone, sipping from her Diet Coke bottle. The hot trickle of vodka in the blood as she grabbed her keys.

'All set,' Phoebe said. 'Come and sit down, Lou-Lou.'

She sat on the floor close to her mother, straight-backed, cross-legged, and her sister, fidgeting and giggling, leaning forward to press a button. There they all were, standing on the wharf at Palmie. She looked at the three of them, the kids: she nearly as tall as Tricia, even then, and strong-looking; Jack smiling but his worry at the ready in that little scowl; Phoebe, head cocked to one side, eyes a bit mad. Lou's hand was on Phoebe's chest and Jack's hand was on Lou's shoulder. Their parents stood one each side and looked stripped bare of all the minute by minute stuff that consumed them. 'Look at us,' Lou whispered.

There was a click; she had not locked the door behind them. They froze as a breathing body came down the corridor in the blackness. 'It's just me.' Jack. Here he was, his hesitant shape in the room. He came and sat down with them and she felt Phoebe's wish for him and Tricia to give up a little of what was inside them, pass it on.

They looked at the photos, all that light and colour laid across the walls of their old house, and she felt the magic of what her sister had made. The photos blurred and Jack was on his feet, sliding open the door. After a while the photos cycled back to the beginning, and she felt herself rise up and drift out there too into the mild night, in the old way they used to find one another, sit out above the sea and check in. She absorbed the ocean, swallowed it down. This nearness was like a drug. She imagined trying to persuade Aart that it was worth the money they would pay for it and felt instantly diminished, given the conversation they had just had. This was as close as she would get.

She realised as she sat down that Jack's shoulders were shaking. 'Hey,' she said, 'Jackie?' His face was slick with tears in the lights from the houses along the ridge.

'Do you ever still think it was him?'

He didn't have to say what he meant. It had always been there, just beneath the surface, all you had to do was dip your finger into the water and you would touch something sinewy and cold. 'Never. Honestly.'

'All this time. They never found her. Nothing ever settled.'

God, he looked like Dad. He could be him now, with his aging face, his fading hair. Not the tears, though; they came from somewhere else. 'They've got the guy,' she said gently. 'That man we saw on the news. He's told them where to find her, and they have.'

'Where was she?'

'In one of the caves up there, behind our school.'

He was crying properly. 'Poor Monica.'

'They reckon it was quick, real quick. They say he got her in the car after hockey and she jumped out again, straightaway, and that's how she died. So then he had to hide her.'

His chest was rising and falling but she didn't think he was having an attack. 'Quick? Okay.' He nodded. 'I do know it wasn't him.' He was barely whispering. 'I just can't look at pictures of him.'

'I'm so sorry I ever put the idea in your head. I was angry with him and he was being so weird. Do you remember?'

He nodded.

'I know he was hard on you,' Lou said. 'And on Feebs.'

'I don't think she remembers that.'

'She remembers how much fun he was.'

'I was scared, even when he was being fun, because you knew what was coming.'

'Not always, Jack. Some of those days were perfect. Remember that last Christmas Day, when he gave us all boards and watched us get up on them? He stayed for hours. Till even Phoebe was up.'

She put her arm around his warm shuddering back.

'It was my fault,' he said.

'No. It was mine. It was mine if it was anyone's. Stupid girl, I was, stirring everyone up. I've tried to put it behind me. What good can it do now?'

'No, Lou. Dad, going into the water.'

Her skin felt something before she could think it. 'How could it be?'

'I went down to find him because I was worried, because Mum had given him something. You told me. Do you remember that? I was the only one who knew about it and that he was going off to do the lanterns. I had to check on him.'

She'd forgotten about that, the pills, long, long before, had just let it slide into the blackness beyond memory. In the car, after Mum had cleaned it like a mad thing, she'd said, 'Sometimes I give him something,' and then she had. Lou watched her crack open the pill casing and pour it into his whisky.

Jack said, 'But I was angry too, when I saw him. Really *burning* mad. It was him bothering the Kazmis. Her mum, answering the door, thinking it might be good news, or something terrible. That was the worst thing. I asked him if he had something to do with it.'

She stared at him, waiting for him to go on.

'He did this strange thing.' He stared at her, as though he could transfer his thoughts into her without saying them. The ocean boomed beneath them. 'He put his hand over my mouth. I still dream about it. It was like he couldn't find the words to stop me talking so he just used his hand.' He placed his hand gently over his own mouth for a moment. 'I pushed him off.'

She pulled him closer. 'Jack, it was an accident.'

'I pushed him. The water was shallow, I went in after him, but there was a rip and he'd just . . . gone.'

He looked out over the beach, into his unchangeable past. 'Well, come on,' she said quietly, breathless. 'Did you mean to? Listen. Did you really mean to go and find Dad and do something to him?'

'No. I don't know. No.'

'I've known you all your life and you didn't.' She knew she sounded angry, she was not sure what she was feeling. 'And then you went in too, right? That was really brave. You were just a kid.'

'I've never even let myself miss him.'

The pool was just visible at the other end of the beach under the streetlight it had now. She imagined Jack there, and Charlie, fighting.

'Let me say something,' he said.

'You don't have to.'

'I need to. I can't do anything until I have.' He paused and she waited, watching the white line of foam at the dark shore. She looked back at his face. 'I'm sorry he's gone. I wish I'd done something different in that moment, anything else but what I did. I'm sorry for you and Phoebe and Mum, that I took him away from you.'

She took his head in her hands and kissed his forehead. Salty and warm. Left her hands on his head as he spoke.

'You don't have to forgive me. You don't have to ever talk to me again. I just needed to say it. I've got to change things in my life.'

You're not the only one, she thought. She felt the beginnings of a headache, an uncomfortable sobering. One last time she let herself imagine: I own the air, from here to the beach. She imagined her father's staircase leaping out in the dark to the water and then watched it disintegrate like a sandcastle at the edge of the surf. Gears engaged in her brain, something Phoebe had always felt about Jack and Tricia. 'Mum knows, doesn't she?'

He held her wrists for a moment then freed himself, nodded.

'She's always known, right?'

'She never took a backward step.'

They looked out towards the black sea and she took his hand, wishing he'd said this then, not carried it around. She imagined him free of this weight, free to make plans, to do whatever he wanted.

What if he had told you? she asked herself. When you were fifteen and had just lost your dad. She knew with complete certainty she would have hated him forever. That's what he had absorbed for her, enough time dragging this awful weight behind him for her to be able to love him still.

~

Phoebe and Tricia sat on the floor watching the photos cycle through, back to the beginning and that girl splashing into the water. Tricia placed her feet gracefully under her buttocks and stretched to her full height. If she had lifted her arms she would have been able to touch the ceiling. 'Lovely, darling. Could you make me a copy for my laptop?'

'Didn't think you believed in looking backwards.'

'It won't kill me at this stage. Leave out that one though, you know, down at the pool.'

'Okay. Bet she's ugly by now, Mum.'

'She wasn't then. She was something to behold. You go and find the others. I'll just stand here for a minute and remember the good old days.'

Phoebe could not read her mother in the dark. She remembered them as good days but her memory of her mother then was of someone holding down a well of subterranean fury. She went out to Lou on the steps and sat next to her, the way Jack used to do when Phoebe was a little kid, room for just the two of them on the stair. Down on the lawn Jack was looking out at the black sea.

'Thanks for the pictures, Feeb.'

'That's okay. I might walk down to the beach before we leave. Have I got time?'

'Why not? Be careful on the path.'

She laughed. 'Okay, Mum.'

Phoebe touched Jack's hand as she passed him and felt her way with her bare feet onto the track, keeping to the side that edged the lawns, away from the black air over the beach. The night was soft and sweet-smelling, the ocean stroking in and out, nudging gently at the sand.

The path down to the sea had metal gridded walkways now. They pressed against her feet as she passed the dankness of the part higher up she used to call the jungle. Something stopped her, as though she were back in that moment that she had not known for what it was, exhilarated by her own courage amid the slippery roots and crunchy fronds in the darkness, not knowing she had seen her dad for the last time, that even now he might be under the dark sea.

She remembered letting go of the first lantern and making her wish: that wanting, to be at the centre of her family forever, to be held close and tight, to be suspended in a moment in which they were all laughing at something she had done. She thought now of the way when they all laughed at her she would take a deep bow, her body folded flat from her middle, to hide her smile. That was all she ever wanted, to be in that moment, getting that smile under control, ready to straighten up and accept the applause.

There was a small platform with benches, where the oldies liked to rest and take in the view. She sat for a while and thought about the pictures, about Charlie, about being the little kid in the family, what pleasure that had brought her, what endless frustration. It was beginning to grow cool, the summer was just about done. She stood and rubbed her arms, said goodbye to the sea.

Then she heard her mother's voice calling her name, from higher up on the path. She turned and they were all there, coming down together. Phoebe waited, watching their shapes take form in the night, emerging into the moonlight. Strange this moment, them descending out of the dark trees silently, all of them watching her, as though she had conjured them, the attention they were paying her. She could not speak, did not want to break the moment open. They finally reached her, standing on the platform above the beach, the sea gently pushing itself onto the sand with the insistence of memory.

'Phoebe,' Jack said, their mother and sister either side of him, 'I have something to tell you.'

CHRISTMAS DAY

One Christmas in late childhood, as the day fades into the mist in the gully, Jack catches the last wave of the day, glances to either side of him and sees that his sisters are up on their boards. He and Phoebe are lurching, laughing, Lou is slightly ahead, the late sun blazing pink on her brown skin, head tilted back as though she is accepting the worship of the crowds.

Mum and Dad are the last people on the beach, watching them come in, standing close together, still, calm. He feels air move through him, taking him with it, as he flies towards his parents and then down, down, tumbling into the wash beyond the bank. Salt water shoots up his nose, replacing the air inside him, and his board thumps him gently, repeatedly, on his spine as his feet find the sand. Another wave knocks him over before he can lift his head clear and it's with him now, the first flutter of panic. Water wants to enter everything, eyes, sinuses, tiny airways into the lungs.

Warm fingers take hold of his arms, there is a hand on each one, pulling him upwards. He finds the sky, the cliff, the beach, and that his sisters are here, on either side of him, lifting him up, setting him on his feet, where he is able to let the water out of him and breathe the good, clear air above the wash.

ACKNOWLEDGEMENTS

Thank you to Pippa Masson for her commitment and excellent advice on early drafts, to Annette Barlow, Rebecca Kaiser, Julia Stiles and Aziza Kuypers for easing me with such care through the editing process, and to all at Allen & Unwin for their ongoing enthusiasm and hard work.

Colleagues and students at the University of Exeter provided enrichment and support during the writing of this novel. Jane Feaver and Sam North were particularly welcoming and I thank Sam too for his most helpful feedback and for making space for me in his screenwriting workshops.

Brad, Ellie and Olive, my treasures, thank you for cheerfully submitting to being dragged across the world and back, for letting me have the computer when I needed it and for being you.